THE BODY FINDER

Kimberly Derting

THE
BODY
FINDER

HARPER

An Imprint of HarperCollinsPublishers

The Body Finder
www.harperteen.com

Library of Congress Cataloging-in-Publication Data
Derting, Kimberly.
    The body finder / by Kimberly Derting. — 1st ed.
       p.   cm.
    Summary: High school junior Violet uses her uncanny ability to sense
murderers and their victims to try to stop a serial killer who is terrorizing
her town, and although her best friend and would-be boyfriend Jay promises
to keep her safe, she becomes a target.
    ISBN 978-0-06-177981-7
    [1. Psychic ability—Fiction.   2. Serial murders—Fiction.   3. Dead—
Fiction.   4. Best friends—Fiction.   5. Friendship—Fiction.   6. High
schools—Fiction.   7. Schools—Fiction.   8. Washington (State)—
Fiction.]   I. Title.
PZ7.D4468Bod   2010   2009039675
[Fic]—dc22

Typography by Andrea Vandergrift
12 13 14   CG/RRDB   10 9 8 7 6 5 4
❖
First Edition

To Amanda, Connor, and Abigail,
for letting me love you

PROLOGUE

VIOLET AMBROSE WANDERED AWAY FROM THE safety of her father as she listened to the harmony of sounds weaving delicately around her. The rustling of the leaves mingled gently with the restless calls of birds and the far-off rushing waters of the icy river that lay beyond the trees.

And then there was another sound. Something she couldn't quite identify. Yet.

She was familiar enough with the meaning of this new, and misplaced, noise. Or at least with what it signified. She had been hearing sounds, or seeing colors, or smelling smells like these for years. For as long as she could remember.

Echoes, she called them.

She looked back at her father to see if he had heard it too, even though she already knew the answer. He hadn't, of course. Only she could hear it. Only she understood what the haunting sound foretold.

He walked casually behind her, at his same slow and steady pace, keeping a watchful eye on his eight-year-old daughter as she ran ahead of him.

The sound whistled past her again, carried on the breeze that sent crisp, golden leaves swirling around her ankles. She stopped briefly to listen, but once it passed she continued on ahead.

"Don't go too far," her father dutifully called from behind her. He wasn't really worried about her out here. These were their woods.

Violet had practically been raised in this forest, learning about her surroundings, learning how to tell which direction she was facing by the lichen growing on the tall tree trunks, and knowing how to tell the time of day by the position of the sun . . . at least on those days when that sun wasn't obscured by the gloom of cloud cover. This was easy territory, even for an eight-year-old girl.

She ignored her father's warning and wandered off the path, still listening to *that something* that was beckoning her forward. Her feet felt propelled by a will of their own as she struggled to make the sound into something coherent, something she could identify. She stepped over fallen branches and walked through a sea of fern fronds that grew up from the damp ground.

"Violet!" She heard her dad's voice breaking through her concentration.

She paused, and then called back, "I'm right here," although not as loudly as she should have, before she started walking again.

The sound was getting stronger. Not louder, but stronger. She could feel the vibrations practically resonating beneath her skin now.

This was how it was with these things. This was the way these *feelings* came to her. They were indescribable, yet to her they made perfect sense.

And when they called to her she felt compelled to answer.

She was close now, so close that she could hear a voice. That was what this echo was, a voice. Single and solitary, seeking someone—anyone—to answer it.

Violet was that someone.

She stopped at a mound of damp dirt covered with a thick layer of rotting leaves. The soil was oddly out of place amid the undergrowth, with nothing living springing up from it. Even Violet knew that the soil was too newly placed to have fostered life just yet.

She knelt down, feeling the pulsating echo coming from beneath. She could feel it reverberating within her veins, coursing hotly through her small body. Without waiting, Violet brushed away the leaves and debris with a sweep of her coat sleeve, before she began earnestly scooping at the soft earth beneath with her hands.

She heard her father's light footsteps catch up with her

and his gentle voice ask, "Find something, Vi?"

She was too lost in her task to answer, and he didn't pry. He was used to this, his little girl searching out the lost souls of the forest. Without speaking, he leaned against the soaring trunk of a nearby cedar and waited without really watching.

Violet felt her fingertips brush against something hard and smooth, cold and unyielding. She shuddered against a disturbing awareness that she couldn't quite name and kept digging.

She sank her fingers into the moist soil once again. And again, they touched something chillingly firm.

Something too soft to be a rock.

And it was back, that nagging something that was trying to get through to her.

She reached in again, this time not to dig, but to sweep away the thin layer of dirt to get a better view of what lay beneath. She had captured her father's interest, and he leaned over her, looking into the shallow hole.

Violet worked like an archaeologist, carefully sifting and brushing across the top of her discovery, so as not to disturb what might be buried there.

She heard her father gasp at the same time she recognized what she had uncovered. She felt his strong hands reaching for her from behind, pulling her firmly by the shoulders away from the fresh dirt and gathering her into his strong, safe arms . . . away from the sound that was calling to her . . .

And away from the girl's face staring up at her from beneath the soil.

4

CHAPTER 1

THE SOUND OF THE ALARM CLOCK WAS AN irritating intrusion into the comfortable haze of sleep that wrapped its arms around Violet. She dragged her hand out from beneath the warm cocoon of blankets to hit the snooze button. She kept her eyes closed; trying to let the haze reclaim her, but the damage had already been done. She was awake now.

She sighed, still not ready to untangle herself from the covers, and she tried to recall what she had been dreaming about before being so rudely interrupted. For a moment, she thought she might remember, but the elusive whisper of her dream escaped her.

She made a disgusted sound to herself as she finally threw off the blankets and sat up in one not-so-smooth motion. She turned off her clock before it could reach its nine-minute snooze interval.

This was the third day of school, and she didn't want to start her junior year with a tardy slip. She rubbed her face with both hands, trying to stimulate the flow of blood in an effort to stay alert. She wasn't much of a morning person.

She stumbled through most of her before-school routine; showering, brushing her teeth, dressing. After scrutinizing herself in the mirror and noting the dark circles beneath her eyes, she once again thought about how badly she wanted to crawl back beneath the mound of already cooling blankets that covered her bed like an inviting nest.

She pulled her hair into a messy ponytail—the only kind of ponytail that her unruly curls allowed—before grabbing her backpack off the floor. She hated it when adults told her how lucky she was to have such gorgeous, natural curls, when she wanted nothing more than to blend in with the sea of shiny, flat-ironed, stick-straight hair with which every girl in her school seemed to have been blessed.

But what did she expect? Life didn't seem to want *her* to blend like everyone else.

After all, how many girls had inherited the ability to locate the dead, or at least those who had been murdered? How many little girls had spent hours of their childhood scouring the woods in search of dead animals left behind by feral predators? How many had created their own personal cemeteries in their backyards to bury the carnage they'd found, so the little souls could rest in peace?

And how many eight-year-olds had been drawn to discover the body of a dead girl?

No, Violet was definitely different.

She brushed aside the disturbing thoughts and hurried out the door, crossing her fingers, like she did every morning, that her ancient little car would sputter to life when she tried to start it.

Her car.

Her father called it a "classic."

She wasn't quite so kind in her description of the small 1988 Honda Civic, with its original factory paint that was fading after years of being battered by the rainy Washington weather.

She called it dilapidated.

Reliable, her father would argue back. And Violet couldn't entirely disagree. So far, despite its morning protests and groans—so much like her own—her Honda had never been the cause of one of her (many) late slips.

Today was no different. The car coughed and spewed when she turned the ignition, but the engine caught on the first attempt and, after a few coaxing moments, the sound turned to something closer to its usual not-so-quiet grumbling.

Violet had just one stop to make on her way to school, the same stop she'd made every day since getting her license six months earlier. To pick up her best friend, Jay Heaton.

Best friend. The expression seemed so foreign now, like an old, comfortable sneaker that once practically molded to your foot but now strained against each step you took because it no longer fit.

The summer had changed things . . . too many things for Violet's liking.

She and Jay had been best friends since they were six years old, when in the first grade Jay had moved to Buckley. It was the day that Violet dared him to kiss Chelsea Morrison at recess, telling him she'd be his best friend if he did. Of course Chelsea had pushed him down for doing it, which Violet had known would happen, and all three of them were hauled into the principal's office for a discussion about "personal boundaries."

But Violet was true to her word, and she and Jay had been inseparable ever since.

In the first grade, they'd played tag on the playground, always ganging up on the other kids to make someone else "it" in order to avoid playing against each other. In second grade, they moved on to the jungle gym, choosing teams and using the tunnels as makeshift forts to defend against their enemies. By third grade, they'd learned to play four square and wall ball. Fourth, tetherball. And fifth was the year they discovered the giant boulder at the edge of the playing field, behind which the recess teacher couldn't see what was happening.

It was the year of their first kiss—or *kisses,* rather—their one and only foray into romance with each other. They tried it once with their lips closed tightly, a small quick peck, and then again, they tried it by touching their tongues together. The sensation was slippery, supple, and foreign. They both immediately agreed that it was gross and swore they would never do it again.

By middle school, their parents, who had become something like chauffeurs, ferrying the two of them almost daily across the mile-long distance that separated their homes, had resigned, maintaining that if Violet and Jay really wanted to see each other, then the exercise would do them good.

But neither of them minded the walk. They had spent years of their childhoods combing through the forested areas that surrounded both of their homes, as they explored and built clubhouses out of old timber. They had mapped and named entire sections of the woods, several of them after themselves or unusual arrangements of their combined names. Things like "Jaylet Stream" . . . "Amberton Woods" . . . "Hebrose Trail."

They also named the makeshift graveyard behind Violet's house, using neither of their names, simply calling it Shady Acres.

They were ten at the time, and the name sounded ominous and dark . . . which was exactly what they were going for. They would dare one another to go out there, to see who could wait alone, until well after darkness had fallen, telling each other tales of the strange occurrences they were sure must be happening out there . . . especially at night.

Violet always won, and Jay never complained that she did. He seemed to understand that she wasn't afraid, even when she pretended to be.

He understood a lot of things. He was the only person, besides her parents, and her aunt and uncle, who knew about her strange penchant for seeking out ravaged animals, and her need to rebury them within the safe chicken-wire enclosure of Shady Acres. It had been an adventure that they'd shared together, combing through fern groves and blackberry thickets in search of the lost bodies. He'd even helped her build little crosses and headstones to mark the tiny graves.

Before they were buried, before they were properly laid to rest, those animals left behind would call out to Violet. They would emit an energy—a sensory echo—in the wake of their murder, like a beacon that only she could find, letting her know where they'd been discarded. It could be anything . . . a smell, a burst of color, a taste in the back of her mouth, or a combination of several sensations at once.

She didn't know how . . . or why . . . It just *happened*.

But what she did know, what she'd learned early on, was that once she placed them in her graveyard, they no longer called out to her. She still felt them, but it was different. She was able to filter them out, until they became nothing more than the comforting static of white noise.

Jay also understood the need to keep Violet's secret, even though he'd never been told to. He seemed to sense, even from an early age, that he needed to keep that secret close to him, like a treasure he protected, saving it just for the two of them. He'd always made Violet feel safe and secure . . . and even normal.

So why, then, had everything changed so suddenly?

Already, as her car sputtered down his driveway, with gravel crunching beneath the tires, her heart rate was racing within the suddenly too-confined space of her chest.

This is ridiculous, she chided herself. *He's your* best *friend!*

She saw the front door opening even before she slowed to a complete stop. Jay was yanking his hooded sweatshirt over his head, dragging his backpack in his wake. He yelled something into the house, probably telling his mom that he was leaving for school, and he pulled the door shut behind him.

It was the same thing every day. There was nothing different from yesterday and the day before that. Nothing different from every single day since they'd met.

Except that now her stomach climbed into her throat as he grinned his stupid sideways grin at her and slid into the car.

Stupid. Stupid. Stupid!

She smiled back, willing her reckless pulse to slow down. "Ready?"

"No, but do we have a choice?" His voice, which had gotten deeper over the summer, was still so well-known to her, so comfortable, that she immediately relaxed.

"Not if you don't want a tardy." She backed out of the driveway, barely glancing in her rearview mirror to watch where she was going. His driveway was almost as familiar to her as her own.

She hated these new, unknown feelings that seemed to assault her whenever he was around, and sometimes even when he was only in her thoughts. She felt like she was no longer in control of her own body, and her traitorous reactions were only slightly more embarrassing than her treacherous thoughts.

She was starting to feel like he was toxic to her.

11

That, or she was seriously losing her mind, because that was the only way she could possibly explain the ridiculous butterflies she got whenever Jay was close to her. And what really irritated Violet was that he seemed to be completely oblivious of these new, and completely insane, reactions she was having to him. Obviously, whatever she had wasn't contagious.

Except that it was. She wasn't the only one that seemed to be noticing him. She almost dreaded the moment they'd step out from the relative peace of her noisy old Honda in the school's overcrowded parking lot. Because that's when the real games began.

Day three of school, but as of day one, girls had begun to wait for them to arrive in the morning.

No, not for them . . . for *him*.

His new fan club, Violet thought sourly. Girls who had known Jay since the first day of his first-grade year. Girls who had never paid him so much as a second glance before now. Girls who seemed to notice the not-so-subtle changes that had taken place over the last two and a half months they'd spent away from school.

Girls like her.

Stop it! she silently screamed at herself.

She slid a sideways glance in his direction, trying to figure out just what it was that was making her so . . . so painfully self-conscious all of a sudden.

He was looking right at her. Grinning. A big, stupid, self-satisfied grin, as if he had been eavesdropping on her all-too-embarrassing thoughts.

"What?" She tried to defend herself, wishing she'd never looked his way as she felt her cheeks burning with shame. *"What?"* she asked again when he just laughed at her.

"Were you planning to ditch school today, or should we turn around?"

She looked up and realized that she'd just driven past the road that led to the school. "Why didn't you say something?" she accused as she pulled a quick, and probably illegal, U-turn. The tops of her ears felt like they were on fire now.

"I just wanted to see where you were heading." He shrugged. "I didn't say I wouldn't skip school. You just have to ask me first." His new grown-up voice seemed to fill all the space of the small car, and Violet found even *that* annoying.

"Shut up," she insisted, even though she couldn't help smiling now too. She couldn't believe she'd passed the entrance to her own school. "Now we really *are* going to be late."

By the time she found a parking spot in the student lot, there were only two die-hard "Jay fans" left waiting for them. Or rather, for *him,* Violet corrected herself again.

She couldn't help but wonder how many others had already given up their watchful post in favor of *not* visiting the attendance office before school started today.

Violet decided not to wait around to watch the flirt-fest begin. She was already half running, with her backpack slung over her shoulder, as she bolted from her car. "See you in second period!" she yelled back to Jay, consciously deciding that this was better anyway. The last thing she wanted to do right now was to watch him with the two girls, who practically assaulted him as he got out of the car.

She dashed through the door to her first class just as the bell sounded.

Made it! she congratulated herself. *Three days down and no tardy slips.*

Just one hundred and seventy-seven to go.

By the time second period rolled around, Violet was already convincing herself that whatever it was she thought she'd been feeling, whatever plagued her ill-advised subconscious, was just an illusion of some sort. It was all smoke and mirrors. A trick of the mind.

And then he sauntered in and fell into the chair beside her, his new size making his desk look like something from a dollhouse. Violet half expected the chair to buckle beneath him.

"Hey, Vi. Glad to see you decided to stay at school after all." He punched her in the arm playfully.

Her heart somersaulted painfully.

Violet sighed. "Ha-ha," she retorted without a trace of humor.

Jay's brow furrowed, but before he could ask her what was wrong, he reached into his back pocket and pulled out a slip of paper. "I almost forgot. Check it out." He held out the paper so she could grab it from him.

She unfolded it and tried to smooth it out a little so she could read it. As it turned out she didn't need to bother; she would have been able to read the unmistakably feminine handwriting if the paper had been on fire.

It was a phone number. For Jay. From Elisabeth Adams,

14

only the most popular girl in the school. She was the odds-on favorite to be Homecoming Queen this year, and most likely Prom Queen too. She was tan, blonde, pretty, *and* a senior. As if that wasn't bad enough, she also had the shiny, straight hair that Violet could only dream of.

This sucked.

Violet tried not to look too deer-in-the-headlights when she glanced back at him. "Wow" was all she could think of.

"I know." Jay seemed as surprised as she was but still managed to appear pretty impressed with himself all the same. "She must have slid it into my locker while I was in first period."

"You gonna call her?" Violet was careful not to sound petulant, but she certainly *felt* that way. She just wanted to be his friend again, to *not* care about whether he called this girl or not. She wanted to listen to the gory details and ask him probing questions that would eventually have them off on some random tangent and laughing at their own stupid, private jokes. But somehow, she just couldn't.

She felt deflated as she handed the note back to him.

The bell, and then the teacher, interrupted before Jay could answer her not-so-innocent question. Jay took the note and stuffed it into his binder as trig class got under way.

Violet tried to concentrate on sines and cosines as she took notes on everything the teacher wrote on the whiteboard in the front of the classroom, but she heard nothing. She couldn't stop thinking about how she was going to get over this . . . this *thing* she had for her very best friend in the whole world.

And she *had* to get over it . . . soon. Because if she didn't, if she couldn't stop feeling so viral toward him, eventually it would infect their friendship, and there would be nothing she could do to stop it. She knew she couldn't let that happen.

He was Jay. He was the best person she'd ever known, and she couldn't imagine losing him.

She allowed herself to look his way, pretending she was glancing at the clock on the wall above the door. He was meticulously lost in the lesson, taking notes well beyond the scope of what was written on the board.

She was grateful that at least one of them was listening, because she knew he was going to have to explain it all to her later.

And he would, without ever knowing that *he* was the reason she hadn't heard a word of the lesson.

Violet avoided Jay at lunch—a first for her—opting instead to linger in her third-period English class under the pretext of finishing up some homework—homework that wasn't actually due until the beginning of the next week. She managed to put off leaving the classroom for almost twenty minutes.

Then she wandered to the bathroom, not really the kind of place anyone wanted to "hang out," by any stretch of the imagination. But she took her time, washing her hands, redoing her ponytail, which didn't really improve the second time around, and then washing her hands again.

Other girls—some she knew and some she didn't—came and went while she was in there, primping and gossiping as they stood in front of the mirrors.

Violet took her cue from them and even put on lip gloss, which she almost never did. She had to dig into the bottom of her backpack just to find some.

When Chelsea walked in, Violet was actually relieved to see someone she could talk to, even if it was only for a few minutes.

"Where have you been?" Chelsea accused in her usual blunt tone. "Jay's been looking for you everywhere." She perched in front of the mirror and began the familiar ritual of preening, starting at her hair and working her way down.

Like Jay, Chelsea had changed over the summer. Not so much developmentally—she'd already had the woman's body—but somehow she'd discovered her femininity overnight. Chelsea had always been sort of tomboy-ish and athletic. But it was as if she now recognized that there was more to life than spiking a volleyball into your opponent's court or pitching a perfect game in fast-pitch softball. She seemed to have finally realized that she was pretty too.

And like every other girl in school, Chelsea had the slick mane that practically gleamed when sunlight reflected off its perfect surface. She had even highlighted her glossy chestnut hair with thin blonde streaks that made her look like she'd spent the summer on a beach in California instead of on a softball diamond.

Next to Jay, Chelsea was Violet's closest friend. She was the friend it wasn't weird to have sleepovers with . . . unlike Jay. And the one she could share clothes with . . . unlike Jay. And Violet had always liked—and was even a little jealous of—Chelsea's tell-it-like-it-is attitude, even when she didn't necessarily want to hear-it-like-it-was.

Now happened to be one of those times.

"Well?" Chelsea asked when Violet didn't answer her. "I swear that boy can't function without you, not even at lunch."

Violet winced, but Chelsea didn't see it as she daintily rubbed the corner of her eye with her pinkie finger, making sure that none of her eyeliner had strayed from place. It hadn't; she looked perfect.

"He'll be fine." Violet answered more glumly than she'd intended. "I'm sure someone else would be glad to sit with him."

Chelsea looked up, finished with her own face, and stared at Violet's. "Well, it doesn't really matter. He's out in the hallway waiting. He asked me to come in here and look for you."

Violet just stared, and then she laughed. Chelsea might actually be the only girl in school who hadn't noticed that Jay had changed, possibly because she was too wrapped up in her own transformation to be aware of anyone else's. Violet was grateful, at least, for small miracles.

When Violet didn't move, Chelsea grabbed her by the arm and started towing her toward the door. "Come on, before he starves to death and wastes away to nothing."

"All right, all right," Violet agreed as they drifted out of the girls' room to where Jay stood in the hallway, looking relieved to see her safe and sound at last.

Violet couldn't help feeling comforted to see that expression on his face. Maybe Chelsea was right after all. Maybe Jay couldn't survive without her.

At least *that* feeling was mutual, because she couldn't imagine getting by without him either.

With just five minutes to spare, Violet and her best friend since the first grade had only enough time to raid the vending machines for chips and a candy bar, before rushing off to their fourth-period class.

But it was okay now. Somehow, realizing that he hadn't outgrown *her* during his summer metamorphosis made her feel better. She felt secure again, just knowing that she was as important to him as he was to her.

Everything was going to be fine.

PREY

THE RAIN MADE IT EASIER FOR HIM TO GET
*around unnoticed. Those who sat inside their own cars had their
views impaired by rain, foggy auto glass, and windshield wipers.
Those outside were too busy trying to stay dry by moving quickly
and keeping their heads down. The darkness only helped add to his
invisibility.*

Unfortunately the rain also kept people indoors.

*Of course he was never truly invisible, not in the car he usually
drove. It attracted attention and stares wherever he went, even on a
dark, wet night like this one.*

*But tonight was different. Tonight he blended. He had become
one of them.*

He pulled out of the busy Wal-Mart parking lot in search of smaller, duskier side streets with less traffic and fewer security cameras. As he drove he listened to the methodical beat of the windshield wipers as they swished back and forth . . . back and forth . . . back and forth.

Two girls, probably in their early teens, dashed across the painted lines of the crosswalk, arm in arm. They leaned in toward each other, and he could practically hear them giggling over some shared secret. He couldn't tell if they were pretty or not, but they were young. He watched their hips sway as they hurried to the other side of the road, and he liked seeing the way they moved.

But there were two of them. One more than he needed.

He silently congratulated them on their safe passage. Lucky girls.

He turned off the main highway onto a side street with older, single-story homes, many of which had been converted into businesses as the city grew and zoning laws changed. The increasing traffic had chased the homeowners away. It was dark and deserted at this hour, which was well past the time a small hair salon or a chiropractor's office would still be open.

He turned again and again. As he drove farther from the highway, the main arterial through town, the roads became more and more narrow, and less and less traveled. Small neighborhood developments began to spring up on either side of him, but the entrances were dark and inactive.

That was when he saw the car. Its hazards flashing through the damp blackness of the night.

He slowed down as he drove past, peering into the interior of the stranded vehicle.

She was alone. Young and pretty, and alone.

This was better than he could have hoped for.

He turned his wheel sharply to the right, parking his own car directly in front of hers. He put on his best nice-guy smile as he got out of his car to see if he could help her.

He approached the vehicle, and he could see the hesitation on her face. She wasn't sure if she should trust him. Smart girl. But he knew he looked innocent enough, like someone she could count on, and within the space of seconds her instincts failed her.

She rolled down the window, not all the way, but enough so he could talk to her.

"Are you all right?" he asked, his practiced voice sounding like soft velvet. If he hadn't been concentrating he might have laughed at the false sincerity ringing through it.

She bit her lip. "I don't know. My tire's flat."

Very pretty girl, he thought from this close up. But he glanced down, trying to look interested in the tires. The two he could see appeared to be fine.

"Other side," she said when she saw him looking. She seemed embarrassed then, and the innocent blush on her face made her even more attractive. She wrinkled her nose. "I don't know how to change a tire."

He glanced around to make sure no one else was coming. The rain was running in small rivers down the back of his neck and soaking his shirt, but he barely noticed.

"Did you call someone?" This was the big question. This was where he found out whether she was the one or not. "Are your parents on their way?"

She didn't even see the trap she was walking into. Her parents must have warned her about strangers, but they should have prepared her better.

22

She shook her head, the pink on her cheeks making her look so pure. "I left my cell phone at home," she admitted.

He thought about that for a moment, making it seem like he wasn't sure how to proceed, even though her words had already set his plan into action. He tapped the base of the window frame with his fingers as though weighing his options before finally speaking again. "Well, I'm not really equipped to change your tire, but I could give you a lift home."

Her instincts kicked back in, and he knew from the look that flashed across her lovely face that she wasn't so sure. Maybe her parents had done a better job than he thought.

He tried to backpedal, to wipe that uncertain look from her face. "My cell phone's in the car. Is there someone you could call?"

She bit her lip again, chewing nervously. "Yeah. Okay, sure," she said, flashing him her best you'd-be-doing-me-a-huge-favor smile. It was a smile that girls learned to do from a very young age, and one that she was particularly good at. "If you're sure you don't mind."

He looked around again, to make sure they were still alone, even though he knew that they were.

He knew how to play this game. He got off on this game. He smiled back at her, trying to look protective and fatherly. "Of course not." And then he said the words that would win her over once and for all. "If my wife knew I'd left you out here without help, she'd have my hide. Besides, you're only a couple of years older than our daughter, and I would want someone to help her if she were stranded."

That was all it took. She was his.

He watched as she unbuckled her seat belt, and he felt a wave of excited electricity jolting through him. He couldn't believe his luck; she was almost making it too easy; she was going to come right to him.

23

He stood back as she opened her car door. "Thank you so much for doing this," she said as she opened up an umbrella over her head. She held it out, offering him shelter beneath it as he led her to the right side of the car. "My parents are going to kill me for forgetting my phone; they're always nagging me about the importance of planning ahead."

He looked down at her, thinking about how wise her parents sounded, and he was grateful that she hadn't taken them too seriously. But again he gave her his protective voice. "They're right, you know. You can never be too careful." He opened the passenger-side door and leaned inside.

She was surprised when he came back out without a phone but with something else instead. Her eyes widened in fear as first recognition and then panic dawned across her exquisitely expressive face.

But before she could even scream, he was on her, shoving her hard against the car's interior and whispering into her ear as he held his hand over her mouth. "Make it easy on yourself. I promise I won't hurt you." He needed to make her understand that . . . it was important to him that she know he wasn't planning to harm her.

He saw the terror in her eyes as she curled up into a protective ball, shivering and silent as the silver duct tape held her mouth closed.

"I swear to you . . . I won't hurt you . . ." He whispered the words over and over again while he popped the trunk and set her inside gently.

His promise made, he smoothed her hair tenderly with his hand before slamming the trunk shut.

He whistled to himself as he pulled his car back onto the road.

It had been a good night.

CHAPTER 2

AFTER THE FIRST FEW ROCKY DAYS OF SCHOOL, at least as far as her feelings for Jay went, Violet started to feel better. Not that the butterflies had vanished or anything, but like so many other things in her life, they faded into the background of her day-to-day activities, becoming more like white noise. And that was something she could deal with.

The girls didn't stop converging on Jay—it was quite the opposite, in fact—they seemed to be multiplying, following him around *en masse*. And while Violet didn't complain outwardly, Jay was starting to, which made Violet feel even more secure in her position at the top . . . for the time being anyway.

He grumbled to Violet about their sudden lack of privacy at school, protesting about the throng of girls that waited for them in the parking lot, or at his locker between classes, and even in the cafeteria at lunch. He began to notice girls individually, and each one had some annoying habit or an irritating personality flaw that grated on his nerves a little more with each passing day.

None of the girls noticed, or cared, that he didn't give them the time of day. But Violet couldn't help feeling smugly satisfied, although she kept her mouth shut and her opinions—even though she agreed with Jay—to herself.

She was grateful that he never seemed to tire of her.

Outwardly at least, nothing had changed between the two of them. They drove to school together in the morning, walked to classes they shared, ate together at lunch, and parted ways when she dropped him off again at his house, only to talk on the phone in the evening. It was nice. And even though Violet silently craved more, it was comfortable.

And this Friday afternoon was no different.

Violet dropped her backpack on the floor inside her front door. It was the area that her mother not-so-fondly referred to as the "shoe graveyard," where everyone who came in left their coats, shoes, umbrellas, and in this case, a backpack.

She smelled dinner already, and she knew that her mom was making lasagna. Not because of the aroma drifting out to meet her, but instead because, when her mom actually cooked something, that was what she made. And it wasn't of the homemade variety either, but one of the prepackaged, mass-marketed frozen ones. That, and a fresh loaf of French bread from the bakery, made up the meal that Violet had eaten more times than she cared to count. Her mom wasn't exactly what you'd call a domestic diva.

"Vi? That you?" her mother called from the kitchen.

Violet kicked off her shoes and followed the scents.

"Hi," Maggie Ambrose greeted her daughter as she stepped into the airy, farmhouse-style kitchen. "How was your day?"

Violet grabbed a pop from the fridge and sat at the table. "Pretty good. How was yours?"

That was all the encouragement her mom needed. "I'm almost finished with the painting I've been working on—you know, the one with the river? I can't wait to show it to you." What she lacked in cooking skills, she more than made up for in enthusiasm for her work.

Violet looked at her mother's paint-covered smock and the rainbow of colors crusted beneath her short fingernails, and she smiled. "Mom, I think you got a little of that river *on* you."

Her mom looked down at her fingernails and grimaced. "Yeah, occupational hazard, I guess." And then she changed the subject. "I hope you're hungry. I'm making lasagna for dinner."

"Great," Violet responded with as much zeal as she could muster under the circumstances. It was probably the only hot meal she would get all week, so she didn't dare complain about it, for fear that her mom might go on strike permanently.

"Oh, and don't forget, you're babysitting for Uncle Stephen tonight."

Violet made a face, but her mom stopped her before she could actually argue.

"You promised, remember? They asked you over a month ago, and you said you would do it."

She was right, and Violet knew it, but it didn't stop her from whining a little. "Yeah, well, a month ago it seemed like a good idea. Now, not so much. Besides, it's the weekend."

Violet loved her little cousins, but they weren't exactly her ideal Friday night dates.

Her mom raised her eyebrows. "Oh, and did you have big plans, Cinderella? Big night at the ball?"

Violet laughed at the sarcasm in her mom's words. "No. But even *nothing* is better than babysitting." She sighed, knowing there was no way out of it. "Fine. I'm gonna go do some of my homework before I head over there."

Violet went to her room and flopped down on the mass of rumpled blankets piled on top of her bed. She thought about studying, but she had all weekend, and right now, with the down comforter reaching up around her, she decided to close her eyes . . . just for a minute. . . .

And then another. Her breathing became even . . . steady . . . and soon she drifted off. . . .

It was the smell that jarred her back to consciousness. Not the familiar smell of melting mozzarella and marinara sauce, but something acrid—harsh—that felt like it was burning the skin inside of her nose.

She opened her eyes and looked around her.

She wrinkled her nose against it. The smell seemed to be right on top of her, but she couldn't begin to imagine what it might be. She winced, holding her breath as she sat up, alarmed.

"What the—?" She scanned the room, not sure what she was looking for.

But there it was. Right in front of her.

The cat had jumped up on her bed while she'd been dozing, and the smell was coming off him in nearly visible, rippling waves, like heat coming off the desert sand.

"Carl!" she accused the fat tomcat at the same time she was scooping him off her bed and racing him toward her bedroom door.

She tried not to inhale as she rushed him down the stairs while he struggled against her hands, trying to wiggle free before she could toss him outside. It was a dance they had done before, and as usual, Violet won, slamming the door in the poor cat's face.

The smell couldn't actually be blocked by the barrier of the door, but the distance created some relief from it, at least enough so that Violet was able to breathe again.

It wasn't the cat's fault, not really. That was the thing about these unusual echoes that only Violet could sense: they worked the other way around too.

The echo, whatever it happened to be for that individual creature, would also attach to the one responsible for the death—forever marking the killer.

Carl had helped her to figure it all out when she was just a little girl. That was when she'd noticed the correlation between the dead mice and the broken birds that he would leave on their doorstep, each one with a distinct color, or scent, or feeling that only Violet could distinguish, a sensation that had nothing to do with the animal itself.

And Carl would carry that very same imprint on him, as if he'd somehow been *stained* by the killing. The sensory imprint was identical to the echo that was left on the body, and as far as Violet could tell, no two echoes were the same. They were distinct. Unique.

She also knew that animals that hunted—like her cat— could often carry several of these sensory markings, these *death imprints*, at once, which would fade only over time but never really vanish.

Carl had been a lifelong hunter, and while Violet knew that it was just part of his nature, she couldn't help being irritated when the sensations he carried with him were unpleasant for her.

Unfortunately, this time it was especially objectionable.

She wandered restlessly around the house for a while, trying to find a place where the pungent odor couldn't find her, but there seemed to be no safe-zone for her . . . at least not entirely. So she decided it might be a good night to get out of the house after all, even if it was to babysit for her aunt and uncle.

She quickly gathered her things, including her backpack

filled with homework, told her mom she'd grab something to eat at her uncle's house, and all but ran to the relative safety of her car.

Her uncle Stephen, her dad's brother, was the youngest of four boys and was at least eight years younger than either of Violet's parents. He was also the chief of police in their small town and was the polar opposite of her father. Namely, he was funny, at least when he was off duty. When he was working, he was no-nonsense and serious . . . exactly like her dad.

His wife, Violet's aunt Kat, was only in her early thirties, but she was one of those women who had a youthful quality about her that made it hard to pinpoint her age just by looking at her.

"How do I look?" she asked Violet.

"Why are you asking *her*?" Stephen Ambrose complained when his wife ignored that he was standing right beside his niece.

Kat rolled her eyes at him like he was a slow-witted child. "Because all you care about is whether I'm done changing or not. You would say I looked good in a flannel nightgown if it meant we could leave."

He smiled at her. "You *would* look good in a flannel nightgown."

Kat shot Violet an apologetic look. "See what I have to live with?"

"I think you look great," Violet told her aunt and meant

31

it. Then she added, "But lose the necklace, it's a little too much."

Her aunt nodded, as though she'd been thinking the same thing, and pulled the long chain over her head. "See? *That's* why I ask her."

"Good God, woman, we're just going to the movies," he teased her.

"No, no, no. *Dinner* and a movie. This is date night, my friend, and don't you forget it." She poked him in the chest as she spoke. "Besides, I don't get out enough. I want to look good."

Uncle Stephen snaked his arm around his wife's waist and pulled her up against him. "You *do* look good. Are you sure we have to go out?"

Her aunt shook her head and ignored him, giving Violet last-minute instructions for cleaning up after dinner, putting the kids to bed, and emergency contact information, all of which Violet already knew.

"Kathryn Ambrose . . ." her uncle announced, trying to get her attention. "Let's go. She'll be fine."

They left in a flurry of good-bye kisses and "be goods," aimed both at the kids and at their niece. When the door was finally closed, Violet went to where her cousins sat and began cleaning up their dinner mess.

Joshua didn't really make a mess, his plate was tidy, and there were hardly any crumbs to wipe away from his spot at the table. Like Violet's dad, he was neat and meticulous.

It was little Cassidy's high chair that looked like a bomb

had gone off. The two-year-old had ketchup on her hands and her face and even in her hair, and it took Violet about fifteen minutes to clean her up.

At least bedtime was relatively painless.

Cassidy was exhausted, and fell asleep in Violet's arms as she rocked the toddler.

Once it was all over with, Violet flopped down on the couch, grateful for a moment's peace. Until the doorbell rang.

She was torn between wanting to be cautious about who was on the other side of the door and not wanting the noise of the doorbell to wake the sleeping children . . . especially a cranky two-year-old.

"Who is it?" she called out in a loud whisper from the inside.

"It's Jay!" she heard him quietly call back.

She smiled and unbolted the door.

The sight of him standing there made her pulse burst. "What are you doing here?"

He shrugged, coming inside without waiting to be invited. Violet knew that her aunt and uncle wouldn't mind; she and Jay had been kind of a package deal for as long as she could remember. Everyone was used to the two of them being together.

"Your mom told me where you were, so I thought I'd come hang out." He made himself at home, sitting down on the couch where she'd just been. "You don't mind, do you?" he asked, even though he already knew the answer.

She didn't bother replying; she just sat down. She was cold, so she leaned against the side of the couch and shoved her feet beneath his legs, letting his body heat warm them. He surfed through the channels until they found a movie they both agreed on, even though it was already more than halfway over.

This was how it was with the two of them—the effortlessness they had.

She made a bowl of microwave popcorn, and they watched the rest of the movie while they joked around, and while Violet tried to forget how close he was sitting . . . and how warm he was beside her . . . and how good he smelled.

Even before the credits were rolling they were already talking about other things, the movie forgotten. They discussed their new teachers, and what they had heard about them from other students who had gone before them. And they gossiped about rumors going around at school, like who was dating who, and who had broken up over the summer.

Violet was purposely avoiding discussions about all the girls who had suddenly noticed Jay, but he didn't seem to have the same aversion to the topic, and eventually he asked, "So, what about that note from Elisabeth Adams?"

Lissie Adams was the last person Violet wanted to talk about right now, but she couldn't just ignore his comment. This time the teacher wasn't there to cut him off.

"Weird, huh?" And then the question that Violet was almost afraid to ask came tumbling from between her cursedly loose lips. "So, are you gonna call her?"

She tried not to care about the answer, and she concentrated on keeping an indifferent look on her face.

"Nah. I'm not really interested."

Violet was stunned and a little afraid that her mouth might actually be hanging open. "Why? Why wouldn't you want to go out with *Lissie Adams*?" She was amazed that she sounded like she was trying to talk him *into* calling the popular senior, but she couldn't seem to stop herself. She couldn't understand why any boy wouldn't want to date Lissie.

He just shrugged. "I'm just not." And then he asked the question that Violet was most afraid of. "Why do you care if I call her?"

"I don't," she lied. "I'm just surprised. I thought you would've called her already."

"Hey, did you hear about Brad Miller?" he asked, already forgetting about the Lissie conversation. "He got his car taken away for getting another speeding ticket. Of course he tried to tell his parents that it was a setup."

Violet laughed. "Yeah, because the police have nothing better to do than to plan a sting operation targeting eleventh-grade idiots." She was more than willing to go along with this diversion from conversations about Jay and his many admirers.

Jay laughed too, shaking his head. "You're so cold-hearted," he said to Violet, shoving her a little but playing along. "How's he supposed to go cruising for unsuspecting freshmen and sophomores without a car? What willing girl is going to ride on the handlebars of his ten-speed?"

"I don't see you driving anything but your mom's car yet.

35

At least he *has* a bike," she said, turning on him now.

He pushed her again. "Hey!" he tried to defend himself. "I'm still saving! Not all of us are born with a silver spoon in our mouths."

They were both laughing, hard now. The silver spoon joke had been used before, whenever one of them had something the other one didn't.

"Right!" Violet protested. "Have you *seen* my car?" This time she shoved him, and a full-scale war broke out on the couch.

"Poor little rich girl!" Jay accused, grabbing her arm and pulling her down.

She giggled and tried to give him the dreaded "dead leg" by hitting him with her knuckle in the thigh. But he was too strong, and what used to be a fairly even matchup was now more like an annihilation of Violet's side.

"Oh, yeah. Weren't you the one"—she gasped, still giggling and thrashing to break free from his suddenly way-too-strong grip on her, just as his hand was almost at the sensitive spot along the side of her rib cage—"who got to go to Hawaii...." She bucked beneath him, trying to knock him off her. "... For spring break ... last ..." And then he started to tickle her while she was pinned beneath him, and her last word came out in a scream: "... *YEAR?!*"

That was how her aunt and uncle found them.

Violet never heard the key in the dead bolt, or the sound of the door opening up. And Jay was just as ignorant of their arrival as she was. So when they were caught like that, in a mass of tangled limbs, with Jay's face just inches from hers, as she giggled and squirmed against him, it should have meant they were going to get in trouble. And if it had been any other teenage boy and girl, they would have.

But it wasn't another couple. It was Violet and Jay . . . and this was business as usual for the two of them.

Even her aunt and uncle knew that there was no possibility they were doing anything they shouldn't. The only reprimand they got was her aunt shushing them to keep it down before they woke the kids.

After Jay left, Violet took the thirty dollars that her uncle gave her and headed out.

As she drove home, she tried to ignore the feelings of frustration she had about the way her aunt and uncle had reacted—or rather *hadn't* reacted—to finding her and Jay together on the couch. For some reason it made her feel worse to know that even the grown-ups around them didn't think there was a chance they could ever be a real couple.

With her spirits dampened, she hoped that at least her cat wouldn't be around when she got home.

CHAPTER 3

SLEEP WAS HARD TO HOLD ON TO THAT NIGHT, elusive and slippery, evading her at every turn. She was restless, and her dreams were segmented and disquieting.

Swaddled in the darkest part of the night, everything suddenly felt wrong to Violet. She couldn't quite put her finger on what it was that was bothering her, but it was there nonetheless, that unnamed distress, looming over her and making her feel helpless . . . powerless.

She knew that the new and improved Jay was partially responsible for these unwelcome feelings. But that wasn't really it . . . or at least, that was only part of what was troubling her.

Violet wasn't sure exactly what the rest of it was. She woke twice to look around for Carl, assuming he was the cause of her midnight discomfort. She thought that maybe he was too near her, too soon after his kill. But when she looked for him, he was nowhere to be seen.

Finally, at just after six o'clock in the morning, as the sun was rising up through the gloom in an effort to conquer the sky, Violet decided to give up. There was only one thing she could do when she was feeling this way, only one way to clear her tangled thoughts.

She dressed quickly and quietly in shorts and a T-shirt. Despite the fact that the September day promised to be warm, it was still early and there was a damp chill in the air, so, as an afterthought, she also pulled a sweatshirt over her head.

She tiptoed out of the house, passing Carl in the kitchen and noting that the reek coming off him was beginning to fade already.

As she stepped outside, she took a deep breath of the dewy air while she put the earbuds from her iPod into her ears.

And then she jumped down from the porch and started running . . . slowly at first, an even, steady pace. She was acutely aware of the gentle rhythm of her feet pounding up from her soles and she concentrated on the tempo, letting it clear her mind as she synchronized her breathing into measured regularity with her footsteps.

As she reached the end of the road, she took a sudden, sharp left, leaving the blacktop in favor of a gravel trail that appeared between the stands of tall cedar and fir trees. She could feel the crunching of the gravel beneath her sneakers vibrating all the way up the muscles of her legs.

As she entered the clearing, at the top of the pasturelands that stretched out before her, the sight of the mountain against the painted backdrop of the dawn made her draw a deep, appreciative breath.

Violet had been born and raised in Buckley, a little nowhere of a town that sat on a stretch of highway that joined the western and eastern halves of the state. Buckley rested in the shadow of Mount Rainier, in the foothills of the Cascades. She had seen the majestic white peak rising high above the Cascade mountain range more times than she could count, and yet she never tired of the magnificent view. The larger mountain dwarfed the smaller ones that surrounded it, making it look as if it was floating above them. It was like a beacon, even against the most brilliant sky.

What made it even more of an extravagance, something not to be taken for granted, was that the mountain wasn't out every day. Of course, Violet knew that it was always *there*; but in an area where the sun found itself cloaked by cloud cover more often than not, it was even more of a rarity to see Mount Rainier in its entirety, unobstructed by fog or the high clouds that often hung over the mountain from the top down . . . or flat-out obliterated by dense, dark clouds that blocked even the most tenacious light that tried to penetrate them.

She ran in the shadow of the mountain for as long as she could, until the trail she followed veered left again, winding around the rich, verdant pastureland that bordered the gravel pathway.

She was surprised that something so small as witnessing

the mountain at sunrise could make her feel so much better. But it did. Already the foreboding feeling that had been hanging over her was lifting, and she felt clearer, calmer.

She settled into an easy pace, allowing her thoughts to drift away, lost in her music and the steady cadence of her body's movements. She liked the feeling of control she had when she ran, that she was in command of her body, in charge of each muscle's perfectly timed movements. She felt strong as she looked down at her long, ground-eating stride, and felt powerful in at least *this* element of her life.

She passed several weak death echoes as she ran. She'd grown accustomed to these, the ones that didn't compel her—didn't *draw* her—and she was able to ignore them easily enough. She didn't know why these forgotten corpses didn't call out to her in the way that others did; she only knew that they didn't.

Not in the way the girl in the woods had when Violet was eight.

Emilee Marquez had been only fourteen years old when she was abducted on her way home from school. She was murdered before being buried in the soft soil where Violet had found her. The draw to find Emilee had been almost overpowering, something beyond Violet's control.

But why?

Maybe it was because not much time had passed, or maybe it was because of the violence of the girl's death. Or worse, Violet thought, perhaps it was because she was so aware of what was happening to her as she died. Maybe she understood

41

too much, and that memory was forever burned on to her body in the form of an echo.

The girl's killer was never found, but Violet would never forget the sound—the haunting voice—that had called her to the body. Sometimes she had nightmares that she would run into him, the man responsible, at the supermarket or at the mall, carrying the imprint of Emilee's death on him like some unspeakable shadow that he could never escape.

Violet pushed the unsettling thought away.

She slowed only once, when the heavy sweatshirt became too warm for her to wear any longer, and she tugged it over her head, tying it tightly around her waist with its sleeves. But she reached her stride again easily and settled back into her rhythm.

By the time she'd run full circle, reaching her house, her T-shirt was saturated in sweat, and she felt relaxed from head to toe.

It was the car in the driveway, and the man-boy perched on the hood waiting for her, that made her lose some of her newfound tranquillity.

He was grinning at her in a way that made her legs feel like they were made of nothing more solid than gelatin. They might have even quivered from something other than her early-morning run.

"What are you doing here?" she asked as she slowed from a jog to a walk and placed her hands on her hips. It would take her a few minutes to get her breathing back to normal. Longer if he kept smiling at her like that.

He shrugged. "I couldn't sleep. What about you?"

She opted for the obvious and filled her voice with as much sarcasm as she could. "I live here, actually."

"Ha-ha, smart-ass. I was asking if maybe you couldn't sleep too." He shook his head at her wisecrack. "You know, since you were running at six-thirty in the morning? I was gonna see if you wanted to go for a walk or something." He eyed her up and down, looking a little disappointed as he hopped down from the car's hood. "But it looks like you already went without me. That's okay, it was a long shot anyway."

Violet didn't like the way she was suddenly so eager to be near him. Even though they'd been nearly inseparable for the past ten years, it now felt urgent to keep him close.

"All right, let's go."

"Are you sure?" He seemed skeptical. "I don't want to talk you into it."

"No, really, I'm not ready to go inside and start my homework yet anyway." She was already leading the way into the trees that surrounded her house, and he was following right behind.

They walked for a long time like that, with him tagging along in her wake, not saying a word to each other. It was normal for Violet to take charge once they'd entered the cover of the woods; she had done so since they were just little kids. And even though Jay was nearly as familiar out here as she was after all these years, he let her lead anyway, comfortably taking second place to her.

It was already getting warm. The forecasts predicted late-summer temperatures in the low eighties. Violet loved this time of year, relishing the lingering sun before it was cast away by the wintry gloom. Summer generally arrived late in her part of the world, usually waiting until July was well under way before making a regular appearance, so the persisting summerlike temperatures were welcome for as long as they wanted to stick around.

"So, are you going to the lake today?" Jay asked, finally falling into step beside Violet as their pace slowed. They headed nowhere in particular when they hiked like this, exploring places they'd been more times than they could add up, both on, and off, the well-known paths.

Violet shrugged. "Are you?"

She already knew the answer; they both did. Today was the big end-of-summer party at Lake Tapps. Kind of a last blast before the sun disappeared for the year. Pretty much everyone they knew would be there.

Jay shrugged too. "I was thinking about it."

Inwardly she smiled at the prospect of spending one of the few remaining lazy summer days with him at the lake. "Yeah?" she questioned, not needing him to actually ask her along. "Maybe I'll go too."

He grinned, practically beaming at her, and an unfamiliar warmth that had nothing to do with the weather crept through her. "Cool. You can drive," he suggested.

She shook her head. If it had been anyone else, she'd probably feel like she was being used, but instead she loved the exhilarating feeling of having something he didn't have, especially in light of the fact that he suddenly seemed to have *everything* that she wanted. "Fine, then you can buy me gas," she added, raising her eyebrows and daring him to say no.

But the accident happened before Jay had a chance to respond.

And it was all his fault. At least that's how Violet would remember it when she replayed it in her head. If he hadn't been smiling at her like that when she'd looked up at him she would never have lost her concentration . . . or her footing.

But he had been . . . and she did. And when her foot failed to clear the thick, gnarled root that crossed the path in front of her, Violet felt herself careening off balance. She kept moving forward even when her foot did not, and before she knew what was happening she was plummeting toward the ground.

Jay tried to grab her, but it happened so fast.

Her hands hit the ground first, scraping against the compacted dirt, followed just milliseconds later by the sensation of the jagged rocks on the pathway ripping at the tender flesh of her knees.

When she stopped sliding, she wasn't sure whether she was hurt more physically or emotionally.

"Vi? Are you all right?" Jay asked, right beside her now, pulling her off the ground.

Tears burned in her eyes, and it wasn't just from the painful sting radiating up through her hands and knees. Humiliation threatened to overcome the hurt.

Jay hauled her up. She could smell his musky scent in his

sweatshirt, and she tried to hold her breath against it. This was bad . . . this was a bad, *bad* place for her to be.

"Are you hurt?" He pulled her away just enough so he could look down at her.

She bit her lip, trying to will the tears away. She blinked and looked back at him. "I'm okay," she responded, but her voice broke, making her words sound puny, pathetic even.

He cringed as he bent down and looked at the angry red scrapes on both her knees. He reached out to lightly brush away some of the dirt from them, but she knew that he was afraid of hurting her, so he barely touched them. "We'd better get you back so we can clean those up." He straightened, and then surprised her by picking her up as he started to carry her along the trail.

She struggled against him. *"I can walk!"* she protested, feeling even more like a baby as he held her in his arms.

He looked down at her in disbelief. "Are you sure? 'Cause I think I just saw you trying, and it didn't work out so well for you." He didn't seem inclined to let her down just yet; he just kept walking.

She laughed but insisted again through her teary giggles, "Seriously, put me down! I feel stupid enough already—I don't need you treating me like an invalid."

He slowed down unsurely before setting Violet on her own two feet. Internally she cursed herself for being so stubborn, and she wished that he'd put up more of a fight. Why couldn't he have insisted on carrying her all the way home?

Instead, he reached out and grabbed her hand. "If it's all right with you, I think I'll keep ahold of you anyway. I don't want to be responsible for letting you fall again."

She didn't argue.

The walk home went way too quickly for Violet. Jay had led her through the trees and into the clearing behind her house in no time at all.

Her parents had already gone for the day before she and Jay arrived back at her house. Her dad was working, as he did almost every Saturday, even when it wasn't tax season, and her mom had rented out a booth at the farmer's market to display some of her paintings.

Jay insisted on carrying her up the back steps and into the kitchen, and this time Violet didn't complain when he lifted her. He set her down gently on the kitchen counter, and then he rummaged through the cupboard while Violet told him where the Band-Aids were. He came back with bandages, gauze, cotton balls, antibacterial wash, and two tubes of ointment. It seemed like overkill to Violet, but she didn't say anything. She wanted to see what he planned to do.

"Okay, this is probably gonna sting," he warned as he leaned over and began cleaning her wounds.

It *did* sting, more than Violet let on, and she had to bite her lip as the tears came back all over again. But she let him keep working without even flinching, which was no small feat as he stripped away the layers of dirt from her skin.

The wounds were big, and round, and raw. She thought she looked like a little kid with the giant scrapes on her knees, and she imagined that they were going to scab over and possibly even scar. She felt like such an idiot for falling over her own two clumsy feet.

But Jay was gentle, and he took his time, being careful not to hurt her. She admired his patience and took perverse pleasure in his touch. He didn't look up to see how she was doing; he just kept working until he was satisfied that her scrapes were cleaned out. And then he picked up the antibacterial wash and some cotton balls.

Violet sucked in her breath when he brushed the soaked cotton ball against the angry red abrasions. Jay looked up at her but didn't stop dabbing at them. Instead he blew on her knees as he labored over them, just like her mother used to do when Violet was a little girl. She thought it was sweet, and she swore that she was even more attracted to him than ever in that tender moment.

When he finished with the wash, he gingerly patted an antibiotic ointment on her knees before covering them with bandages.

"There," he said, admiring his own handiwork. "Good as new."

Violet glanced at the ridiculously huge Band-Aids on her knees and looked at him doubtfully. "You really think so? 'Good as new'?"

He smiled. "I think I did pretty good. It's not my fault you can't walk."

She narrowed her eyes at him. She wanted to tell him that it *was* his fault, that she would never have tripped if he'd just stayed the same old Jay he'd always been, gangly and childlike. But she knew that she was being irrational. He was bound to grow up eventually; she'd just never imagined that he'd grow up so well. Instead she accused him: "Well, maybe if you hadn't *pushed* me I wouldn't have fallen." She made the out-landish accusation with a completely straight face.

He shook his head. "You'll never be able to prove it. There were no witnesses—it's just your word against mine."

She giggled and hopped down. "Yeah, well, who's gonna believe you over me? Weren't you the one who shoplifted a candy bar from the Safeway?" She limped over to the sink while she taunted him with her words, and she washed the dirt from the minor scrapes on her palms.

"Whatever! I was seven. And I believe *you* were the one who handed it to me and told me to hide it in my sleeve. Technically that makes you the *mastermind* of that little operation, doesn't it?" He came up behind her, and reaching around her, he poured some of the antibacterial wash onto her hands.

She was taken completely off guard by the intimate gesture. She froze as she felt his chest pressing against her back until that was all she could think about for the moment and she temporarily forgot how to speak. She watched as the red scrapes fizzed with white bubbles from the disinfectant. He leaned over her shoulder, setting the bottle down and pulling her hands up toward him. He blew on them too. Violet didn't even notice the sting this time.

And then it was over. He released her hands, and as she stood there, dazed, he handed her a clean towel to dry them on.

When she turned around to face him, she realized that she had been the only one affected by the moment, that his touch had been completely innocent.

He was looking at her like he was waiting for her to say

something, and she was suddenly aware that her mouth was still open. She finally gathered her wits enough to speak again. "Yeah, well, maybe if you hadn't done it right in front of the cashier, we might have gotten away with it. Instead, you got both of us grounded for stealing."

He didn't miss a beat, and he seemed unaware of her temporary lapse. "And some might say that our grounding saved us from a life of crime."

She hung the towel over the oven's door handle. "Maybe it saved *me*, but the jury's still out on you. I always thought you were kind of a bad seed."

He gave her a questioning look. "Seriously, a 'bad seed,' Vi? When did you turn ninety and start saying things like 'bad seed'?"

She pushed him as she walked by, even though he really wasn't in her way. He gave her a playful shove from behind and teased her, "Don't make me trip you again."

Now more than ever, Violet hoped that this crush of hers passed soon, so she could get back to the business of being *just friends*. Otherwise, this was going to be a long—and painful—year.

CHAPTER 4

THE LAKE HOUSE WAS CROWDED WITH TEEN-
agers, and they seemed to be coming *and* going in waves. The
lawn leading down to the water was littered with towels and
blankets, water bottles and pop cans, bags of chips, and kids of
all shapes and sizes basking in the warmth of the summer heat
as they soaked up the last of the season's sun.

The house belonged to the grandmother of Gabrielle
Myers, a friend of theirs from school. Violet didn't even
recognize all of the kids who were there that day, and she
doubted that they all knew Gabrielle or her grandmother,
but instead were tagging along with friends, or friends of
friends, who had invited them to come.

Violet had carefully chosen some long-hanging, loose-fitting basketball shorts to wear over her swimsuit, in hopes of keeping her injuries at least partially hidden. But it didn't take long before one . . . and then two . . . and then at least twenty of her friends had noticed her bandages peeking out from beneath the swishing fabric, and she was forced to recount her morning accident.

Jay loved hearing her tell the story, and every time he heard her talking about it, he would come over so that he could interject, and of course embellish, his role in the events. In his version, he was her champion, practically carrying her from the woods and performing near-miraculous medical feats to save her legs from complete amputation. Violet, and annoyingly every other girl within earshot, couldn't help but giggle while he jokingly sang his own praises.

Violet happened to walk up just in time to hear Jay recounting his version once more to a group of eager admirers.

"Hero? I wouldn't say *hero* . . ." he quipped.

Violet rolled her eyes, turning to Grady Spencer, a friend of theirs from school. "Can you believe him?"

Grady gave her a concerned look. "Seriously, are you okay, Violet? It sounds like it was pretty bad."

Violet was embarrassed that Jay's exaggerations were actually dredging up real sympathy from others. "It's fine," she assured him, and when Grady didn't look convinced, she added, "Really, I just tripped."

She reached out and shoved Jay. "Will you knock it off, *hero*? You're making an ass out of yourself."

Jay laughed and followed her to a spot away from the crowd

on the lawn. But even as they began to settle in, several of the girls who had already spread out their towels and blankets in other places casually began to migrate in their direction. She found that even *she* was getting more attention than usual from his crowd of admirers, and she felt conspicuously like she was being used in their attempts to get closer to him.

But Jay's fans were easy enough to ignore, especially since several of her *real* friends were already there. Violet left Jay among his groupies and headed toward where Chelsea and some of her other friends from school were sunning themselves.

Chelsea scooted over when she saw Violet coming, making room for her on the big, colorful beach towel. "What's up? I heard you practically broke your legs this morning."

Violet sat down next to her friend, who looked like perfection personified in her deep purple bikini, her body well toned from sports. "Ha-ha," Violet mumbled, curling her lip in a mock sneer. "It was nothing." She flashed the tops of her gauze-covered knees from beneath the hem of her shorts. "See? Just a couple of scrapes."

"Well, to hear Lissie and Valerie tell it, Jay practically saved your life." The way Chelsea said the other girls' names reminded Violet that Chelsea didn't care much for the cheerleader crowd. In fact, she didn't try very hard at all to hide the fact that she thought they were vapid and useless.

Violet knew she liked Chelsea for a reason other than her friend's obvious athletic talents.

"Nah, it was just me being clumsy as usual," Violet admitted, smiling.

"Yeah, well, good thing Jay was there to catch you." Chelsea leaned back on her elbows and looked out at the lake. "You gonna take a turn on the Wave Runners today?"

Violet followed Chelsea's gaze and saw one of the brightly painted watercrafts pulling up to the dock. There were actually two Wave Runners, both belonging to Gabrielle's parents, who left them at the house for most of the summer, where they stayed available and were used frequently. Violet loved riding them out into the water and trying to catch the cresting waves that were spit out in the wake of a boat speeding by, while the wind whipped at her hair and face. It was exhilarating.

"Probably later, but I think I'll just kick back for a while. Do you mind if I stay here with you guys?"

"Sure. But it looks like your boyfriend's about to take a spin," Chelsea said in her usual unimpressed voice.

Violet saw what her friend was talking about. Jay was buckling up one of the life jackets and getting ready to take out the Wave Runner that had just returned. She saw a group of girls from another local high school follow him like lost puppies down to the dock. She'd seen them before, at parties she'd been to, and she wasn't surprised that they were at the lake today. *Everyone* seemed to be there.

One of the girls must have gotten up the nerve to ask Jay for a ride, because she too was picking up a life jacket and slipping it over her barely-there bikini. She bounced up and down excitedly as she waited for him to straddle the seat, and then she climbed on behind him, grinning widely and grabbing him tightly around the waist. Violet vaguely recognized the girl, whose name she thought was Savannah. She looked like she'd just won a beauty pageant as she waved at her friends who were still standing on the dock.

Violet tried to ignore the sudden stab of jealousy she felt as she watched the girl wrapping her arms around Jay. She turned away so she didn't have to see the two of them together. "Whatever . . . he's not my boyfriend."

Chelsea just ignored Violet's comment as she eased herself back down and slipped her sunglasses over her eyes. "If you say so."

Violet tried to follow Chelsea's lead, as she stretched out on the towel that was more than big enough for the both of them. She closed her eyes and listened to the sounds around her until she could no longer fight the exhaustion that was clinging to her after a long night of chasing sleep. Soon she began to drift away, and the sounds around her shaped her dreams. She dreamed of music and friends, and of sun and smoke. She dreamed of her best friend's smile, and of waves and beaches.

She was dragged from the haze of sleep by something tickling her arm. She thought that an ant must have crawled onto her, and she tried to shake it off without opening her eyes to look. But when she laid her arm back down across her stomach, she felt it slowly moving from her wrist to her elbow and back again.

She squinted, with one eye still closed, and lifted her head halfheartedly to see what it was. Someone was dragging a piece of grass back and forth along the sensitive hairs of her forearm. She followed the trail from the grass to the hand to the face and saw Jay grinning down at her.

"Hey there," he said, tossing away the grass. "I thought you'd never wake up."

Violet sat up all the way. "How long was I sleeping?"

Jay shook his head. "Not long, less than an hour probably. I wanted to see if you want to go out on one of the Wave Runners with me."

"What about your girlfriends?" As soon as the words were out of her mouth, Violet was embarrassed for sounding so petty. She tried to make it seem like she was only kidding as she added, "I thought maybe Savannah's friends were all waiting for their turn down on the dock."

He just laughed. "No, Savannah was the only one. She wanted me to show her how to drive one." Violet was glad that he hadn't seemed to notice the irritation in her voice before.

"So, did you?"

He shrugged. "I tried to, but I don't think she was really paying attention. I think she just wanted someone to give her a ride."

Not someone, Violet thought to herself. *You. She wanted you to give her a ride.* Sometimes she wondered if he was really that dense, or if he just wasn't interested in returning the girls' attention. But when she saw the clueless look on his face, she realized that it had to be the former. He was such a *guy.*

She looked around her then and realized that she'd been abandoned by her friends while she'd been sleeping. "Where'd Chelsea go?" she asked.

"I saw her taking off on one of the Wave Runners with Jules. So, you wanna go with me?"

Violet was reluctant to take off her shorts in front of every-one and expose her knees like a clumsy little girl, but she *did* want to go out on the Wave Runner with him. She weighed the option of staying where she was, covered up from her hips to her knees in the baggy gym shorts, or cutting a vicious path through the water sitting atop the powerful watercraft in search of a wave to jump.

Her daredevil side won out. "I'll go, but *I* get to drive," she insisted with a grin.

Jay didn't argue. He never did; he was too easygoing to care whether he was the driver or the passenger.

On the dock, Violet self-consciously dropped the shorts, baring her knees and the swimsuit beneath. She looked around to see if anyone was staring, but no one seemed to notice. She plucked up a life vest and buckled herself into it before straddling the Wave Runner's seat. Jay followed right behind and casually gripped her hips as she started the engine and attached the coiled key fob to her life jacket, a safety measure that would cut the engine if the driver was thrown from the vehicle.

She leaned forward and began easing the watercraft through the cove, watching cautiously for other vehicles or for people who might have wandered too far from the water's edge. But once she reached the end of the cove and passed the buoys that signaled the end of the five-mile-an-hour speed limit, she grabbed the handle that controlled the gas and she pulled it, gunning the Wave Runner into high speed. She leaned farther forward and let the wind cool her face. For the first time in weeks, since well before school had started, she was no longer aware of Jay's proximity to her. He became any other passenger on the back of the vehicle as she got lost in the punching accelerations over the short, choppy waves.

They bounced across the top of the water, sometimes jumping high, reveling in those moments when they caught a larger wave and felt the Wave Runner surge beneath them as it hopped above the water, catching air.

Violet felt so free. She could hear Jay laughing from behind her as he held on tight. She spun the craft first sharply to the right and then quickly to the left. He knew she was trying to buck him free, testing him to see how long he could hold on to her before being tossed into the frigid water of the lake as she maneuvered the miniature speedboat back and forth. But he was stronger now than ever before, and his reflexes were sharper. He seemed to know which way she was going to go even before she did.

After a while, Violet slowed down near a floating dock in the lake and parked the Wave Runner.

"Do you want to jump in?" she asked as she pulled the key from the ignition without waiting for an answer, making it more of a statement than a question.

Jay stood up and hopped from the Wave Runner onto the dock. Violet joined him and instead of diving into the water, she sat down and dangled her feet in.

"It's quiet here," he commented absently. He sat down beside her.

"Mm-hmm," she sighed, kicking her feet and splashing up water.

"How are your knees?" He reached out and brushed his

fingers across the damp bandages.

Violet shrugged. "They're fine . . ." and then she added with mock adoration, " . . . thanks to you, of course." And to show her gratitude, she kicked water in his direction.

He nudged her with his shoulder but didn't say anything. They stayed like that for a while, enjoying the silence of being alone and enjoying each other's presence. It was easy . . . and comfortable.

Violet sighed when it started to feel like too much time had passed. "We should get back. I'm sure someone else is waiting for a turn."

Jay stood up, silently agreeing with her, and Violet reluctantly followed. Without asking if he wanted to trade places, Violet again got on in front.

They took their time getting back, meandering lazily along the shoreline and staying out of the way of faster vehicles. It took Violet longer than it should have to realize that the path she was taking wasn't random at all, that she was being pulled . . . drawn.

Something was calling to her.

Something dead.

She didn't say anything to Jay, mostly because there wasn't anything to say yet. Instead she concentrated on where it might be coming from. It was strong, whatever it was, stronger than she would have expected from something out here in the water, and she wondered if that meant it had died recently. Today, even.

She followed the pulling sensation, the tugging that had propelled her almost without her awareness, as she scanned the waters for some sign, some sensory input to guide her.

She didn't taste or smell anything out of place. There were no unexplained sounds coming from any direction . . . at least not that she could hear over the engine of the Wave Runner.

She thought she saw something in the water ahead of her. It looked like a large oil slick licking across the top of the lake's surface. It was near a thick stand of grasses and reeds that sprang up from the waters near the shore. It wasn't completely out of place there, a boat could have leaked the substance into the water, but she eased forward anyway, wanting to get a better look.

Jay didn't ask her what she was doing; he was just happy to be along for the ride, as usual.

But the closer Violet got to it, the less it looked like oil. It had the same greasy sheen as oil, casting a rainbow of hues across the plane of the water as it was rippled gently by the waves. But there was something different about it, something she couldn't quite put her finger on.

Until she was practically right on top of it.

She was careful not to catch the weedy plant life in the Wave Runner's engine, and she leaned over the edge as she slowed down to make sure she didn't take the craft into the too-shallow water.

She *needed* to see what was there.

"What are you looking at?" Jay finally asked with only a little interest. He was used to Violet's wandering ways.

"I don't know" was all she answered, too caught up in her curiosity to attempt any more of an explanation than that.

Violet stood up on the watercraft as she came to a stop. Multihued light seemed to be radiating up from beneath the water, centered among the reeds, and then diffusing outward as it reached the surface. Violet had never seen anything like it, and she knew that the spectrum of light was defying its very nature by behaving in that way.

It could only be one thing.

There was something dead down there.

Her first thought was a duck or maybe even a large fish that had drifted into the cluster of grasses. The vibrant light continued to play off the waves from below, fading into a fine, colorful mist as it broke through the surface of the water and then vanished into the air. Violet strained to see through the plant life, as it grew thicker where it reached toward the water's edge.

She thought she saw something bobbing in between the weedy greens, but she couldn't be sure, so she hopped off and waded toward it. She felt a sharp twinge of fear, but still couldn't stop herself from moving forward.

"What is it, Vi?" Jay asked, and now his interest seemed genuine, concerned even. "Come back here. *I'll* see what it is."

But it was too late. Violet had already seen it. And she was in the water, wading toward whatever was hiding among the reeds along the lakeshore.

Thick, pale, and bloated skin surrounded milky-white eyes that stared out at Violet. A deathly echo created a halo of watery light as long hair radiated in tangled waves from the girl's head.

Violet screamed at the same time that Jay reached her and saw what she was looking at. He wrapped his arms around her from behind and dragged her away in search of help.

CHAPTER 5

HELP ARRIVED FIRST IN THE FORM OF THE
Bonney Lake Police Department and East Pierce Fire and
Rescue, the first responders in this part of the lake.

Violet was wrapped in itchy wool blankets and perched in
the back of the big red ambulance with an emesis basin hovering on the tops of her knees. She had puked twice since Jay had
dragged her away from the watery grave she'd discovered. She'd
never been bothered this way by any of the animals she found,
but somehow the image of the dead girl, lying lifelessly beneath
the water's surface, made her feel sick. It wasn't until the immediate shock had worn off that her stomach finally settled down.
The bowl she now held was just a precaution.

Besides, there were other distractions to take her mind off her weak stomach.

Being in the presence of so many men—and women—who carried guns for a living was a little disturbing for Violet. Not because she was afraid of them, but because in general, those who carried weapons had a higher probability of using them. And those who used them had a greater potential for bearing the imprints of death on them.

Innocent people carried imprints too.

Hunters, occasionally. War veterans, possibly. Police officers, certainly . . . maybe not all, but definitely some.

The ones she could sense at the moment, aside from the obvious echo from the girl in the water, were faded and bland, but in general, this was the kind of scene Violet would avoid whenever possible.

Unless, like now, she was the one who had discovered the body.

Her uncle Stephen had been called, at Jay's request, and even though his jurisdiction was almost a half hour away, he'd arrived in less than fifteen minutes. Violet wondered how many stoplights he'd blown through, with his sirens blaring, to get to her so fast.

She didn't ask, because she didn't care. She was just so grateful that he was there. She had felt immediately better when she saw him rushing toward her, and she'd let him wrap her in a bear hug like when she was a child. Having him there made her feel safe.

When he finally released her so she could breathe

again, he slipped an arm loosely, but protectively, around her shoulders. "Geez, Vi, sucks to be you sometimes, doesn't it?" He squeezed her once again, quickly, and then added more seriously, "I'm really sorry you had to see that."

Violet shrugged.

Her uncle seemed to understand that she didn't want to talk about it. "I think they're almost finished taking Jay's statement. I'll stay with you while they talk to you, okay? I promise I won't leave you alone."

Her parents arrived separately since her dad had come straight from work. They were both stressed and worried, and they too buried her in embraces, and whispered gentle reassurances, as she endured recounting the events several times to several different people from several different agencies.

She and Jay had each given the details that led up to, and included, finding a corpse floating in the shallow waters of the lake, cradled in the willowy grasses. Although in Jay's recounting there were no lies to tell, no stories to fabricate. Violet wished that her account could have been so simple.

But it wasn't.

Coincidence. Chance. These were the words she counted on to create a veil of deceit, to keep her "gift" a secret.

She must have been convincing enough, though, because she could see the sympathy in the eyes of everyone who heard her story. Sincere looks that conveyed compassion directed at the poor girl who had stumbled upon such a horrific scene.

Her uncle Stephen's presence was reassuring to her on many levels, and eventually, maybe sooner than was usual, she was released to her family. He also took responsibility for getting Jay home, since Jay's mother, the only woman in the known universe who didn't own a cell phone, couldn't be reached.

Violet rode with her dad, but Stephen insisted on taking Jay with him. Jay didn't complain as he climbed into the front of the police cruiser, asking if he could turn on the siren.

He was like an eager five-year-old. It was kind of childish. But also really adorable.

Violet was glad for the relative calm that riding with her dad afforded her. He was a still sort of man, and sometimes just being within arm's reach of him could soothe her most frayed nerves. Besides, unlike her mom, who was a little New Agey and was always encouraging Violet to "share" her feelings, her dad wouldn't press her for information before she was ready. He would wait her out, listening silently when she *did* decide the time was right.

Violet leaned her head back and tried to absorb some of her father's tranquillity.

After a time, though, she couldn't not speak. "There was a light," she explained. Her voice sounded strange, as if it were echoing up from a long, vacant tunnel. She cleared her throat and tried again. "I saw a rainbow of lights coming up from below the water."

He knew, of course. Not about the light, but that she had in some way been called by the girl's lifeless body.

Her dad was quiet in his usual way. He was serious, stable, solid. As always, he was Violet's rock.

"I didn't say anything about it to Jay. I just followed it, so I could get a better look. Jay didn't even realize what I was looking for until it was too late." She kept her eyes closed as the car drifted over the familiar highway toward home.

Her dad reached over and squeezed her knee. That was all it took.

The tears finally came, crushing the breath from her with a surprising intensity. Her dad didn't say anything, but she felt the car pulling off the road, and then he hauled her close to him. She cried like that, leaning against him inside of the parked car, for what seemed like hours but was probably only minutes. She didn't care that they were parked along a busy highway, or that she was clinging to him like she was a child. She let herself sob, crying for herself and crying too for the girl in the water, and for whomever that girl had left behind in the wake of her tragic death.

It bothered her to know that the girl had been murdered. That she, and Jay, and her father, and her uncle all *knew*, based on the echo that Violet had discovered, but that they couldn't tell anyone. She was sure the police would figure it out, that they would find evidence to support that fact, but still, she hated *knowing* for certain. She hated lying about it, and forcing others—those she cared about most—to keep her secrets.

She held on to her father, even when the tears were nearly gone. She felt safe in his arms. "I don't want to be able to do that anymore," she mumbled hoarsely into his damp shirt. "I don't mind the animals, I can't explain why, I just don't. But why did I have to see . . . *that* . . . *her*?" She whispered the last word so softly that she wasn't even sure he'd heard it.

He patted her back, and when he finally spoke Violet jumped a little. Every muscle fiber in her body felt bundled and tight.

"I'm sorry, baby," Greg Ambrose said, his voice sounding strained. "I would do anything in the world to protect you from seeing things like that, your mother and I both. We never wanted you to go through anything like this again." He pulled her away from him so that he could look at her. His eyes were red.

"When you were little, we were worried when you first started finding dead animals in the woods. That was when we knew you'd inherited Grandma Louise's special *skill*. We were afraid of what that would do to you, how it would make you feel to be drawn to so much death. We knew there was nothing we could do to *stop* you from sensing them there, but we used to try to discourage you from digging them up—we would try to distract you with diversions and bribes. We offered you gum and candy; we would even ask if you wanted to go for ice cream instead of digging up one of those animals. You were so little, but even then you were determined . . . you were *so* stubborn. And you would go out of your way to get to them, not satisfied until they'd had a proper burial. It seemed to give you a sense of . . . *serenity*, I guess, to know that they were taken care of. You even used to make up funny stories about those poor little lost creatures of yours. Remember Bob, the squirrel banker who forgot to pay his electric bill so he froze to death?" He laughed and wiped her cheek with his thumb. "I was always afraid we were going to get a call from the school psychologist. But your teachers just thought you were *creative*."

What Violet remembered was that her dad was the one who helped her when the local animals—dogs mostly—discovered the shallow graves of her cemetery and began to dig up the little bodies. He was the one who taught her to dig deeper and to cover the graves with heavy stones to prevent the scavengers from getting through to the animals buried below.

And when the dogs remained persistent, he even helped her build a small fence from chicken wire.

"When you found that girl, the one in the woods, I thought it would be your undoing. Your mom and I worried that it was too much for such a little girl to deal with. But you did it. You cried at first, and you even had some nightmares, but you didn't fall apart. And as soon as that poor girl was buried, safe and sound in her own proper resting place, you seemed to just"—he shrugged—"*move on*."

He lifted her chin with his finger. "You'll do it again. I know you, Violet. You *will* be okay. *Better* than okay. Trust me." He smiled at her then.

Violet tried to smile back, but she still felt miserable. She couldn't explain it entirely, but it *was* similar to the way she would feel before she'd buried one of her animals—she felt restless and unsettled. Only this was worse . . . much, *much* worse. She felt like she was buried beneath a stiflingly heavy cloak of darkness that was suffocating her, and she desperately needed to claw her way out from underneath it. She didn't share her dad's optimism. To her it felt like she might never break free. But somehow, even if she didn't entirely buy into it, it made her feel better just to hear him saying the words. *She would be okay.*

"We should get home," she reminded him, suddenly wanting to shift the focus away from her. "Mom's probably getting pissed that we're taking so long."

"Yep, I'm sure I'm going to get an earful about it." He patted her leg and then started the car.

Violet couldn't shake the melancholy feelings that clung to her, infiltrating every pore of her body. She leaned back and closed her eyes, wondering if the nightmares from her childhood were about to return, to haunt her sleep once more.

WATCHING

THE CHAOS OF THE SCENE WAS DELICIOUS. IT created the perfect amount of disorder so that he was completely hidden amid the confusion. Undetectable.

Just the way he liked it.

He loved the hunt; it was what kept him going. But this . . . this was his guilty pleasure.

Watching his work—the aftermath of a kill—exposed to the world.

Of course he'd known it would be. Eventually anyway.

After all, it was a water dump . . . in a busy lake. Somebody was bound to come across it sooner or later. The only surprise was how quickly she was found.

But it was hot today, and people had flocked to the lake in droves. So not such a surprise really.

It was okay, though. It was a clean drop. He'd made sure of that. As usual, he'd been careful. No witnesses, no evidence, nothing to tie it back to him.

Spotless.

Police and fire crews worked in unison to keep the scene contained as they dredged the waters and searched the shores.

He watched as onlookers pushed and shoved, trying to get a better view of what was happening along the water's edge. He liked their energy, their insatiable craving for the gory details, no matter how gruesome or unsettling they might be.

And right now, they were ravenous.

He stood as close as he could, listening to them, reveling in that need.

They were talking about his work, about what he'd done, never realizing that he was standing among them.

It excited him. He felt powerful. Alive.

He knew he was taking a chance. He wasn't supposed to be here. He'd already caught fleeting glimpses of people who knew him, who could, given the chance, identify him. He was glad he was hidden beneath a hat and sunglasses, and he was careful to stay near others in the crowd who were similar to him in size so he wouldn't stand out too much. And in a crowd this large, they came in all sizes.

He let his mind wander as he surveyed those around him, pressed against him. It wasn't hard to find girls he liked, girls he could use. In their skimpy bikinis and ultra-short shorts, revealing smooth expanses of unblemished skin, they were particularly delectable to him. Perhaps *someday he would see them again, in another place, at another time.*

But he knew he couldn't stay. The longer he waited, the greater his chance of being discovered, especially in a setting like this.

He ducked his head low and eased his way toward the back of the people straining to get closer. Behind the dark lenses, his eyes darted in every direction, absorbing as much of the scene as he possibly could, so that later, when he was alone with his thoughts, he would be able to recollect each aspect. Each dirty little detail.

Today was a good day.

He had seen enough to hold him. For now.

CHAPTER 6

THAT DAY, THE ONE AT THE LAKE, WAS LIKE THE last day of summer . . . not just for Violet, but for everyone. And even though the calendar didn't support that argument, the weather cooperated, ignoring the forecasts that had predicted summerlike temperatures, and turning sad and dreary by the following day.

Violet struggled to get through that first twenty-four-hour period. She continued to feel smothered, first by the darkness of night, and then by the oppressive gloom of that endless Sunday. She kept mostly to herself, staying in her room as much as possible, only half listening to the music coming from her headphones, and only half sleeping when exhaustion overcame her.

Jay called several times, and as much as she wanted to hear his voice, she avoided his calls. She felt like she owed him an apology for what she had forced him to witness, but she wasn't sure what she could possibly say to him to make it better.

She felt like she was sleepwalking through those first painful hours.

The second night came, and sleep finally defeated her. She'd tried to avoid it, spending countless hours laying in bed and playing the what-if game over and over in her head. *What if she had never seen those haunting colors echoing up from the water? What if she had chosen not to explore them further?* Or best of all, *what if she had just been normal, going through life in ignorance . . . blissfully unaware of the dead?* She was exhausted from her own self-deprecation and inner turmoil.

But just like when she was eight, when sleep finally claimed her, it came at a cost. Nightmares of the dead girl drifted through the waves of her subconscious. Pale, lifeless eyes watched her closely whenever she closed her own. And no matter how shocking the images were, she couldn't avoid them as sleep reclaimed her, again and again, until the dawn.

She went back to school too soon, but didn't realize it until it was too late.

That Monday, as she ventured out, she thought the diversion would be good for her. Jay was relieved to see her, and even though Violet was still unable to ask for his forgiveness, his presence made her feel better . . . almost alive again.

74

He reached out to her and held her cold hand as they walked to class together. At any other time that simple gesture would have caused her heart to skip beats, but at the moment, it simply reminded Violet that she was still awake.

What she hadn't bargained for was that what had happened over the weekend, at the lake, hadn't happened only to her, or to the two of them. It was as if it had happened to the entire school. And every student who could get close enough wanted to talk about the events.... They wanted her to relive it for them, over and over again.

How did Violet see her, the dead girl?

Did she recognize her?

What was it like seeing a dead body?

Did she think the girl had drowned? Was there blood? Did she see bruises?

Was she missing body parts?

The questions were endless.

Those who really knew Violet, her friends, were more sensitive but no less chatty on the topic. And their questions, for some reason, bothered Violet more than the predictably grim curiosity of the others. They were too personal.

Was Violet all right? Did she want to talk about it? Did her uncle say if they knew who the girl was?

She felt like concern for her was being paraded around like an exhibition, and even when she tried to change the subject, which she did as often as she could, they always managed to bring it back around to the topic they really wanted to discuss: the dead girl in the water.

Jay was the only one who understood her, the only one who seemed to know that she wasn't ready for this yet. He stayed as close to her as he could throughout the day, and even though Violet thought that *she* should be trying to offer some sort of comfort to him, she doubted that she could have brought herself out of her own well of self-pity long enough to try. He didn't seem to mind, though. He didn't appear to be damaged the way she was.

At home, her parents were patient. They listened when she talked, and she *did* talk to them, but when she was finished they would leave her alone again. It was a cautious dance as they took great care to stay out of her way, and she wondered if they thought she were fragile or breakable. Instead of being grateful for the space they gave her, she felt annoyed that they considered her so weak.

Her uncle Stephen made regular appearances during that first week too, checking in on her and dropping off cookies that her aunt Kat had baked, the real homemade kind that didn't come in a roll from the refrigerated section at the grocery store. Violet tried but couldn't seem to find it in herself to appreciate the effort her aunt had made.

And then, almost simultaneously, two things happened that changed everything.

Just one week after Violet found the body in the lake, another dead girl was discovered.

It was *exactly* one week to the day.

Then, on the following day, and two cities away, on a Sunday afternoon, the girl from the lake—Carys Kneer—was buried by her family . . . laid to rest in proper fashion.

Once and for all.

And despite the fact that another body had just been found, Violet was suddenly at peace with the world again. She seemed to abruptly wake from the haze that had claimed her.

And she stayed that way. . . .

Until the next girl vanished.

CHAPTER 7

BY MONDAY, EVERYONE AT SCHOOL HAD HEARD about the discovery of a second body. The news was bigger this time, not just because another girl was dead, or because she'd been found so close to home. It was bigger news because of *who* the girl was.

Brooke Johnson might not have attended White River High School, but she *had* been a student in the next closest town. And as happens with kids in small towns, their social circles had overlapped: they attended the same parties, dated the same boys, and hung out in the same places. Brooke had been popular, which didn't necessarily translate into being well liked, but which definitely made her more important

78

on the gossip ladder. Violet hadn't known Brooke personally, but she knew who Brooke was, in the same way that kids from Brooke's school would know who Lissie Adams was.

The other thing that made Brooke's death more newsworthy was that it established a pattern . . . at least in the eyes of the community at large.

They knew now what Violet had known all along: that the girl in the lake had been murdered before being dumped in the water. And despite the fact that the authorities could neither confirm nor deny a connection between the two bodies, locally, no one really doubted it. Two girls abducted, and then subsequently murdered and discarded so close to each other, in such a short period of time, hardly seemed like a coincidence.

If it walks like a duck, seemed to be the sentiment regarding the assumed correlation, and people were reacting accordingly.

Grief counselors had been made available at several area schools, including White River in Buckley. There were assemblies and after-school classes scheduled about personal safety, stranger danger, and self-defense. Suddenly every girl in school was preoccupied with concerns over her own well-being. And despite the fact that they were not actually *permitted* under the school's "no-tolerance" environment, tiny cans of pepper spray became something of a staple—like lip gloss and tampons—in nearly every purse in school.

But by the middle of the week, conversations began to feel more normal again, and while safety was still a real issue, even Brooke Johnson's death was eventually eclipsed by the trivial quest for lighthearted rumors to cut through the gloom.

Jay, on the other hand, was neither eclipsed nor forgotten. And as the last days of summer drifted toward fall, the number of lovesick girls trailing behind him on any given day seemed to multiply.

While she'd been locked in the grip of her own troubles, Violet had temporarily forgotten to be jealous of those other girls and had finally remembered how to just be Jay's friend again. During those days before the girl from the lake was finally buried in her hometown, Jay had been the one who kept Violet sane. He slipped candy bars into her backpack for her to find and left little notes in her locker just to let her know he was thinking about her. She leaned on him every step of the way, and he never once complained. And afterward, when she felt back to her old self again, at least mostly anyway, he was still there.

She wondered what she'd done to deserve a friend like him, someone who never wavered and never questioned. Someone who was always *there* . . . being supportive, and funny, and thoughtful.

Violet stood in the hallway and watched him. He was digging through his locker looking for his math book, and even though she knew it wasn't there, Violet just let him search, smiling to herself. Crumpled wads of paper fell out onto the floor at his feet.

He seemed to sense that she was staring and he looked back at her. "What?" he asked.

"Nothing," she responded, the smile finding her lips.

He narrowed his eyes, realizing that he was the butt of some private joke. *"What?"*

She sighed and kicked a toe at his backpack, which was lying crookedly against the wall of lockers. "Your book's in your bag, dumbass," she announced as she turned away and started walking toward class.

She heard him groan, followed by the sound of his locker slamming, before he finally caught up with her.

"Why didn't you say anything? Sometimes you really piss me off."

It was easy to ignore the harsh words when his tone was anything but scolding.

She shrugged. "It's fun to watch you scramble."

"Yeah, *fun*. That's what I was thinking."

Grady Spencer fell into step beside Jay.

Grady had started out as one of Jay's friends but had quickly become Violet's too. When they were younger, in fourth grade, she'd had a crush on Grady, passing him notes in school that asked him whether he "liked" her too. One even had boxes to check "yes" or "no." He'd picked yes, and they were officially boyfriend and girlfriend for the rest of the year, which only meant that she chased him at recess, and he pretended he didn't want her to.

Later, after the first day of fifth grade, she'd cried when she'd realized that they wouldn't be in the same classroom that year. And that had pretty much been the end of that particular childhood crush. He had moved on to Miranda Grant, a new girl in his class, and Violet fell in love with her fifth-grade teacher, Mr. Strozyk.

"What's up?" Jay asked Grady.

It was funny to see Grady now, because, like Jay, he'd grown nearly six inches since the last school year, and now he towered over her. Half of the boys in her class had suddenly sprouted and developed into men; the other half were still lingering in boyhood. The girls had been waiting for the boys to catch up for a couple of years, and those who had were considered fair game. It was like open season at White River High School.

"Not much, man," Grady answered in a deeper voice than she remembered. "You guys going to the game on Friday?"

"'Course. Right, Vi?" Jay said, pretty much answering for her.

"Sure." She shrugged.

She didn't mind; she knew they were going. It was autumn, which meant football season. And home games were practically a religion in her town.

They got to the classroom she and Jay shared this period, but it wasn't Grady's class. Instead of walking on, Grady paused.

"Violet, can I talk to you for a minute?" His deep voice surprised her again.

"Yeah, okay," Violet agreed, curious about what he might have to say to her.

Jay stopped and waited too, but when Grady didn't say anything, it became clear that he'd meant he wanted to talk to her . . . *alone*.

Jay suddenly seemed uncomfortable and tried to excuse himself as casually as he could. "I'll see you inside," he finally said to Violet.

She nodded to him as he left.

Violet was a little worried that the bell was going to ring

and she'd be tardy again, but her curiosity had kicked up a notch when she realized that Grady didn't want Jay to hear what he had to say, and that far outweighed her concern for late slips.

When they were alone, and Grady didn't start talking right away, Violet prompted him. "What's going on?"

She watched him swallow, and his Adam's apple bobbed up and down along the length of his throat. It was strange to see her old guy friends in this new light. He'd always been a good-looking kid, but now he looked like a man . . . even though he still acted like a boy. He shifted back and forth, and if she had taken the time to think about it, she would have realized that he was nervous.

But she misread his discomfort altogether. She thought that, like her, he was worried about being late. "Do you want to talk after school? I could meet you in the parking lot."

"No. No. Now's good." He ran his hand through his hair in a discouraged gesture. He took a deep breath, but his voice was still shaking when he spoke. "I . . . I was wondering . . ." He looked Violet right in the eye now, and suddenly she felt very nervous about where this might be going. She was desperately wishing she hadn't let Jay leave her here alone. "I was wondering if you're planning to go to Homecoming," Grady finally blurted out.

She stood there, looking at him, feeling trapped by the question and not sure what she was going to say.

The bell rang, and both of them jumped.

Violet was grateful for the excuse, and she clung to it like a life preserver. Her eyes were wide, and she pointed to the door behind her. "I gotta . . . can we . . ." She pointed again, and she knew she looked and sounded like an idiot, incapable of coherent speech. "Can we talk after school?"

Grady seemed relieved to have been let off the hook for the moment. "Sure. Yeah. I'll talk to you after school."

He left without saying good-bye, and Violet, thankful herself, tried to slip into her classroom unnoticed.

But she had no such luck. The teacher marked her tardy, and everyone in class watched as she made her way to her seat beside Jay's. Her face felt flushed and hot.

"What was *that* all about?" Jay asked in a loud whisper.

She still felt like her head was reeling. She had no idea what she was going to say to Grady when school was out. "I think Grady just asked me to Homecoming," she announced to Jay.

He looked at her suspiciously. "The game?"

Violet cocked her head to the side and gave him a look that told him to be serious.

"No, I'm pretty sure he meant the dance," Violet clarified, exasperated by the obtuse question.

Jay frowned at her. "What did you say?"

"I didn't say anything. The bell rang and I told him we'd have to talk later."

The teacher glanced their way, and they pretended *not* to be talking to each other. Violet decided that she didn't need to get in trouble for not listening, especially after being marked late, so she made an effort to pay attention to the lecture. It was nearly impossible to concentrate, though.

She had thought about going to the dance even before

Grady had asked her, and she'd hoped, probably in vain, that Jay might ask her to go with him, even if it meant they only went as friends. She would rather spend an evening in his company, even innocently, than in anyone else's. But now that she'd been asked by Grady, she had to at least consider the possibility of going with him. Why not? She and Grady had been friends for almost as long as she and Jay had been, and as long as he understood that was all they *would* be, it might be fun to go with someone else.

When class was over, Violet practically had to run to keep up with Jay, who had left the classroom so fast she barely had time to put her books away. She hurried after him, frustrated that he was making her chase him.

By the time she caught up to him, Violet didn't bother to hide her annoyance. "Why are you in such a hurry?"

He started to say something, and then he seemed to change his mind. "No hurry. I just don't want you to make me late too."

Violet shook her head as she watched Jay disappear into the crowd, irritated that he'd left her feeling like she'd done something wrong. Between Grady and Jay, she was more than a little confused about guys in general.

When school was out, Violet wondered if Jay would still want a ride home. He'd spent the entire day snubbing her. That's what it felt like anyway. He even ate his lunch with some of his guy friends instead of sitting with her and Chelsea. She thought about leaving him at school without waiting to find out what was up with him, but she wasn't quite mad enough to be that bitchy. So instead, she waited in her car for nearly twenty minutes.

When she heard the tapping on the passenger-side window, she looked up, expecting to see Jay standing outside, waiting for her to unlock the car's doors and let him in.

But it wasn't Jay. It was Grady Spencer, and suddenly Violet wished that she hadn't waited, that she'd followed her first malicious thought and left Jay behind altogether.

She rolled down the window, trying not to look horrified by the prospect of talking to Grady. "Um, hey there," she said as cheerfully as she could. "What's up?"

"You're not waiting for Jay, are you?" Grady asked, surprising her with his question.

"Sort of." She cringed, suddenly feeling foolish for sitting in her car for so long. "Why?"

Grady looked embarrassed to be the one to tell her, and he hesitated before blurting it out. "Jay got a ride with Lissie Adams and a couple of her friends."

Violet wouldn't have been more surprised if Grady had just slapped her across the face, and the sting of his news was just as vicious. She sat there for a stunned moment, completely dazed and unsure of what she should say or what she should do.

And then a jealous, bitterly hot anger flashed through her, and she wasn't sure which was worse . . . that Jay had gone home without even telling her why he was avoiding her . . . or that he'd gone home with Lissie Adams.

It didn't really matter, though, because suddenly she wasn't just annoyed with him . . . *she was furious.*

She was also acutely aware that Grady was still anxiously watching her, and she didn't want him to see how upset she was, so she shoved her hands beneath her legs so he couldn't see them shaking. She took a breath before rolling her eyes and saying, "It would have been nice if he'd said something to me." Somehow she managed to say it in a voice that sounded teasing and light, even though she was filled with angry frustration.

Grady was visibly relieved, and that seemed to give him the courage he needed to do what he'd come there for. "So, I was wondering if you'd thought about the dance at all."

Violet looked at his hopeful face. He was smiling at her as he leaned down and peered at her through the passenger window. It was just a dance, just one night, and it was a chance to dress up and hang out with someone she genuinely liked.

And then she thought of Jay, and bitter resentment washed over her.

She smiled back at Grady's handsome face, making her choice right then and there. "Yeah," she said, feeling unexpectedly decisive about her last-minute decision. "I'd love to go to Homecoming with you, Grady. In fact, there's no one else I'd rather go with."

Grady grinned back at her. "Cool. I'll give you a call, and we can figure out the details later."

As she pulled out of the parking lot, thirty-three minutes after school had let out, she waved at Grady, who looked like he'd just won the lottery and needed to find someone he could gloat to.

He waved back at her, but she never even saw him. She was already lost in her own thoughts, trying to figure out why Jay had blown her off so unexpectedly.

CHAPTER 8

VIOLET SPENT THE REST OF THE AFTERNOON brooding . . . getting angrier and angrier, and feeling worse and worse. She'd hoped that her homework might provide some sort of diversion, occupying her thoughts with something other than being annoyed with Jay.

But there hadn't been enough homework for her to do, there probably wasn't enough homework in the world, to distract her for very long. She thought about Jay while she was doing her trig assignment, she thought about him while she wrote her English paper, and she even thought about him when she was reading about the Lewis and Clark expedition. And not a single one of the thoughts she'd had was very pleasant at all.

Violet knew that her parents were concerned about her from the way they kept asking if she was feeling okay, or if everything was all right at school, casually trying to coax her problems out of her. She felt a little guilty that she didn't want to talk about it, especially after all the worry she'd put them through when she'd discovered the dead girl in Lake Tapps. But she couldn't help it, and as soon as she finished dinner, which consisted of a delivery pizza and a bag of prepackaged Caesar salad, she hurried up to her room where she could be alone.

She turned on the stereo and tried to finish her math homework. But instead, she ended up doodling along the edges of her paper and replaying the day's events through her head. She wished again that she had just left after school let out, without waiting there like an idiot for Jay.

And now, with a little distance from the moment, she also wished that she hadn't agreed to go to Homecoming with Grady. She wouldn't have done it if she hadn't been so angry with Jay, so somehow even *that* became his fault.

She was sprawled across her bed on her stomach, trying to concentrate on the next equation, when she heard her mom knocking on the door. She tried to pretend she didn't hear it. She just wasn't up for a lecture about how holding her feelings inside wasn't healthy and would block her chakras. But her mom didn't give up easily and she knocked again . . . louder this time.

Violet pressed her forehead against her palms, trying to ward off the headache that was starting to pound behind her eyes, probably from her backed-up chakras, and she sighed her answer, half hoping it wouldn't be heard. "Come in."

She listened as the door opened, but she just couldn't bring herself to look up. She didn't have the energy to have this conversation right now, so she decided to lie to her mom. "I have a lot of homework," she said before her mom could ask her what was wrong again. "I'm fine. *Really.* And I need to get this done."

When her mom didn't say anything right away, Violet felt hopeful that maybe she'd bought it and had decided to leave her alone after all. She waited to hear the sound of the door closing again. Instead she heard Jay's voice.

"Really . . . you're fine? Because I'm not."

Violet looked up in surprise. Jay was the last person she'd expected to find in her room tonight.

He gave her an apologetic smile when she didn't say anything right away. "You're not gonna kick me out, are you?"

Violet wasn't sure how she should react. She really *wanted* to stay mad at him; it was easier than admitting, even to herself, that her feelings had been hurt today. But, somehow, seeing him standing there—in person—took some of the wind out of her sails. She suddenly wished she could read his thoughts.

She shrugged, trying to keep her fragile hold on her already disintegrating anger. "No" was all she said, still waiting to see why he'd come. She sat up, watching him cautiously.

He sat down on the edge of her bed, and she felt herself shifting toward him as her mattress sank beneath his weight.

"Look, Violet, I'm really sorry about today. I shouldn't have left without you. *You* didn't do anything."

When she looked at him, listening to his explanation, she felt her heart foolishly clamoring inside her chest.

He paused, and then continued. "It's not like I'm mad that you're going to the dance. I was *hoping* you'd go to the dance." He grimaced, and Violet thought he seemed to be choosing his words carefully, and she wondered what it was that he *wasn't* saying. He let out his breath and admitted, "I guess I just didn't expect it to be with Grady."

So this was about Grady? She opened her mouth and started to say something, to tell him that she hadn't planned on telling Grady yes, but before she could interrupt him, he plunged on. "I know . . . it's stupid, and it's really none of my business, and we've all been friends for so long, and . . . and I don't know, Violet . . . I guess I didn't want the fact that you two are going on a date to mess things up."

Violet could no longer hold on to her frustration; now she was struggling with unspoken regret for not being able to tell him how she really felt about him. But he kept talking. "I realize that I had no right to get pissed off about it, though, and I acted like a total baby by leaving school today without telling you. I guess I just didn't want to run into the two of you since you said you were meeting him after school."

She picked at a piece of fuzz on her blanket. Violet wished now, more than ever, that she'd told Grady no.

"It's okay, I guess. But it's not like Grady and I are dating or anything. It's just a dance—*one night*—it doesn't mean *anything*. I promise it's not going to ruin friendships. Especially not *ours*."

"I know. I don't know why I got so bent about it. For some reason it just caught me off guard and I acted like a total jackass. I'm really sorry, Violet." The sweet sincerity of his voice caressed her.

She grinned at him. "Yeah, I know, you said that already." She nudged him with her sock-clad foot. "I forgive you . . . you know, for being such a *jackass*."

He grabbed her foot and yanked it until she was lying on her back. She giggled, feeling better already just knowing she didn't have to spend any more time being angry with him.

But she also decided that this was as good a time as any for her to say something she'd been meaning to tell him for a while now . . . something that she hadn't been able to bring herself to say before.

"Hey," she said seriously, "since we're apologizing tonight, I want to say something too."

He flopped down on the bed, lying right beside her. She waited for the sense of calm that his nearness usually brought to her, but it never came. She wasn't exactly sure what she was so nervous about, but somehow lying here, with his face only a breath away from hers, she was more uncomfortable than ever, and her uneasiness, and quite possibly the heat of his body against hers, made her hesitate.

Once again, Jay seemed to be reading her mind, and Violet wondered if she were really that transparent. She hoped he couldn't read *everything* that was going on up there.

"Go ahead, Vi. You can say anything to me." His lazy half-smile was mesmerizing, and she found herself staring at his lips for too long. "Anything," he reassured her gently, and she wondered what those lips would feel like against her own.

It was now or never, she thought wryly, and she blinked to break his mind-numbing spell over her. "I . . . I'm really sorry . . . about that day at the lake. I didn't mean to make you see that. . . ." Now that she was in the middle of it, the words seemed even harder to find, and she wasn't sure just how to say what she was trying to say. Inside her head she always sounded so confident and sure of herself, but somehow when the words reached her lips they fell out in a stammering mess. ". . . I shouldn't have gone there . . . especially since I was pretty sure there was . . . you know, *something* there."

Jay shook his head and propped himself on his elbow so that he was looking down at her. "You don't have to apologize for that. I know that what you *find* is out of your control." He reached out and brushed a stray piece of hair out of Violet's face. His words were as gentle and thoughtfully sincere as his touch. "Besides, if you'd have told me ahead of time that you were sensing something there, I would have gone with you anyway. It's not your fault it happened to be *a girl* and not some animal in there.

"I just don't want you to shut me out when you're *feeling* something. We've been friends for too long, Violet. I *want* you to tell me if you're ever sensing anything strange."

His hand fell away from her face, and Violet had to fight

the urge to shudder in the wake of the electric charge she felt from his touch. Where his fingertips had brushed against her flushed cheeks they were still tingling. She decided to keep that *strange sensation* to herself.

"I know it's not my fault, but I should have at least warned you." She wanted him to understand how badly she felt about making him a witness to something he never should have seen. "Anyway," she continued, "I'm sorry for that."

"I'm pretty sure you said that already," he responded, using her earlier words against her.

She smiled, desperately wishing he'd touch her again. She hoped he couldn't see that in her face too. "I just don't want anything bad between us," she offered by way of an explanation.

"I know." He reached out, capturing her hand in his. He laced his fingers casually through hers.

Violet leaned against him and the calm finally came, settling over her peacefully.

And then he kissed her. Gently. Softly. Not on the lips, as she'd imagined so many times before, but on her forehead.

The gesture was sweet and a little possessive.

Violet hoped, maybe, it was a start.

ADRENALINE

EACH HUNT WAS AS UNIQUE AS THE GIRL HERSELF.

It was better if no two girls were extracted in exactly the same way. Or from the same area.

But that had become increasingly difficult, as absences from his job became more and more conspicuous. So he'd been forced to hunt closer to home recently, and that meant taking more precautions than he had in the past. It meant being even more diligent. Meticulous.

Not that he'd been sloppy before. He was never sloppy; it went against everything he believed in.

He ran his finger along the razor-smooth edge of his KA-BAR tactical knife. He knew he wouldn't have to use it; the terrifying effect of the weapon in the presence of the girls was enough to cause total submission. Just stroking the steel blade stimulated him in ways no woman ever had.

He stuffed the military-grade knife in his "briefcase," a nondescript duffel bag he carried whenever he went out on a hunt, next to the duct tape and the zip ties.

He didn't mind the extra safety measures he had to take. In fact, for some reason it added to the excitement of it all, the increased risk of searching out girls who lived in such close proximity to where he lived and worked. It was like pissing in his own backyard. Sick and wrong. And he liked it.

He checked himself in the mirror one last time before heading out the door.

The hunt was on.

By a quarter past twelve, he was in a shitty mood.

Nothing had gone well. He hadn't spotted even one promising prospect out on the streets after dark.

He'd been afraid this might happen. Not so much that he wouldn't find a girl, but that his choices would be limited, his options less attractive. Literally. He preferred the pretty ones.

He knew that word of the disappearances had spread, and families were watching their daughters a little more closely. But there were exceptions to every rule. The stupid and weak always separated from the herd eventually.

All of the girls he'd seen tonight had either been traveling in groups or weren't worth his effort.

He was about to call it a night when he spotted her. Crossing the dark street. Alone. And pretty.

He didn't waste any time.

"You need a ride?" he asked through his open window, his car slowing to match her pace.

"It's okay," she answered, glancing up just long enough to acknowledge him. "I just live down the street."

"I don't mind at all. In fact, I'd feel better if you let me drive you."

She slowed down a little but didn't stop. He knew she was wavering, but not enough, so he added, "With everything that's going on lately . . . you know, with the girls that have been found . . ." He left the sentence hanging, hoping to strike some fear in this one, but he must have misjudged her.

There was fear, all right, but not the kind he'd hoped for. He saw the alarm flash across her face, and he couldn't help but wonder what she recognized in him that the others hadn't.

Her pace quickened, and he could see her fumbling nervously for something in her pocket. He saw what it was the second she had it free. Her cell phone.

She wanted to call for help.

He couldn't let her, but he'd have to act fast if he planned to stop her.

He slammed on his brakes and shoved the transmission into park. The girl started running before he was even out of his car.

The little bitch was fast!

He raced after her, his heavy boots falling loudly against the pavement. The advantage she'd gained in her head start was quickly lost to his superior agility.

Plus, it was always easier to be the predator than the prey. Prey panicked.

He hit her from behind, and he heard her squeal as the air was knocked from her lungs beneath his weight when he crushed her to the ground. The cell phone skittered across the street.

His hand shot out, before she could find her breath again, covering her mouth. It was bad enough she'd run; he didn't need her screaming too.

He rolled swiftly onto his back, taking her with him so that she was lying on top of his chest as he surveyed the area for possible witnesses. This had the potential for true disaster; this could be the mistake he'd avoided making for so long.

But they were still alone. Just the two of them.

She fought him, thrashing violently against his grip, even though he knew she was aware of his strength as he restrained her. She was like a rag doll flopping helplessly in his arms. He tightened his grip on her anyway, struggling against an instinct to smother her with his hand.

In one rapid motion, he jumped to his feet, hauling her up with him. His car was still running, and was far too easy to spot with its headlights filling the darkened street.

He was angry with the girl. She shouldn't have run. She wasn't supposed to do that; they were never supposed to do that.

She had ruined the hunt for him . . . ruined the mood.

He reached inside the open car door and released the trunk. He didn't take care with this one—this girl—she didn't deserve his concern or his gentle reassurances.

When she saw where he was taking her, she kicked at him with her legs. He slammed her against the hard edge of the trunk's opening, letting her head smack against the metal exterior of the car before throwing her inside. In the split second that her mouth was uncovered she tried to scream for help, but his fist found her jaw before the sound could gain any momentum. It came out in an injured whimper instead.

Some of his mood was restored.

He worked quickly, grabbing his tool bag, and ripping a piece of duct tape from the roll. She thrashed sideways, away from the silver adhesive, but he tangled his fingers into her hair and jerked her back, sealing her mouth shut once and for all.

The zip ties made her hands and feet useless, forcing her to be the kind of docile victim he preferred. He watched as he saw some of the fire fading from her eyes. She stared back at him pleadingly.

He felt much better.

In a moment of compassion, he tried to stroke her face comfortingly, but the instant he touched her, the panic returned, and she struggled all over again, straining against the plastic strips that bound her wrists and ankles.

Bitch, he silently cursed her. Stupid little bitch!

He slammed the trunk hard, glad to be done with her. He was tired of looking at her. He didn't care if she was afraid or if she suffered.

He knew one thing for certain . . . the next time he saw her, she wouldn't be fighting.

CHAPTER 9

"OOH, I LIKE THOSE ONES," CLAIRE EVERTON gushed as Violet lifted the hems of her jeans to show off another pair of shoes.

Chelsea rolled her eyes, her lush black lashes giving the gesture dramatic effect. "Claire, you've liked every single pair you've seen so far. Show me the ones you *don't* like."

Claire's shoulder slumped as she pouted. "All I said was I liked them. I didn't say she should get them."

Chelsea shot Violet a frustrated look before turning back to Claire to take pity on the girl's fragile ego. It seemed like a near-monumental act for Chelsea, who rarely checked what she said before saying it aloud.

For the most part, it was one of the things Violet liked about Chelsea, but sometimes, like now for example, Chelsea had to do a little damage control.

"I know, Claire-bear," Chelsea cooed in a patronizing baby-talk voice. "I didn't mean to snap at you."

Claire didn't seem to feel patronized at all and cheered up immediately. She turned away and plucked up another pair of shoes and gazed at them longingly, and they heard her saying, "I like these too . . ." as she wandered deeper into the Nordstrom shoe department.

Chelsea glanced back to Violet and wrinkled her nose as she looked at the shoes Violet had on. "I don't like them," she stated in her matter-of-fact tone, all traces of the baby talk long gone.

Violet shook her head. "Me neither."

The shopping trip had been meant to distract Violet from thinking about the recently discovered dead bodies. There was something about the two dead girls, something besides concerns over her own safety, that kept her feeling on edge.

She assumed that was natural considering that she'd been responsible for finding the girl in the lake. But she was struggling to concentrate on even the simplest of tasks, even one as easy as shopping.

Jules appeared then, practically from out of nowhere, carrying an armload of shoe boxes. "Here," she insisted, handing Violet two boxes. "I found you the perfect pair. I wasn't sure how the sizes ran, so I got you a seven and a seven and half." Then she turned to Chelsea. "These are for you." One box. Apparently she was pretty certain about the size. "Hey, A-D-D," she called out to Claire, "come over and try these on." She set two identical-looking boxes on a chair that she'd obviously designated for Claire.

And then she sat down in an empty seat and waited impatiently.

"What about you? Aren't you going to pick out a pair for yourself?" Chelsea asked Jules.

"I'm done. In the time you guys wasted looking for the 'perfect' shoe, I found mine *and* all of yours. I even paid already. . . . They're holding them up at the counter for me." She leaned forward in her chair, balancing her elbows on her knees, which were spread apart, making her look extremely out of place in the upscale ladies' shoe department.

There wasn't a feminine bone in Jules Oquist's body, although you wouldn't necessarily know it from her outward appearance. It wasn't until she moved, or spoke, or pretty much even breathed, that you couldn't help but notice what a tomboy the athletic girl really was. Outwardly, however, she was kind of pretty. But unlike Chelsea or the other girls, Jules didn't try to be. Hers was an understated prettiness that didn't need makeup or hair dryers. She had great coloring, soft honey-colored hair, and generously full lips. But that was where any comparisons to the female gender ended. This extended shopping trip wasn't exactly her cup of tea.

Chelsea opened her box and her eyes widened in surprise. "Oh my God, they're *exactly* what I've been looking for," she breathed. Chelsea plopped down in one of the overstuffed chairs and slid her foot into the delicate silver sandal, look-ing like Cinderella. And just as in the fairy tale, it fit perfectly. "Thanks, Jules." Chelsea beamed, thrilled by her friend's choice.

Violet opened hers next, curious now to see how Jules had fared for her.

She hadn't been exactly ecstatic about going to the Homecoming Dance with Grady, but she had to admit she'd had a blast choosing a dress, and now, finding the right shoes to go with it. The strappy black sandals inside the box were striking. And even though Violet hadn't thought of wearing sandals, now that she saw them, she knew they would look great with her simple, elegant black dress. She loved the strap that crossed over the front of the ankle and clasped together with a subtle jeweled buckle on the side. The first pair she tried on was *exactly* her size.

So far, Jules was two for two.

Claire was next, and she was having a hard time waiting for her turn. As soon as Violet agreed that she had found her shoes, Claire dug into her box.

They were all a little surprised by the bold choice . . . a pair of shiny, red, patent leather, peep-toe pumps.

"What's up, Julia?" Chelsea asked, knowing that Jules hated to be called by her given name. "Have you gone all girlie on us?"

Jules looked offended by the mere suggestion and gave Chelsea a disgusted look. "I just wanted to give you guys a kick in the ass to move things along. Anything wrong with that?"

"Not at all," Claire sighed breathlessly, looking at the shoes and not at Jules at all. "These are . . . they're . . . *hot*," she finally said, finding the right word.

They were pretty hot, Violet thought, and they would look amazing with Claire's shoulder-baring halter dress.

Three for three was pretty impressive, especially for a girl who professed to hate shopping.

Jules stood up and stretched gracelessly. "Let's hurry up and pay before she"—she indicated Claire with a flick of her thumb—"sees something shiny and we lose her again."

Violet was fine with the suggestion.

The mall was crowded for a Friday night, and because of that Violet had noticed at least a couple of sensory inputs that were strangely out of place in the shopping environment. With two girls found dead so recently, she seemed to be acutely aware of everything out of the ordinary lately, as if she were *searching* for the echoes, even in the most mundane places.

She'd recognized one, in particular. It was the odd scent of seawater coming from an older, distinguished-looking gentleman who was shopping with his wife in the shoe department. She only noticed it when he walked right by her, and she doubted that the smell had anything to do with the ocean at all. It was old, probably very old, and she wondered if the man had fought in a war in his lifetime. Or if he'd once been a hunter.

Either way, she doubted he was the killer.

After they paid and left the department store, Violet and

her friends decided to grab a bite to eat. Chelsea talked them into trying a Thai restaurant just down the street from the mall. Violet didn't need to be convinced. One thing she wasn't picky about was food—the more exotic the better. She especially liked anything that wasn't frozen lasagna or pizza delivery.

They shared orders of pad Thai, Swimming Angel, and some Vietnamese spring rolls that came with both a sweet garlic *and* a peanut dipping sauce. The smell of their jasmine-infused rice mingled with the scents of coconut sauces and chili peppers. By the time they were finished, Violet was stuffed and wondered if she'd even fit into her dress anymore.

On the ride to Chelsea's house, Claire chattered on and on about the upcoming dance. Violet was busy tuning out the incessant babbling until she heard Chelsea's voice, and Violet realized that she was talking to her.

"What?" Violet asked, pretending she just hadn't heard what Chelsea had said, instead of letting on that she wasn't listening to any of them at all.

"*I said*, is it weird for you that Jay's taking Lissie Adams to Homecoming?" Chelsea repeated it slowly, as if Violet were a dull-witted child.

Oh God, not this, Violet thought. This was a subject she'd been hoping to avoid. She suddenly wished she were an ostrich so she could just bury her head in the sand and ignore the question entirely.

Unfortunately three sets of eyes, including Jules's, who was peering at Violet from the rearview mirror, were now staring back at her.

Okay, Vi, just play it casually. "Weird? Why would it be weird? Jay and I are just friends. And Lissie seems okay."

Eyebrows raised.

"*Ri-ight.*" The word was dragged out skeptically. Of course it was an unconvinced Chelsea who asked, "Why would *you* be jealous that he's taking a senior . . . no, no, check that, *the most popular senior in school*, to Homecoming?"

"Yes," Violet answered, making it sound like Chelsea had made a statement rather than posed a damning question. "That's right, I would have no reason to be jealous . . . since we're *just friends*." Now she was the one speaking slowly, as if they might have trouble comprehending her words.

They did, but not because they were too slow to understand them. They just weren't as clueless as Violet wanted them to be.

Claire reached over and patted Violet's leg in what was supposed to be a comforting gesture. Instead, Violet was annoyed by the condescending quality to it.

"Seriously, why is that so hard to understand?"

Why? Probably because it wasn't true. Or at least because even she didn't really want it to be true.

Jules turned her attention back to the road, and Claire shrugged her narrow shoulders delicately but unconvincingly. Chelsea glanced back over her shoulder at Violet, giving her a look that said she wasn't buying it at all, but at least she didn't say it out loud.

Violet was glad when Claire begin prattling on again, filling the awkward silence that had settled inside the car.

Violet knew, of course, that she had no business being jealous that Jay was going to the dance with Elisabeth Adams. He hadn't even actually asked the It-Girl until after he'd found out that Violet had agreed to go with Grady, and she'd been regretting *that* particular moment of weakness every second of every day since. And somehow the perfect shoes, to go with the perfect dress, didn't make her feel any better . . . even now. Because in the end, she was going to have to stand across the dance floor from the boy she really wanted to be there with and watch him dance with his own perfectly perfect date.

She closed her eyes and tried to concentrate on the endless stream of words dribbling from Claire's never-silent mouth.

She was really starting to worry about what she had gotten herself into.

Violet didn't have much time to think about the dance and how disappointed she was to be going with Grady instead of Jay. All worries about herself, and her own insignificant problems, were overshadowed by the news that greeted her when she arrived home the next morning, after staying the night at Chelsea's house.

Both of her parents were waiting for her in the living room when she walked through the front door.

Her mother was pacing in front of the fireplace, and her dad gave the impression that he'd been relaxing as he leaned back into the couch, his long legs stretched out in front of him. But it was the preoccupied look on his face that gave away his discomfort.

Violet immediately felt her guard go up when she saw them like that. The hairs on the back of her neck prickled involuntarily. "What's wrong?" she asked, closing the door behind her.

They looked at each other, an unspoken conversation passing between them, before her father stood up and crossed the room to where she stood. He reached out and squeezed her upper arms in a gesture that, coming from him, was meant to be reassuring.

Violet could feel the panic rising within her.

"What?" she wondered aloud, looking past her father to her mom, knowing that her mother had never been good at hiding things from her. Her mom was as incapable of disguising her thoughts and feelings as her dad was good at concealing his.

"Sit down, Vi. We need to talk," her mom instructed, brushing past her husband and pulling her daughter toward the sofa.

Violet didn't fight her. *"What?"* she asked again. This time her voice felt like a hoarse whisper being ripped from her throat as she pled with them to tell her what this was all about.

Her mom spoke first. "It's Hailey McDonald . . . she's been missing since last night." She sat next to her daughter and put her arm around her. "Her mom called Uncle Stephen in the middle of the night last night to say that Hailey never made it home. They've checked everywhere they could think of . . . at all of her friends' houses, the places where she was last seen . . .

and no one knows where she could be."

Violet felt sick. Her hands started to shake in her lap, and the shuddering spasms moved up her arms and coursed through her body like electric currents.

Hailey McDonald was only in middle school, she was *maybe* thirteen, much younger than the other two girls whose bodies had already been discovered. And Violet knew Hailey, she used to babysit her when the younger girl was only in grade school. Hailey's older brother, Jacob McDonald, was a year younger than Violet at White River High School.

This was close. *Too close.*

"Do they think that . . . you know, do they suspect . . ." She took a breath to stop the quivering in her voice. "Do they think *he* took her?"

Her dad sat down on the other side of her. "Yes." His voice sounded too calm to be saying something so horrendously unacceptable. "Stephen said she was supposed to be walking home from her best friend, Elena Atkins's, house, but that she never made it. Her parents waited for over an hour past the time she was due back before they started calling around, but by then it was probably too late."

"Maybe she's just pissed at her parents and she's hiding out at another friend's house." Violet tried to sound convincing even though she didn't believe a word of it herself. And then, because she couldn't think of anything else to say, she just covered her mouth with her own trembling hand. "Oh my God," she whispered.

Violet wanted to cry, to let out her frustrations and fears. It would be healthier that way, and she might even feel a little better if she could release her feelings . . . *share*, as her mom would say. But instead she felt herself shriveling up, drawing inward. Shutting down.

It was the same way she'd felt after discovering the dead girl at the lake. A hopeless feeling that sucked her deeper into the mire of her own inner turmoil. She felt vulnerable and despondent.

And determined.

Everything had just changed for Violet. Knowing this girl . . . and knowing what she was capable of doing to help, even if it was futile, and even if it turned out to be dangerous, she knew she could no longer just sit around and wait to see *if*—or when—they found Hailey.

Violet was done waiting around for someone else to find the psychopath who was preying on these girls. She was going to do something, even if she had to sneak around to get it done.

She excused herself to her bedroom, telling her parents that she wanted to be alone, and grabbing the house phone as she passed it on her way.

She *was* going to do something. But she wouldn't do it alone.

She was going to ask for help.

CHAPTER 10

JAY CAME OVER AS SOON AS VIOLET CALLED HIM; she didn't even have to give him a reason. He was there in less than ten minutes.

Of course, he'd heard about what had happened to Hailey. Everyone had. Buckley was a small town, and news traveled fast . . . especially *bad* news.

When he got there she told him what she was thinking about doing. It was nothing dangerous, at least as far as she was concerned, and she hadn't expected Jay to disagree with her about it. So when he did, she was more than a little bit surprised by his stubborn reaction.

"No way," he insisted, and his voice left little room for

argument. "There is no way you're going to go around look-ing for this guy."

Violet was shocked by the tone in his voice, and by the harsh look he shot at her. She thought maybe he misunder-stood her plan, so she tried to explain it to him again. "Jay, I'm only going to public places, like malls and parks, to see if I can *get a feeling* for who this guy is. Who knows, maybe he goes to places like that to find them, maybe he hangs out there wait-ing to pick out a girl to . . . you know, kidnap." She tried to make her argument sound logical, but there was a desperate edge to her voice. "I'm not going alone . . . *you* can go *with* me. We'll just hang out at different places to see if we can find him. And if we do, we'll call my uncle. It's not like we'd do anything stupid."

" '*Anything stupid*' would be going out to look for a killer. I won't let you go looking for trouble, Violet. This guy is dangerous, and you need to leave it to the cops. They know what they're doing. And *they're* armed." He sounded like he thought she'd lost her mind, and maybe she had, but she had already made her decision.

"Look, I'm doing this. I was just asking you to come along with me."

"You're not," he insisted. "Even if I have to tell your uncle and your parents what you're planning. I promise you, you're *not* doing it."

She could feel her temper flaring. "You can't stop me, Jay. If you tell on me, then I'll lie. I'll bat my eyes innocently and promise *not* to go looking for this guy. But I swear to you that every chance I get, even if I have to sneak out of the house to do it, I *will* be trying to find him." She stood up, meaning to glare back at him, but instead found herself craning her neck just so she could see his face. The awkward position didn't steal any of her thunder. She refused to back down. "I mean it, Jay. You can't stop me."

Jay glared incredulously back at her. Emotions ranging from disbelief to frustration and back to disbelief again flashed darkly across his face. He seemed to be fighting with himself now. But when she heard him sigh, and then saw him raking his hand restlessly through his hair, she knew she'd won. His icy determination seemed to melt right before her eyes.

"Damn it, Violet." He sighed brusquely, wrapping his arms around her and holding her tightly. "What choice do I have?" he asked as he practically squeezed the life out of her.

She wasn't sure how to react to him now. It definitely wasn't a tender hug, but the close contact made her undisclosed desires stir all the same. She couldn't help wondering if he felt even a fraction of what she did.

His arms were strong, and she felt safe in the circle of them. She'd never imagined that she could feel so comfortable and so *uncomfortable* at the same time. She waited within the space of his embrace to see where this was going.

"So, how is this going to work?" he demanded roughly against the top of her head.

She froze. "What do you mean?" she asked as her heartbeat sped up.

He released her, and she realized that he wasn't talking

about *them*—he was talking about her plan to find a killer. She tried to ignore the sharp stab of disappointment she felt.

But she recovered quickly. "I was thinking that we would start going out, you know, to places where our friends, and girls from other schools, might hang out. We can go after school and on weekends, for as long as it takes, until either the police catch him, or until I cross paths with him. Either way, he needs to be stopped, Jay." She looked up at him again, this time feeling vulnerable for an entirely different reason. "I just don't think I can sit by while more girls are abducted, or worse, found *dead*." Her voice fractured on the last word, even though she was trying to stay composed. She hated feeling so helpless and weak, and she hated admitting that she needed help. But she did.

She needed Jay to go with her. Because despite her bold words about doing it by herself, it was all just a bluff. She really wasn't sure if she could do it on her own.

"All right," he finally agreed, flashing her the same stupid grin that always made her heart stutter, even though he still seemed uncertain. "How 'bout we start by going to the movies tonight? We can make sure the theater is safe."

It took some doing to convince her parents to let her go out after the news of Hailey McDonald's disappearance. If it hadn't been for Jay's promise not to let her out of his sight, they would never have agreed at all. They seemed to feel even better when Jay insisted on driving, since his mom's car was infinitely more modern than her beater Honda.

115

After checking the movie times online, they decided on an action flick that had just opened and was playing at the nearest theater, in Bonney Lake, the city where Brooke Johnson had lived.

If someone *had* been searching for teenage girls to abduct, Saturday night at the multiplex would have been the perfect place to go. Clusters of kids, ranging from probably eleven or twelve all the way into young adulthood, moved in swarms around the freestanding building and drifted aimlessly around the crowded parking lot. Inside the lobby, they were like energetic herds as they moved into, and out of, the theaters.

Violet had never really stopped to watch the groupings before, and it was a bit like watching spastic monkeys at the zoo. But they weren't really what she was interested in tonight.

She was there to find a killer. It was only a bonus that she was there with Jay.

They ran into a group of friends from school who were seeing the newest gross-out comedy release, and they stopped to chat for a few minutes. The girls in the group perked up the moment they realized that Jay Heaton was around, and Violet felt a twinge of satisfaction that he was *her* date tonight . . . even if it wasn't really a date.

Once Jay was in her sights, Amanda Kaufman's appreciative gaze never left him. "Hey, Jay," she said, practically purring at him, ignoring everyone else around her—including her boyfriend, who wasn't paying any attention. "You look great." She reached out and rubbed his chest. "I like your jacket. It's *sooo* soft," she cooed.

Violet looked at it, wondering if she'd missed something special. She hadn't. It was just a plain gray hoodie—pretty much like every other hoodie that every other boy in school wore every single day.

Violet looked at Jay and raised her eyebrows. She knew he noticed her glance, even though he was pretending to ignore her.

"Thanks," he said to Amanda in a voice that was a little too congenial, and Violet realized that he liked the attention.

Amanda giggled, and Violet nearly laughed out loud at the high-pitched sound that came out of her mouth. Amanda's boyfriend, Cameron, a senior football player, was too busy talking about next week's game with his buddies to even notice that his girlfriend was flirting right under his nose.

Violet tried to pay attention to her surroundings, concentrating on sensing anything unusual.

She already knew that one of the imprints would be a glowing, oily sheen like that from the girl in the lake, and she would easily recognize it on the killer if she saw him. She just didn't know what his other imprints would be.

But it didn't take Violet long to realize that there was nothing out of the ordinary in the lobby, so instead she sipped her Coke and watched the girls fawn over Jay. She kept thinking that she should be jealous of all their attention, but she just couldn't manage it because she was having too much fun watching them make fools of themselves. And that included Jay.

The other two girls in the group were encouraged by his reaction to Amanda. Yvette Siegel tried next, and her boyfriend was just as clueless as Amanda's. "I bet you'll look great in your tux," she praised Jay.

"Did you already pick one out?" Alexandra Yates asked. She was the only one without a boyfriend, and she stepped forward, practically shoving the other two girls—*her friends*—out of her way to get closer to him.

Violet would have laughed out loud, but instead she choked on her soda when it went down the wrong way. All three of the girls suddenly noticed her standing there for the first time. She tried to suppress the coughing fit, but she couldn't stop it.

Jay reached out to smack her on the back harder than he really needed to. "You okay?" he asked, and Violet shot him a deadly look as she coughed into her closed fist.

"I'm fine," she gasped, barely getting out the words in between her own choking. She nudged his *helping* hand away and glared at him.

He grinned back at her.

"Hey, Violet." Alexandra was the only one who actually acknowledged her there. "What about you? Have you picked your dress for the dance yet?"

Violet cleared her throat once more as she nodded her head. "I'm all set, I think."

"Where are you guys eating that night?" Amanda's voice had taken on a pouting quality that didn't suit her at all. "Have you made reservations?"

Violet realized that the girls thought that she and Jay were going to Homecoming with each other. "Oh, no"—she corrected the mistake—"we're not going together."

That seemed to immediately cheer up Amanda again, even though Violet was pretty sure that the other girl was already going to the dance . . . with *her boyfriend.*

"Really?"

"Really. Violet's going with Grady Spencer," Jay told all three girls as he smiled oh-so-innocently at Violet.

"And Jay's going with Lissie Adams," Violet revealed to the trio, smirking back at him.

"Oh," Amanda whined again, sounding completely dejected. And from the tone of her voice, Violet was a little surprised that Amanda didn't stomp her foot when she said it.

"Hey, we gotta get going, our movie's about to start," Cameron reminded Amanda as he reached out and pulled his girlfriend away from Jay. "It was nice talking to you." He actually said that last part with a straight face, even though he hadn't spoken so much as a single word to either Violet or Jay.

Violet watched them go, while all three of the girls, at different times, glanced back over their shoulders to get another look at Jay before they left. Jay nudged Violet conspiratorially.

Violet's eyes widened as she glanced up at him. "What the *hell* was that all about?"

Jay looked serious for a moment, and then he winked at her. "It's good being one of the beautiful people, that's all."

"Oh my God, Jay, they were practically slobbering on you." For the first time in a long time, Violet was nothing but amused by another girl's antics around her best friend. It felt good . . . *not* feeling even a little bit resentful about the attention they were showering on him.

Jay laughed, nudging her again. "Jealous?"

Violet almost choked on her drink again. "How could I be? They were acting like complete idiots. I'm serious—I think Amanda might have actually drooled on herself a little."

Jay handed the woman at the entrance to the theaters their tickets, and after he pocketed the stubs he reached over and took Violet's hand. It was a friendly gesture, something they used to always do, and it felt nice.

The theater was only about half full, so they were able to find a spot off to the side that was relatively private. Once the credits rolled, Violet's mind began to wander again, to their real purpose for being here tonight. To catch a murderer.

So far she'd sensed nothing . . . or rather, nothing but the outlandish behavior of other girls around Jay. She'd sensed no echoes of the dead all evening, and she supposed she might have been expecting too much to think that it would happen so quickly . . . so easily.

She resigned herself to the fact that this might take a while.

In the meantime, she and Jay sat shoulder to shoulder throughout the movie, and the warmth of him pressed up against her made it difficult for Violet to concentrate. She tried to remember when *exactly* he'd started to smell so good to her, or when his touch had become like a mood-altering narcotic.

She glanced sideways to see if she could tell what he was thinking, if their casual contact was affecting him the way it was her, but his face was blank, completely unreadable, as he watched the action on the oversized screen.

She leaned toward him and whispered, "I have to go to the bathroom."

She stood up to go. And so did he.

She gave him a questioning look. "I'll be right back," she said quietly.

He followed right behind her.

"What are you doing?" She was starting to get irritated.

"I'm going with you."

"Yeah, I got that," she said, her voice getting louder now. *"Why?"*

He pushed her along from behind until they were out of the darkened theater and standing in the dimly lit hallway.

"I can go to the bathroom by myself," she insisted, putting her hands on her hips and cocking her head to the side.

"No, Violet. You can't. I told your parents I wouldn't let you out of my sight, and I meant it. Besides, until you decide to stop hunting for this guy, I'm not letting you do *anything* by yourself." That stubborn set of his jaw was back. "Now, hurry up," he said as he leaned casually against the wall outside the ladies' room.

Violet didn't want to waste her time arguing, so she just shook her head as she opened the door. "You're crazy! You know that, don't you?" She didn't wait for him to answer as she disappeared into the empty bathroom, but she swore she heard the sound of his laughter following her inside.

There was something mildly creepy about the pale, washed-out bathrooms at this theater. They were usually empty while the movies were running in the multiplex, and the cold, ghostly lighting cast an almost menacing pallor across the small, white, hexagonal tiles of the floors. The fluorescent tubing even made an ominous humming sound that echoed against the walls around her. She was actually kind of glad that Jay was waiting outside the door.

Violet hurried in and out of the stall, catching a glimpse of herself in the mirror as she washed her hands. Even in this lighting, she had to admit that she didn't look too terrible. She'd never really thought of herself as pretty, but she knew she wasn't unattractive either. She never wanted to be one of those girls who looked for flaws, picking themselves apart with unjust criticisms.

She turned on the air dryer hanging on the wall, but got impatient with how long it was taking and finally dried her hands on her jeans as she went back out to where Jay was waiting for her, still leaning casually against the wall.

She didn't stop to wait for him, and he had to rush to keep up with her. "What took you so long?" he whispered as they looked for their seats in the dark again.

She didn't respond to his question; she was still annoyed that he thought she needed an escort just to go to the restroom. But once they were sitting, Jay reached out and took her hand once more.

Violet didn't complain about it. She liked it too much to complain.

His hands were strong and so much larger than hers now. His skin felt thicker—tougher—than her own, and the contrast was exhilarating. Just his touch made her feel warm all over.

She was disappointed when the movie came to an end, even though he showed no signs of releasing his grip on her hand. And she was more than a little embarrassed to realize that she'd barely paid attention to the show at all. She'd had other, more interesting, things on her mind. She desperately hoped that Jay didn't ask her any questions about the movie she was supposed to have watched.

They saw Amanda's little group on their way out to the parking lot, but this time Jay barely acknowledged them, simply nodding his head in their direction as they passed. Violet was aware of the looks exchanged by the three girls as they made it clear that they'd noticed he was holding her hand.

Jay must have seen it too, because he gave her hand a quick, reassuring squeeze.

It made Violet curious about all the times that she thought Jay was completely clueless about the attention he'd been getting from the girls at school. She wondered if he was more aware than he let on about how much interest he'd stirred in the female population at White River High.

And then her blood ran cold as another thought occurred to her. If he wasn't entirely ignorant about what he was doing to the other girls, what did he know about her own thoughts and fantasies? Could he possibly suspect how she really felt about him? Was she as transparent as Amanda and the other girls at school had been?

That would be terrible! Violet thought miserably. She was going to have to be more careful around him and stop obsessing over him like one of his little groupies.

She decided that, from this point on, despite the fact it was something she desperately wanted, she couldn't risk ruining what they had. Their friendship, which had been a part of her life for almost as long as she could remember, was far too important to her to do anything that might jeopardize it.

She pulled her hand away from his, feeling suddenly decisive and strong. But it turned out to be less a show of resolve than she'd meant it to be, considering that they'd reached the car and she would have had to let go anyway. Jay opened the passenger-side door, and she slid inside.

She looked down at her hand, which was still warm from his touch, and she could already feel herself missing the contact with him. She didn't entirely understand the sense of loss she felt about something that she'd never really had in the first place.

Besides, Violet thought, she had more important things to worry about right now.

She needed to find the killer, to stop him before he could hurt anyone else.

How was she ever going to do that if she was too busy crushing on her best friend?

CHAPTER 11

SUNDAY, VIOLET AND JAY SPENT MOST OF THE DAY at the local mall. They wandered in and out of the stores, had lunch at the food court, and even spent some time playing video games in the arcade, which, as it turned out, was more for Jay's benefit than for hers. She was so terrible at all of the games she tried that she'd spent ten dollars in less than ten minutes. Jay was still on his first two quarters by the time she was finished.

She decided that she couldn't afford to spend too much time in the arcade.

Violet stood beside the game Jay was playing—*very well*, she had to admit—and she looked around her. The electronic sounds of the games were almost deafening, especially to someone who was so hyper-aware of her senses. But Violet already knew that the man she was looking for wasn't here. It would have been easy for her to spot the radiant imprint she was looking for, especially in the dark confines of the arcade.

She looked back to the video game monitor and tried to feign interest in what was happening on the screen, but soon she was bored, and she decided she would rather wait for Jay in the mall. He didn't look up from what he was doing long enough to notice that she was leaving.

She left the sensory overload of the arcade behind her as she stepped into the wide-open space of the atrium. They'd already had lunch, and Violet had no desire to eat again, so instead she started to wander the storefronts near the food court.

She glanced around her. The mall was crowded, and there were lines at several of the eateries. Women with toddlers and preschoolers in tow converged on the McDonald's. The smells from the different fast-food restaurants, all lingering together, were strong but not entirely unpleasant.

And then she noticed something strange.

Suddenly it wasn't the smells that Violet was acutely aware of but rather the *taste*. She had the strangest sensation of garlic in the back of her mouth . . . it was pungent and thick, and nearly overpowering.

This was it. This might be the something she'd been looking for.

An echo of some sort.

Violet looked around her, trying to imagine where it might be coming from, but there was really only one way to be sure.

She started walking, leaving the food court behind her and moving farther into the mall. When the pungent taste grew stronger, Violet knew she was heading in the right direction.

Her heart rate increased and her other senses heightened as she looked around her, wondering if she might be walking right toward the killer. She was terrified and at the same time exhilarated. She knew Jay would be mad at her for wandering off.

She reached the end of the offshoot of the mall that housed the food court and arcade, and met the larger inner space of the shopping center, where big department stores dwarfed the outlets and boutiques. She had to decide which way to go now.

She chose to go left and found herself heading toward two of the larger department stores. It seemed like a fine choice, a busy section of the mall, but after walking past several stores she knew she'd picked the wrong direction. The garlicky taste in her mouth began to fade. She turned around and headed back in the opposite direction.

She passed her starting point and kept going, moving toward Sears and Macy's. She concentrated on the sensation inside of her mouth, savoring the garlicky flavor . . . not because she enjoyed the taste, but because it was acting like a compass . . . guiding her way.

The taste grew stronger, and more tangible, the farther

she walked. Her pulse quickened and her breathing began to feel hoarse and erratic. She looked everywhere, at everyone, trying to decide who it might be . . . where the echo, or imprint, was coming from. She had to weave around mothers pushing strollers and couples holding hands.

And then, without warning, the taste began to fade again, and Violet felt herself spiraling into a frustrated panic. She stopped right where she was, in the middle of the mall, in the middle of the heavy pedestrian traffic, looking around her for a clue as to where she should go next. A shopper passed her, bumping Violet with the overflowing shopping bags that hung from her arms. Violet ignored the woman.

She walked back the other way, trying to recapture the taste.

When she did, it only grew stronger for several long strides, before disappearing again.

Violet watched the people around her, trying to see where he was . . . and just *who* he might be. But there were so many people, moving in so many directions, that she couldn't tell who it was coming from. She glanced at the nearest stores and tried approaching each of them, one at a time, but the taste only faded when she did.

He wasn't in the stores. So where was he, then?

She turned around, feeling waves of disappointment washing over her, and just when she decided that she might have to give up, the taste hit her again . . . stronger than before. And she realized that he had to be close.

That was when she noticed it . . . the long, narrow hallway

leading off the main drag of the mall, with the sign hanging above the entrance that read RESTROOMS.

Violet approached the poorly lit hallway slowly . . . cautiously, feeling overwhelmed by the unexpected apprehension. She couldn't be sure, but she thought that her legs might be shaking as she made her way toward the public bathrooms.

She approached the men's room, and when her taste buds nearly exploded from the burst of hot garlic that shot through them—her mouth felt like it was on fire—she knew that whoever he was, he was inside.

She paused, suddenly unsure. She didn't know if she could do this. She was so close to discovering whoever it was that carried the imprint of death, the one who was making her mouth feel like she'd just eaten an entire plate of warm, buttery-soft garlic cloves. But she couldn't help thinking that maybe she was too close. Maybe Jay had been right. Maybe this *was* too dangerous.

She felt frozen in place as time slowed down. She could hear the beat of her thundering heart in her ears, and her mouth was suddenly parched. She tentatively stepped closer to the door in front of her, just one small step. She was still trying to decide whether she should go inside or just stay put until whoever was in there came out. Goose bumps prickled up and down her arms, and she held her breath, afraid that if she let it out, somehow he might hear her behind the door . . . waiting for him.

She took another tense step forward.

It wasn't until she felt a hand close around her wrist that she realized someone was standing right behind her. A strong arm pulled her backward before she even had a chance to react. Her eyes widened, and she tried to remember how to scream, but her voice was frozen, and for a moment, she thought she might have forgotten how to breathe as well.

"What the hell are you doing here?" She was stunned to hear Jay's voice whispering against her ear. He didn't sound happy.

She turned to face him and wasn't quite sure what she saw there. Concern? Irritation? Annoyance? *Definitely* annoyance.

But before she could even try to explain why she'd left the arcade, he put his finger to his lips, dragging her close to him so he could speak in a voice that was quieter than a whisper. "Did you sense something?" The words were just a sliver of sound.

Violet nodded, a little surprised by the rigid expression she saw on his face.

Again, his voice was nearly inaudible but it was filled with purpose. "Is he in there?" Jay asked, indicating the public restroom.

She nodded for a second time.

"You." He barely said the word, but Violet felt the gravity of his frustration. "Go wait in the center of the mall, by the benches. *And don't move until I get there."*

Violet started to protest, finally realizing that he meant to go into the men's room by himself. "What if—?" she began, but he cut her off with an unwavering stare that silenced her before she could finish her argument.

"Seriously, Violet. *I mean it."* He nudged her back toward the mall, and Violet decided that now wasn't the time to argue with him. She knew from the look on his face that he was determined, and that nothing she said was going to change his mind.

She was certain that she was shaking now as she made her way back through the endless stream of shoppers. She was suddenly all too aware of what she'd been about to do, of what Jay had just stopped her from doing, and she realized how absurdly dangerous it had been. *Had she really been about to do something so foolish?*

The unfortunate answer was yes. And Jay had known it too, which was why he was so angry with her. He'd told her not to leave his sight; he'd made a promise to her parents that he would take care of her, and she'd ignored all of it.

She sat down on a bench in the middle of the bustling shopping center and tried to focus on something other than what Jay might be doing at that very moment. She felt raw with terror. What if the killer was in there? What would Jay do? And worse, what could the killer do to Jay?

Violet wrung her hands nervously in her lap as she waited for what seemed like an eternity, watching the entrance of the hallway anxiously and hoping for a glimpse of Jay.

When she finally saw him, and he appeared to be all in one piece, she jumped up and nearly shoved passersby out of the way to get to him. The look on his face hadn't changed in the minutes that had passed, but Violet didn't care, because even though he was still mad at her, he was obviously safe.

"You're okay." It was a statement, not a question, and her words were filled with relief. "What happened?"

Jay pulled her aside, to where they were out of the way of the foot traffic. His touch was comforting to Violet despite the fact that it completely lacked any trace of tenderness.

"There were just some punk kids in there . . . smoking. So unless the guy's in junior high, it wasn't him." Violet was surprised to hear an edge of frustration in his voice that had nothing to do with her. She'd assumed that Jay was there only to humor her and to keep her out of trouble. She hadn't believed that he had any real interest in finding this guy. And yet, when he'd told her that the killer wasn't in there, he seemed genuinely disappointed.

Suddenly a wave of garlic burst freshly across her tongue. She spun around in time to see a group of boys exiting the hallway where the restrooms were, and walking right toward where she and Jay stood.

Violet reached out and grabbed Jay's arm for support, feeling nauseous from the fiery blast that assaulted her mouth.

As they passed, a boy, maybe only thirteen or fourteen years old, looked up at her. The contrast of his dyed black hair against his pale, sallow skin made him seem anemic and sickly at first glance. But when his eyes met hers, in that split second, she felt a level of cruelty coming from deep within him that practically blistered her with its intensity. The searing flashes of garlic were like explosions that angrily scalded her tongue as he stared back at her.

Whether real or imagined, Violet could envision this boy, who was probably accustomed to hurting small creatures at random, growing into the kind of man who *could* actually kidnap and murder young girls.

But for now, at least, he wasn't the person she was searching for.

Violet had to look away first, closing her eyes until he'd passed her by completely.

"Was that who you sensed?" Jay asked.

Violet could only nod, waiting until the queasiness, and the lingering flavor of the boy's particular brand of evil, faded away.

Jay didn't ask her if she was ready to go or not; he just put his arm around her. There was nothing gentle or reassuring about the contact, it was meant more to guide than to comfort her, as he led her out of the mall to the car.

They drove home without speaking—Jay was too angry, and Violet too exhausted from her brush with malevolence. She was still reeling from the intensity of the sensations she'd experienced from the hate-filled boy.

She knew she couldn't do that again, just go randomly looking for a killer in their midst. It had been too hard on her today. She was used to trying to buffer herself from those kinds of feelings; she had practiced building up walls to shield herself from experiencing that kind of intensity. Especially when she wasn't even sure exactly what she was looking for. She didn't think she could take much more of that.

If she was going to try again, she was going to need a better game plan, she decided. And this time it was going to require some serious preparation.

CHAPTER 12

THE ATMOSPHERE AT SCHOOL WAS MUCH MORE somber than it had been after the previous disappearances. Violet suspected that it was because Hailey McDonald was not a casual acquaintance met in passing at a party or social event. To the vast majority of the student body, Hailey McDonald was someone they knew.

Hailey was the sister of a fellow student, and her family was well known by many of the kids at White River High. Her absence in the community was almost palpable, and it was being taken much more personally than the deaths of the other girls had been.

The other thing that was obvious at school on Monday

morning was the conspicuous increase in security. And it wasn't just the unarmed school security guards that patrolled the campus maintaining order; there was now also a visible police presence, with at least two uniformed officers standing guard around the hallways outside of the classrooms.

One of the officers carried several imprints on him, which Violet just assumed were occupational hazards. Fortunately, none of them were particularly offensive to her, and she could easily ignore them whenever he was nearby.

The grief counselors were back as well, which struck Violet as a little premature, since there was no evidence—not yet, at least—suggesting that Hailey McDonald wouldn't be found and brought home unharmed.

The counselors made themselves available to those students who felt the need to unburden their fears and frustrations in a safe environment. But many of the kids at school also found them to be a convenient excuse to ditch class, since passes to see the counselors were being handed out like candy.

Violet had opted to keep her concerns to herself rather than visiting the counselors. And since Jay still wasn't speaking to her, she really had no one to confide in.

He had dropped her off on Sunday evening, after their disastrous day at the mall, and had waited in the driveway just long enough to make sure she'd gotten safely inside. When Violet tried to call him later that night, he hadn't even bothered answering the phone, and he didn't respond to her e-mails. She didn't press the matter. She knew he was mad, and just needed some time to get over it.

Her parents, however, surprised her when she'd arrived home by giving her a brand-new cell phone of her own.

Violet had been begging them for a phone since she was fourteen years old, citing the names of all the other kids her age who had already gotten one. Her parents had always refused, ignoring her Christmas and birthday requests for the phone and stating that there was no "good reason" for her to have one.

Apparently they'd changed their minds.

Violet should have been ecstatic with the cell phone, but somehow it didn't hold the same appeal it once had. Now it felt more like a necessary tool for survival than the new toy she'd always hoped for. She'd shoved it away in her purse . . . right next to her can of pepper spray.

She made her way through her class schedule on Monday, trying to ignore the fact that Jay, who sat next to her in several of her classes, was still giving her the silent treatment. He sat impassively, staring forward and doing a good job of at least pretending to pay attention to the teachers, in an effort to avoid mistakenly making eye contact with Violet. She knew he was still furious with her.

She really didn't mind that he was so upset since she felt as though she deserved it, at least to some extent. She'd acted like an idiot yesterday, she realized, recalling that she'd basically planned to confront a killer in a public restroom at the mall. So instead of letting it get to her, she pretended not to notice his intentional slights.

But something else happened Monday that caught Violet off guard.

After PE, her first-period class, she was surprised to find Grady waiting for her outside of the locker rooms. He walked with Violet to her second-period class. They made casual small talk, which was easy with Grady since they'd been friends for so long. And she liked that he didn't seem to be pushing her, despite the fact that they were still planning to go to the dance together, to be anything more than that. Violet actually found herself enjoying his company and was glad that he'd decided to walk with her.

Jay didn't look up as he passed them on his way into class, but Violet was sure that he hadn't been clenching his fists until he'd spotted her and Grady together.

Still, considering that they were "just friends," Violet was even more surprised when Grady was waiting for her, again, after each of her next two classes.

She'd planned on having lunch at her usual table, with the same friends she and Jay sat with almost every day. Grady usually sat at another table with a bunch of his jock friends, but today it was like he somehow sensed that Violet was going to be alone and he'd decided to tag along with her. Violet didn't complain.

She carried her lunch tray to the table where Claire and Jules were already sitting. Grady sat down next to Violet . . . in the spot where Jay normally sat.

Jay's absence was glaringly obvious.

Violet glanced as discreetly as she could around the

cafeteria, wondering who Jay had decided to spend his lunch hour with, but he was nowhere to be seen. She was a little irritated with herself for the twinge of disappointment she felt at not seeing him, even from a distance.

"Hi, Grady," Violet heard Chelsea say knowingly as she joined the group, squeezing in between Claire and Jules. Violet knew that the tone was meant more for her benefit than for Grady's.

"Hey," Grady said, nodding at the other girls at the table.

There were a few moments of awkward silence, made even more awkward by Chelsea's not-so-subtle quizzical glances in Violet's direction. Chelsea was about as understated as a jackhammer. Ultimately, though, it was Claire who made things worse when she asked where Jay was today.

Violet really didn't want to tell them that Jay was mad at her, and it wasn't like she could explain their fight to them anyway, so she made up some lame excuse about Jay needing to stay after class to get some work done. She had no idea if Jay would corroborate her stupid lie if he was asked, and for now she really didn't care . . . as long as it kept anyone else from mentioning his absence from lunch again.

When Andrew Lauthner, a lunch-table regular and long-time Chelsea admirer, joined them, Grady thankfully turned his attention to the other boy. Since they started talking about cars, a subject about which Violet knew absolutely nothing, she didn't feel too bad about ignoring their conversation . . . and the two of them.

Chelsea flashed Violet another meaningful look, telling

her that she wasn't buying the Jay's-got-work-to-do story. And Violet played dumb, pretending she hadn't noticed Chelsea's perceptive looks.

When the bell finally rang, Violet was glad that Grady was still too involved in his conversation with Andrew to walk her to her next class. Unfortunately Chelsea's curiosity hadn't diminished throughout the meal, and she jumped up to follow Violet out of the cafeteria.

They walked for almost a full sixty seconds before Chelsea actually said anything, even though Violet knew, without a doubt, that it was coming.

"I like *new*-Jay," Chelsea finally announced, as though she was making a simple observation rather than trying to pry information out of her friend.

"Shut up." Violet groaned, unable to completely hide her smile at Chelsea's absurd comment. Still, she didn't feel inclined to share her problems with Chelsea.

"Don't get me wrong, Vi. I still like old-Jay better; I'm just saying that new-Jay's not so bad. Plus, at least *he* had the balls to ask you to the dance. That's something that old-Jay couldn't seem to manage."

"He's not *new-Jay*," Violet insisted, stopping at her locker to grab her notebook. "Jay's just pissed off at me right now. He'll get over it. Besides, I already told you that we're just friends."

"Which one? New-Jay or old-Jay?"

Violet rolled her eyes as she slammed the metal door shut. "Both." She turned on her heel and left Chelsea standing alone by the row of lockers. And then she called back over her shoulder. "Besides . . . there is no *new-Jay*."

It took Violet only a moment to register the fact that Jay was standing right there in the hallway, just a few feet away from her and within earshot of her entire conversation with Chelsea, although she couldn't be sure how long he'd been standing there. Still, she was mortified that he'd caught her talking about him at all.

She ignored the blazing look he flashed in her direction as she hurried past him, escaping to her next class . . . and trying to ignore the fact that he would be sitting right next to her.

The next two days went by with Jay giving her the silent treatment and Grady paying her extra attention. It was like some bizarre alternate universe, where up meant down and yes meant no.

Violet didn't mind Jay avoiding her, because, for the time being, it gave her time to work on the new plan she'd come up with, one that she knew he would never help her with. But the extra attention from Grady was another story altogether. He was starting to get on her nerves, following her around like some hyperactive puppy that was always underfoot. And it always seemed that he was one step ahead of her . . . reaching her classrooms before she could slip past him and disappear into the crowded hallways, waiting for her at her usual table in the cafeteria, and even meeting her at her car after school so he could have just a few more minutes with her.

It was starting to become obvious that Grady wasn't

completely interested in being just another one of Violet's friends. She was sure now that he wanted more, and she blamed Jay's absence for Grady's increased bravado in searching her out during school hours. She was afraid that if Jay didn't start talking to her again soon, Grady might decide that the school day wasn't enough and start making after-school visits to her house. As it was, he'd started calling her all the time. She wasn't sure how many messages her voice mail could hold.

Recently, the very thought of going to the dance with Grady made Violet's skin itch, as if she might be breaking out in hives—or more likely a bad case of second thoughts.

In an effort to ignore Grady's enthusiastic interest, Violet turned her own attention to the details of her new plan. The idea had first occurred to her during the unusually quiet ride home from the mall with Jay. She knew for certain that just wandering through public places in search of echoes was a mistake. There were too many variables involved, too many people who had killed *without* malice, either by occupation or by sport. She realized then that she was going to have to narrow her search somehow.

She already knew she would recognize the imprint left behind by the girl at the lake. She had seen it for herself, and she knew that whoever he was, he would be carrying that radiantly oil-like film around him, the same way the girl in the water had. But that was a visual echo, which meant it would be useful only if Violet found herself face-to-face with the killer. It would be nearly impossible to track from any distance.

She needed more information. And there was only one way to get it.

She was going to have to figure out just what echo the other girl, Brooke Johnson, had left behind. And, in turn, had left on the killer.

For someone like Violet, someone who could sense the energy remnants of murder, a graveyard was a difficult place to go. So far, at least as far as she knew anyway, burying a body seemed to bring a sense of peace, releasing its echo into something less . . . *intense.* But her experience was limited, experimental at best, and she'd always been afraid that maybe her theories were wrong.

So Violet generally tried to avoid places where the chances of encountering echoes would be the greatest—graveyards, hospitals with morgues, funeral homes—on the off chance that she might sense something there that was more than she could bear. Her parents had shielded her from that possibility, even going so far as to leave her at home when they went to her grandmother's burial. And that had been just three years ago.

But now, with Hailey McDonald still out there some-where, Violet felt a sense of responsibility that far outweighed any fear—*real or imagined*—of her own potential sensory dis-comforts. She might just be the only person who could find this guy, and she wasn't about to ignore that possibility.

If she was going to find out what Brooke's echo was, she would have to go to the cemetery where Brooke was buried.

The concept was simple enough, but actually pulling it off was another thing altogether. Her parents practically had her on maximum-security lockdown. She felt like she was doing hard time. And with the absence of Jay as her guardian and protector, they didn't seem to be inclined to let Violet out of their sight for more than five minutes at a time.

Jay would have been the perfect accomplice, except for the annoying fact that he refused to speak to her. That, and after her little stunt at the mall, there was no way she was going to convince him to help her again. She was more afraid that if he knew what she was still planning to do, he would try to stop her . . . even if it meant ratting her out to her parents.

Violet had gone around and around with ideas of how she could sneak away for an afternoon, discarding each one in turn as she realized that if she got caught in a lie—even one of omission—she would probably never see the light of day again.

Okay, maybe a little dramatic, but not completely implausible.

When the answer finally came to her, she felt a little dense for not thinking of it sooner. It was the perfect excuse, and no one, not even her parents, would know the truth. Even her companion would be oblivious to his role in her deceit. It was foolproof.

She dialed Grady from her brand-new cell phone, the first useful purpose it had served since she'd gotten it.

He answered his phone on the first ring, his voice enthusiastic. Violet cringed a little. After they exchanged some small talk, she plunged right into her plan.

She laid out her words carefully, following the script she'd prepared in her head before placing the call.

"Anyway, I was calling because with everything that's been going on, I haven't even had a chance to visit Brooke's grave yet, and I feel terrible about it," Violet explained as sincerely as she could.

"Man, I didn't even know you guys were friends."

"Yeah. We played softball and soccer together when we were younger, and even though we didn't see each other much, I was still devastated when I heard . . . you know . . ." She tried to sound broken up, like she couldn't finish her sentence. She wished she were one of those girls who could cry on command, just for dramatic effect. "Do you think . . . would you mind . . . taking me? So I don't have to go alone . . . ?" Her voice trailed off, and she waited for his answer.

She nailed it perfectly, from form to execution. And even with the high degree of difficulty, she had to give herself a perfect 10 for her performance. Jay would have seen right through it, but Grady was clueless.

"When do you want to go?" he asked.

"Can you be here in an hour?"

She probably could have told him to be there in two minutes, and he would have been there in one.

When Violet hung up, she was surprised that she didn't feel even the slightest hint of guilt over her deceit, and she wondered if she would have felt differently if it had been Jay she'd lied to.

The next part of her plan was a little trickier. She had to convince her parents to let her go.

Her dad was still at work, but her mom was in her studio.

144

Violet wandered across the lawn to the small shed that had been converted into an art studio, and when she pushed the door open she was assaulted by the familiar linen-y scent of canvas and the more vaporous fumes of paint thinner.

Her mom smiled in greeting as she was cleaning brushes in an old Mason jar filled with the caustic cleaners. "What's up, Vi?"

Violet hesitated, and her first real pang of guilt battered at her conscience. But there was no turning back now, she decided, and she forged ahead anyway. "Grady Spencer called and asked if I could go to the cemetery with him."

Her mom's eyebrows rose at the unusual request, and she stopped stirring the brushes, wiping her hands on her paint-smeared smock. She seemed concerned, and Violet knew why. This wasn't something Violet would normally ask.

Violet plunged into her rehearsed explanation. "I guess he was friends with the girl that was killed, the one from Bonney Lake. He wants to take flowers to her grave but he doesn't want to go alone." She could scarcely believe she'd said that without flinching. "I didn't think it would be a big deal, especially since he'll be with me, so I told him I would." She forced herself to appear as relaxed as she could manage at the moment, while her heart hammered nervously against her rib cage. "It's okay, isn't it?"

Maggie Ambrose studied her daughter thoughtfully. "Are you sure, Violet?"

Violet nodded and held her breath as she looked at her mom warily, watching for any signs of what she might be thinking. For a moment, she thought she saw a fleeting look of skepticism, and she wondered if maybe she'd laid it on a little too thick.

Finally, though, her mom went back to cleaning her brushes and shrugged. "I suppose it's fine. As long as you two stay together." She gave Violet a look that said she was serious. "I mean it, Violet Marie . . . stay together. *And be careful.*"

"We will, Mom. Thanks." She ran up and gave her mom a quick kiss on the cheek, surprising them both a little. Violet hadn't done that in ages, and she couldn't help thinking that the impulsive action was brought on by her own burning sense of shame at having flat-out lied to her mother. Maybe the affectionate gesture made her feel a little less remorse for what she was about to do.

But even with the heft of her conscience weighing on her, Violet practically skipped away from the converted shed and waited impatiently in the house for Grady to arrive.

CHAPTER 13

VIOLET SAT IN THE PASSENGER SEAT OF GRADY'S souped-up, five-year-old Nissan Sentra. It was a strange car to have "pimped out," although she kept that thought to herself since Grady was so obviously proud of it, puffing up as he pointed out the new spinners and the iridescent-purple paint job he'd put over the stock champagne silver it had worn from the factory. The engine was ridiculously loud, another thing Grady was enormously pleased by.

But for Violet, the noisy ride couldn't ease the tension she felt now that she was actually following through with her plan. She couldn't believe she'd pulled it off. But it came with a price.

She could feel the muscles in the back of her neck bunching

up the closer they got to the small downtown cemetery where Brooke Johnson had been buried. Grady must have mistaken her anxiety for grief—over the loss of her invented friendship with Brooke—because he'd stopped bothering her with his constant stream of small talk once they rounded the bend on the winding riverside road.

But for once, Violet had the opportunity to do something useful with her ability, and she refused to shirk that obligation.

The heavy, black, wrought-iron fencing came into view as Grady made the final left-hand turn toward the cemetery.

Violet was surprised when they reached the entrance and she hadn't yet felt, or rather *sensed*, anything from within the gated walls. She worried that maybe she'd been wrong about all of this. That maybe this was similar to what happened with the animals she'd discovered in the woods, when their individual echoes seemed to vanish into a nearly imperceptible static noise once she'd reburied them in her own personal graveyard.

And if it was just static, maybe she wouldn't be able to distinguish Brooke Johnson's echo from the rest.

Grady pulled the car into a small lot and turned off the deafening engine.

When she stepped out of the car, Violet was immediately immersed in an electric crackling. It was all around her, only slightly different from the staticky hum she'd become accustomed to in her own improvised graveyard . . . but definitely there nonetheless. The tension in her neck was back, and she braced herself for a sensory onslaught.

Grady couldn't hear a thing.

He rounded the car and walked quietly beside her as they began to wander, little by little, through the rows of headstones and grave markers. Small American flags sprang up from the ground in several spots, and Violet was careful not to disturb any of the homemade memorials that filled the cemetery with vibrance and color, taking on a life of their own.

"Do you know where she's buried?" he asked, his voice acquiring a somber quality, echoing the solemn atmosphere of the cemetery that stretched out before them.

She didn't know. For some reason, Violet hadn't even considered that it might be a problem *finding* the girl's grave; she'd just assumed that she would know where it was . . . that she would somehow *sense* Brooke's location among the others buried here. She shook her head in answer to his question.

"That's okay," Grady said, taking it in stride, and suddenly Violet felt like she was with her old friend again. She'd missed him. "We'll just walk around until we find it," he reassured her.

Violet supposed he was right; it shouldn't be too hard. It was a small cemetery, taking up less than a few square blocks. But when she looked out at the sea of headstones, many covered with flowers and balloons, she was amazed by how many grave sites seemed to fit into the relatively small space.

Violet soon realized that the white noise wasn't just static after all. As she concentrated, trying to find her way toward Brooke Johnson, she could *feel* fluctuations in the energy of it. She took a deep breath, trying to relax herself enough so that she could work on separating one energy from another.

There were definitely echoes of the murdered here.

She heard a shrill explosion of fireworks somewhere very nearby, and she flinched, turning nearly full circle to see where it had come from. The crisp crackling sounds were familiar, reminding her of hot July days and summertime picnics.

"What's wrong?" Grady asked, eyeing her curiously.

Violet realized that she'd just separated her first echo from the others.

"Nothing," she answered honestly as she moved in the direction of the sound. She needed to find where it had come from, hoping she'd gotten lucky and found Brooke already.

She stopped at a stone marker, with a bronze engraved faceplate that read:

EDITH BERNHARD
June 19, 1932—May 2, 1998
Adored Wife and Mother

The banging and popping sounds were so clear here, as Violet stood in front of the simple headstone, that she could almost smell the sulfurous smoke of fireworks that was conspicuously missing. She wondered about Edith Bernhard, dead at age sixty-five. She wondered who she was and how she'd died . . . and who she'd left behind. It wasn't a natural death, not for Edith . . . not with her echo. But what then? Murder? Euthanasia for a woman sick and suffering? Suicide? Could suicide even leave an echo? Did Edith carry the imprint of her own murder?

"Did you know her?"

For a moment Violet had forgotten that Grady was still there, but he was standing right behind her now, reading the woman's headstone over her shoulder. Somehow, Violet felt as if he was intruding on the dead woman's privacy simply by being there.

"No. I was just looking," she answered as she drew Grady away from the grave site.

They wandered around like that, Violet stopping abruptly at several distinct echoes that managed to unravel themselves from the rest. She stopped at the strong smell of coffee to read a marker for a man who had died in his early thirties . . . over forty years ago.

She had the feeling that every inch of her skin was being softly raked by a thousand downy feathers, making her pause at the site of an infant who had died just days after he was born . . . eleven years ago. Violet felt a sense of sadness as she thought about what might have happened to the baby to give him a tragic echo of his own, and she had to walk away, feeling uneasy and dissatisfied.

When she first heard the sound of the bells, they were so clear, so crisp, that she was sure they were part of the real world. She was certain that she must be near a clock tower, somewhere in the cemetery, as it chimed the hour. There was something hauntingly melodic about the sound, though, something too heartrending to be real. She glanced around her, sweeping a quick look over to Grady to see if he'd noticed it too.

Not surprisingly, though, there were no clocks to be seen,

no towers, and from the look on Grady's face it was clear that he hadn't heard what she had.

It was an echo.

And more than that, Violet was certain that this was Brooke's echo. Compelling and strong.

Violet brushed past Grady, consumed by the need to find the source of the bells.

It didn't take her long. The musical chiming served as a beacon, making it easy to locate the grave. Fresh flowers cascaded down from the top of the headstone, avalanching onto the grass below. Silvery Mylar balloons, still suspended by the helium within, swayed back and forth in the autumn breeze. Violet had to bend over once she'd found the site to clear the mementos out of the way just so she could see the name on the marker.

It was her:

BROOKE LYNNE JOHNSON
Treasured Daughter
Beloved Friend

Just seeing the date of her birth, followed by that of her death, made Violet's knees feel weak and unsteady, and she sank to the ground, ignoring the cool dampness that saturated her jeans. They had been so close in age, and had once lived so near each other. As comfortable with death as Violet had always been, this girl's brutal murder was just too real to her.

She closed her eyes and listened to the bells. They

resonated sweetly, reaching to her core, very nearly reaching her soul, the sound vibrating throughout her as it moved with a life of its own.

She memorized it.

It was an *auditory echo*. And it was still strong, not yet faded from the passage of time. Violet would be able to track it. She would recognize the sound anywhere. Anytime.

And the man who wore this imprint was oblivious to that fact.

She suddenly felt like the predator, carrying the most powerful weapon of all. Now she would become the hunter . . . and he, the hunted.

She waited only a few moments longer than she needed to, silently thanking Brooke for sharing this time with her . . . for sharing her heartbreakingly beautiful echo.

Grady was waiting for her at a respectful distance.

When they walked back through the graveyard, Violet let all the echoes, including Brooke's, fall back into one harmonious static hum, filling her with tranquillity once again.

They were bodies at peace. Ripped from this world before their time, but laid to rest by those who loved them most. And they were in harmony.

INVISIBLE

HE WORE THE COVER OF DARKNESS LIKE A NIGHT-time shroud. But even though the blackness shielded him, he couldn't help glancing around one last time as he closed the trunk of his car as softly as he could.

He didn't need a flashlight out here, even if he'd had a free hand to hold one with. He knew his way by heart; he had practiced this route many times before, in anticipation. He had memorized each step until he could pace it with his eyes closed. That was how it needed to be, because his load was heavy, and he didn't have time to spare finding his way.

He hauled the musty military-grade duffel bag up from the ground, the unwieldy contents shifting, straining his back even before he started moving. He slung the long strap across his chest, using his upper body to help balance the weight. His pace was stable and sure, despite the burden he carried, his feet finding their way around the natural obstructions hidden in the blackness.

He counted each measured step until he reached his destination, and then he dropped his cumbersome load. His pulse had quickened, and his breathing, which had already been labored, now grew even more ragged and unsteady. He felt a familiar eagerness, something he hoped he would never grow accustomed to. . . . It thrilled him to his very bones.

He loved this part of the game.

He bent down, savoring the work ahead, and he unzipped the bag at his feet.

The unmistakable metallic scent of blood lingered with the wispy trace of barely decaying flesh. He inhaled it all deeply. In a moment it would be over, and he would never smell this particular girl again.

He turned and dropped to his knees. He used his hands to sift through the soft soil and the leaves where he'd previously prepared the dump site. The dirt was heavier now, after a fine autumn drizzle, making him labor a little more than he'd anticipated. But he didn't mind; this too was a part of what he appreciated about the hunt . . . this final act, in which he released the girl, once and for all, burying his secrets along with her.

By the time the hole was ready, he had broken out in an icy sweat that was chilled by the night air. He lifted one end of the canvas bag and jerked it so that the body inside shifted, falling through the open zipper and landing with a heavy thud inside the superficial grave. He felt nothing for the girl as he used his hands to cover her with the freshly sifted earth.

When he finished burying her, he reached for a loose pile of leaves that he'd left nearby and he layered the exposed terrain with them, making the scene look as natural as possible. Not that it would be necessary way out here.

He stood up and shook the soil from his hands and clothes, using the back of his sleeves to wipe the sweat and dirt from his face before gathering the bag and folding it into a meticulously tight roll, which he tucked beneath his right arm. He reached out in the darkness and put his hand against the trunk of a tree to his left, a guide he used to calculate his way back, and he began to follow his premeditated path back toward his car.

Once he was safely inside, he surveyed the area as best he could, and satisfied that he'd gone completely unnoticed, he started his engine.

As he pulled away from his hiding place amid the overgrown brush and trees, he checked his face for any grimy remnants in the mirror before turning out onto the main road. He waited for some sense of relief to catch up with him, some feeling of accomplishment of a job well done . . . some sense of achievement . . . of conclusiveness.

But it never came. Instead all he felt was a restless stirring coming from deep within him.

He wouldn't be able to wait this time. The familiar feelings were coming faster and faster after each girl, the impatience to find another . . . to start the hunt again.

He was insatiable, he decided. Unquenchable. Ravenous for the chase.

Soon, he assured himself. Soon.

CHAPTER 14

BY FRIDAY, DAY FIVE OF JAY'S EVASION OF VIOLET, she was starting to feel abandoned for good. It wasn't as if she didn't have other friends, but it just so happened that *he* was her favorite one. Besides, it was hard seeing him all day long, sitting so close to him in classes and passing him in the hallways, unable to talk to him. She supposed she could try, but the idea that he might give her the silent treatment in return was devastating to Violet, and she wasn't quite willing to set herself up for that kind of rejection.

Story of my life, she thought miserably. She was never willing to put herself out there.

She bit into her apple just as Chelsea was sitting down

beside her at the lunch table.

"Where's new-Jay?" Chelsea asked, unable to let the joke die. She'd been singing that same ol' song for the past week, and every time she did, it bugged Violet a little bit more. That was probably why Chelsea hadn't given it up yet; she could probably *smell* Violet's irritation.

Instead of correcting Chelsea, yet again, Violet looked around the cafeteria and realized that Grady was nowhere to be seen. That was a first, at least in the space of the past five days, and Violet found it strange that she hadn't even noticed his absence.

Violet shrugged in answer to Chelsea's question.

She felt a mild pang of sadness for Grady, who had been running around in circles in an effort just to be near her. But more than any regret she had over Grady's misplaced affections, she was grateful for the moment of peace.

At least it *had* been peaceful . . . until Chelsea sat down.

It wasn't long before Jules and Claire were joining them.

"Where's new-Jay?" Jules asked, and then she and Chelsea exchanged a look and started cracking up at their own joke.

Even Claire, who was generally so serious about everything, giggled a little.

Violet rolled her eyes. "How long did it take you geniuses to plan that little gem?" she accused her friends, which only made them laugh harder. She shook her head. "You two are idiots," she said, biting into her apple again and deciding to ignore them.

"Which is it, Violet?" Claire asked. "Are they geniuses or idiots?"

Chelsea leaned into Jules now, laughing so hard at their

stupid joke that no sound was even coming out of her mouth anymore.

Violet looked from Chelsea to Jules and then back to Claire. "Idiots," she stated flatly.

There was another long moment as the Two Stooges struggled to regain their composure.

"Come on, Vi. If we can't joke about new-Jay, who *can* we joke about?" Chelsea asked, finally getting herself under control. She used a paper napkin to dab at her watering eyes.

"Joke about whatever you want," Violet stated as blandly as possible. "It's not your fault you're not funny."

"Oh, I'm funny all right. I'm freakin' hilarious. You're the one who's lost her sense of humor," Chelsea lobbed back at her.

Violet was about to argue the point with Chelsea, but her comeback got lost in her throat when she saw Jay walking in.

"Oh, look, there's old-Jay," Claire said nonchalantly. "And he's with Lissie Adams."

Violet had seen that too.

They walked in like they were old friends. Jay was smiling down at Lissie while he carried his tray of food. Lissie was walking as close to him as she could get and still maintain her balance. Lissie's best friend, a girl who had spent her entire high school career being socially eclipsed by Lissie's über-popularity, seemed content to be trailing behind the two of them. As a couple, Jay and Lissie looked like they'd been clipped from the pages of a Hollywood gossip magazine, with their faultless good looks and their perfect smiles. Lissie even had her own entourage. The only thing missing was the red carpet.

But they weren't a couple, Violet argued to herself, *were they?*

Violet's chest suddenly felt heavy, crushed beneath the weight of her own unanswered questions. What if they *were* a couple now? What if her stupid stunt at the mall last weekend had pushed Jay far enough away that he'd replaced her with Lissie? Had that really been less than a week ago?

What if she'd lost her chance with him?

As if there'd ever really been a chance for her at all.

Violet looked wistfully their way once more, wondering if she'd just been fooling herself. They were sitting side by side, at the table where Lissie sat every day with those she deemed good enough to be her friends. She was snuggled up against Jay and saying something that was obviously meant only for his ears.

He truly was a great guy; especially in the ways that really counted beyond his new gorgeous exterior where he was still Jay . . . smart, funny, sweet. Why had she never seen him more clearly before he'd metamorphosed into the very image of hotness that every girl in school was catfighting one another just to get close to?

But he wasn't perfect, she reminded herself as she watched him sitting at Lissie's table. He was incredibly stubborn and pigheaded. Plus, she didn't miss the way he stole the remote when they watched TV or how he always ate all of her chips at lunch. At least she tried to tell herself she didn't.

He never looked up from his conversation with Lissie. He didn't even glance her way, although Violet was sure he knew she was there . . . sitting in the same old place, with the same old friends. While he tested his weight on the delicate ice of new and upwardly mobile social circles, she was still just the same old Violet.

Chelsea seemed to sense that this was no time for joking, and she backed off the new-Jay, old-Jay thing . . . at least for the moment. She put her arm around Violet. "Hey, don't worry about them. Elisabeth Adams is no different from any other girl in school who's been dying to get her claws in him. She's shallow and boring," Chelsea tried her best to reassure Violet. "She's just another brainless cheerleader."

"Besides," Claire piped in, "I hear she's a slut. I hear that she gives it up to all the guys. Half the football players call her 'Kneepads,' if you know what I mean."

Of course she knew what Claire meant; how could she *not* understand the barely subtle innuendo? And why on earth did Claire think that *that* little tidbit of information would make Violet feel better?

Claire might have been the only one at the table who didn't notice the icy glare and the scathing tone that Chelsea shot her way. *"No way,"* Chelsea disagreed. "Prissie Lissie is all that virginal, pure crap. She's one of those girls who wears a promise ring to her daddy that she won't give it up till she's married or some shit like that. There's no way that Jay could even get to third base with her tight, Christian ass."

It was supposed to be a pep talk; Violet knew that and tried not to fault her for it. It was Chelsea's way of showing her unconditional support for her friend. But somehow, Violet ended up feeling even worse than before. Now she couldn't stop picturing Lissie and Jay making out in his mom's car, with his hand beneath her shirt . . . rounding first base and heading for second. She felt sick.

That was definitely a mental image she could live without, and she wished at that moment that she could gouge out her own mind's eye to make it go away.

"So, that pretty much settles it, Violet. You are *definitely* going out with us tonight," Chelsea insisted. "Olivia Hildebrand throws the best parties, and you could use a night out. It's BYOB, but I'm having my older sister buy for us, so if you just pitch in a coupla bucks I'll take care of the booze."

Violet had already told Chelsea that she didn't want to go to the party. What she really wanted to do, all she could even imagine doing tonight, was putting on her most comfortable sweatpants and crawling into bed to watch old movies.

She started to object, but Chelsea interrupted her. "Trust me, Vi. Don't sit around by yourself tonight. Tell your parents you're staying at my house and we'll go out and get stupid. Forget about Jay. Forget about Lissie." She put on her best pout and gave Violet a doe-eyed look that was more sarcastic than serious. *"Pretty, pretty plee-eease!"*

"Come on, it'll be fun," Jules cajoled in her usual brief manner. She was nearly as incapable of tagging multiple words together as Chelsea was at any form of true sincerity.

"Ooh, and if you don't have anything to wear, you can borrow something from me," Claire added, as though that was Violet's only hang-up about going.

It was Violet's turn to laugh as she looked at her friends,

each trying in her own pitiful way to make Violet feel better about losing Jay. She wanted to say no, but suddenly she couldn't. Maybe they were right; maybe what she needed was a girls' night out, even if it would end up being at a crowded party with a bunch of her drunken classmates.

"Fine." Violet finally succumbed to the pressure. "But you'll have to pick me up. My parents won't let me out of the house by myself. They think we're safer traveling in packs."

"That's my girl." Chelsea crumpled her empty brown lunch sack into a ball and tossed it toward the garbage can at the end of the table. She missed by a mile, but ignored that fact completely, leaving her garbage where it landed on the ground. "I'll call you when I'm on my way."

She and Claire took off to their next class, leaving Violet to walk with Jules, who was heading in the same direction she was.

They had to walk past Lissie's table on their way out, and Violet was surprised to see that Jay was no longer sitting there with the senior girls. She'd never even seen him leave. But somehow, Violet realized, she had attracted Lissie's attention, and as Violet and Jules walked past, the cheerleader stopped talking to her friends and watched Violet intently.

It was strange, the look in the other girl's eyes, kind of defensive . . . almost *challenging*. It was as if *Lissie* was jealous of *her* . . . and was really pissed off about it.

Violet wanted to tell her that she had nothing to worry about just to make her stop glaring like that. She wanted to tell her that she and Jay weren't even friends anymore, let alone anything beyond that. But there was no point in it. From what Violet had seen in the cafeteria that day, Lissie was already getting her way, and she'd soon realize that Violet was no competition for her.

Suddenly the party seemed like a great idea.

By the time Violet had dressed and re-dressed several times, she was starting to think that maybe Claire had been right, that maybe she should have borrowed something from the self-proclaimed "fashionista."

She finally landed on a pair of her better jeans, coupled with a cute black top and some black flats. She added a beaded necklace and matching earrings and checked herself out in the mirror. She rarely wore makeup but had decided that this was a special occasion—her night out with the girls to forget Jay—so she'd sparingly accented her green eyes with a touch of eyeliner and gingerly applied a coat of black mascara.

The effect was somewhat dramatic, making her eyes look exotic rather than ordinary.

She glossed her lips. *Not bad,* she thought, tucking a wild wisp of hair behind her ear.

Her cell phone rang with the standard, preprogrammed ringtone that had come with the phone. Violet hadn't even bothered to change it, feeling a little like she would be dancing on the graves of the girls who had gone missing— figuratively, of course—if she were to enjoy her new phone for anything other than the utilitarian purpose for which it had been purchased.

She flipped it open, and before she could say hello, Jules

was yelling into her ear, "Get your fine little ass in gear, girl! We're out in your driveway!"

Violet could hear screams and shrieks of laughter in the background. She decided she'd better get out there fast before they alerted her parents, and they changed their minds about letting her go out tonight.

"Keep it down, or I'm not going anywhere," she insisted into the phone, and then snapped it shut without so much as a good-bye.

She grabbed her purse and hurried down the stairs two at a time.

"Chelsea's here. I'll see you in the morning!"

"Be careful!" her mom yelled back.

"Keep your phone on," her dad called out without raising his voice. "Just in case," he added.

CHAPTER 15

THEY COULD HEAR THE PARTY LONG BEFORE they ever reached Olivia Hildebrand's house. Music similar to what had been playing inside Chelsea's car was booming . . . only much, *much* louder. The four of them climbed out of the tiny Mazda and trudged up the long driveway that was over-flowing with cars. Violet scanned the vehicles, silently hoping against hope that she would see Jay's mom's car parked among the rest. But it wasn't there, and she decided to set that impossible wish aside.

Still, Violet found herself smiling when they reached the front door, her arms filled with cheap alcohol that she probably wouldn't even drink. The music was loud and her friends were louder. She could hear kids from inside the party calling out to them as they walked up to the front doors. Their enthusiasm was contagious.

Violet loved going to parties, mostly just so she could see what everyone was like outside of school. They became different people when they were away from campus. These were the same kids she'd gone to school with ever since she was a little girl. But here, at night and away from that familiar institution they attended five days a week, away from the cliques that governed where they sat and who they hung out with on a daily basis, they were free to be whoever they wanted to be. Of course, the booze helped to loosen those sharply defined social lines a little.

"Violet! *Vi-o-let!*" she heard a boy's voice screaming to her from the other side of the kitchen as she set her load down on the counter. Swarming teens began to reach in and take what they wanted even before she'd taken her hands off the alcohol she'd carried in.

"Oh, good," Chelsea yelled above the noise without even looking to see who was screaming Violet's name. She set her bags on the counter with the rest. "Your fan club's here."

Violet looked in that general direction to see who it was, and when she saw him her stomach dropped.

Grady was there, weaving his way through the crowd of noisy teens and heading right toward her.

"Oh God," Violet breathed, leaning in close to Chelsea so that only she could hear what she was about to say. "It's *new*-Jay."

Chelsea couldn't contain her laughter, as Violet finally came over to the dark side, and it came out in kind of a half snort, which made her laugh even harder. "Here," she said, grabbing Violet by the arm and practically dragging her in the opposite direction . . . *away from Grady.* "We'll pretend we didn't see him."

They ducked quickly through a hallway that wrapped past the bedrooms and back around to the family room behind the kitchen. They were near the spot where Grady had been when he'd started yelling for her, and now he was nowhere in sight. The two girls were giggling as if they'd pulled off some great stunt by dodging him.

"Think we lost him?" Violet asked as they tried to blend into the crowd.

Chelsea grabbed two clear bottles of the tastes-more-like-juice, fruit-flavored drinks from the counter and handed one to Violet. She twisted off the little metal cap and then clinked the top of hers against Violet's. "Here's hoping," she said and guzzled her drink.

Violet took a swallow of the Kool-Aid-like wine cooler. She couldn't imagine why she'd thought she wanted to stay home by herself tonight. Chelsea had been right; the party had been *exactly* what she'd needed.

As the night went on, Violet immersed herself in the music and the laughter, letting the noise become a riotous screen that made it impossible for her to think of anything beyond the present. She couldn't find the time to feel sorry for herself in this raucous, self-indulgent environment of kids with too much alcohol and no parental supervision.

She watched beer games in the kitchen, a fight in the front yard—which wasn't really a fight at all, more like an overblown shoving match—and she saw two people puking before the night was over. One was Todd Stinnett, a boy from her second-period class, who had chugged one too many beers at the Quarters table. The other was a freshman girl, Mackenzie Sherwin, who wandered outside to throw up in the bushes. Unfortunately for Mackenzie, she didn't get her hair out of the way in time and ended up walking around for the rest of the night with the matted strands dangling around her face.

A group of stoners thought the poor girl was hilarious and made puking noises at her every time she stumbled past them.

By the time Grady finally caught up with Violet, it was nearly midnight, and when he got close to her she wasn't even sure *how* he was still standing upright. He was completely wasted.

"Where've ya been? I've been lookin' everywhere for you." His words were a slurred mess, and he wrapped an arm heavily around her shoulders. Violet wondered if it wasn't so much a gesture of affection as it was a means of maintaining his precarious balance.

But she was worried about him, even though she played innocent, pretending that she *hadn't* been avoiding him all night. "I've been around," she answered with a straight face. "Besides, it looks like you had plenty of fun without me." She tried to move out from beneath the weight of his arm. He was leaning on her so hard that it felt like he was trying to push her down to the ground.

Her sudden shift made him lose his shaky balance, and he ended up hanging on even tighter, putting most of his unstable weight on her. "Don't go," he pleaded, his hot breath thick with the pungent smell of stale beer and tequila.

The combination was foul.

On the other side of the room she saw Chelsea talking with a group of girls. She flashed Violet a questioning look with her eyes. Violet just rolled her own in response and then looked back at Grady. She wanted to get away from him and go back to her friends, but she didn't want to leave him alone in his condition. He was a mess. And he *was* her friend.

"I think we should get you home," she finally offered. She hadn't had anything to drink since that sip of wine cooler earlier in the night, so she knew she was fine to drive him. "Give me your keys."

He closed one eye as if it were easier to focus that way as he reached into his pocket and pulled out his keys. He stared at her as he jiggled them in front of her face. "I can drive. . . ." His mouth made his words sound like mush.

Violet reached out and snatched them from his hand. His reflexes were way too slow to stop her, and when he finally tried, he was about five seconds too late. The sudden movement nearly made him fall over, almost taking Violet with him.

Violet struggled to keep them both upright. "Come on, Grady. I owe you one anyway."

He gave her his one-eyed squint again. "What d'ya mean?"

She didn't bother explaining that he'd bailed her out the other day by taking her to the cemetery when she'd needed to go to Brooke Johnson's grave. In fact, she didn't say anything to Grady, and he didn't ask again or argue about driving himself. He seemed to give up as he leaned on Violet and she led him out of the house. She lifted the keys up as they passed Chelsea, silently letting her know where she was going.

The air had cooled as the night had gone on and the brisk snap to it seemed to have a *mildly* sobering effect on Grady . . . which at this point was a vast improvement. His car was farther down the road than Chelsea's was, thanks to Chelsea's small car and her creative definition of "parked," which to her consisted of lodging it, cockeyed and nose first, into a gap between two other parked cars.

The tall cedar and fir trees towering overhead all but blocked most of the light cast by the nearly full moon, creating ghostly shadows that fell across them as they walked, or in Grady's case, stumbled, toward his car. But by the time they reached it, he was walking mostly on his own accord again . . . he was no longer swaggering from side to side.

Violet helped him around to the passenger-side door and held it open for him.

But Grady wasn't ready to go just yet.

"Thanks a lot, Violet. I really appreciate this." Even his words sounded a little less sloppy now.

"It's no problem. I was getting a little bored anyway." And then when he gave her a look that said he didn't believe her, she added, "Seriously. I'm kind of tired too." She made an effort to sound convincing.

He straightened up from where he'd been leaning against the doorjamb and took a step closer to her. He was standing over her now, and she suddenly felt somewhat trapped between him and the open car door . . . stuck between a rock and a hard place.

"We could hang out here for a while." He slid his arm around her waist.

She wasn't sure how she should react; even though she knew what he was trying to do, she had no doubt that she did not want him doing it. But she was frozen to the spot where she stood.

He leaned in, moving toward her, his other arm snaking around to pull her up against him. His grip was tight . . . *too tight* . . . and Violet didn't like the feeling creeping over her, the sensation that he wasn't *asking* her if he could do this. The feeling that this was all out of her control.

The goose bumps that broke out on her arms had little to do with the nighttime chill.

He dipped his head down, and all at once Violet found her voice again. "No, Grady!" she insisted, turning her head away before his lips were on top of hers. *"Don't!"*

She tried to duck beneath his arms but his grip tightened, squeezing her even harder against his chest. Her heart felt like it was tripping over itself now, and she was suddenly afraid of where this was going.

He put his mouth against her ear and whispered hoarsely while his lips clumsily caressed her earlobe. "It's okay, Violet. I won't tell anyone if you don't want me to." He made it sound like an invitation, but the forcefulness of his actions was making it feel more and more like a command. His tongue flicked out and stroked the side of her neck in what Violet feared was his version of seduction.

Violet was vaguely aware of the sound of tires approaching, and she could see headlights getting closer. She thought about calling out for help, but she was also afraid that she might be overreacting.

She was sure she could handle this herself.

Grady tried once again to kiss her, searching out her mouth, and this time she pushed him with both hands pressed against his chest, shoving him back as she tried to crane her head out of his way. "*Stop it*, Grady. I mean it!" She was surprised that she sounded so strong. At least her voice wasn't as shaky as she felt.

But he was bigger and stronger than she was, and his hands reached up behind her to the back of her head, ignoring her denials and pinning her in place. When his mouth finally landed on hers, the combination of his alcohol-soaked breath and his brutish unrestrained actions made her quiver sickly beneath him. His lips were moist and soft, but not in the way that Violet would have hoped for in a kiss, and as his tongue tried to find its way into her mouth it reminded her of a warm, slippery slug.

She felt like she was going to puke.

She struggled against it . . . *against him* . . . and her fists pounded uselessly against his chest. She was no longer so sure that she *could* handle this. She writhed her head away long enough to dislodge his mouth from hers, and she took the opportunity to shove her hands upward, covering her face in an effort to block him.

"*Please! Stop!*" she cried, hoping that something would get through to him and he would stop trying to force himself on her. She hoped that he would snap to his senses and realize, once and for all, what an ass he was being.

What she really wished was that he would just let her go.

173

And then he did. But not in the way she'd imagined.

He jerked away from her, and she heard a strangled sound escape from him as his body slammed against the side of his own car. She was pushing so hard against him, trying to keep *away* from him, that when his arms actually released her, she banged her head on the doorjamb. She heard a loud, dull thud, and then a whimper that could have been any wounded animal.

Violet tried to keep up with what was going on, but her brain still felt fuzzy—muddled—from Grady's unexpected groping. At first she thought that he must have slipped and fallen, or that maybe she'd shoved him harder than she thought, even though she doubted she could have knocked him down on her own.

When she realized what was really happening, she almost couldn't believe her own eyes.

Jay was there, and he was standing over Grady, who was now lying in a crumpled heap at his feet. The look on Jay's face was as murderous as Violet had ever seen on anyone before, and he was clenching and unclenching his fist as he glared violently at Grady.

She looked down and saw that Grady was holding one hand over his mouth, and there was blood seeping from between his fingers. He held his other hand up in surrender. "Stop! *Stop!*"

Jay seemed to have a difficult time deciding. And then he leaned over, his fist balling up again, ready to strike, as he reached in and jerked Grady forward by the collar of his shirt. "Isn't that what Violet said to you, you jerk? Didn't she tell you to stop?"

Grady recoiled, curling up as tightly as he could and

pulling his arm around his face. "Please! Don't—" But he didn't finish his sentence as his voice cracked vulnerably.

Violet was stunned. Silent and dazed, she could only stand there and watch, a million unanswered questions spinning in her head.

Where had Jay come from? How long had he been there?

And the one question she was afraid to ask: *where was Lissie tonight?*

She hated the conflicting feelings that plagued her at that moment. She was grateful that someone had saved her from Grady's unwanted advances, and even more grateful that that someone turned out to be Jay. At the same time she was appalled that he'd punched Grady, and she felt sort of sorry for Grady despite his overzealous hands and mouth. She was also shocked by the undisguised fury she saw on Jay's face, but she had to admit that she kind of liked that she could stir such a reaction in him. It meant that he cared.

Even if it wasn't in the way she'd hoped for, he still cared.

She watched as Jay let Grady fall back to the ground. Well, not *fall* exactly, it was more of a shove, releasing him and making him smack his head against the car as he collapsed backward.

But he wasn't quite finished with his warning to Grady, and he snarled at him from between gritted teeth, "If you ever . . . *ever* . . . touch her again, I swear to God, Grady, I'll fucking kill you. Do you hear me?"

Violet was stunned by the rage in Jay's voice as well as in his words.

Grady just nodded, wiping his bloody hand on his jeans. He looked like he wanted to say something more but couldn't quite find the words.

Jay didn't wait for him. "There's no way you're driving tonight, Grady. Give me your keys," he demanded then, holding out his hand impatiently.

Grady started to dig in his pockets and then had second thoughts. "How'm I supposed to get—?" he started to ask, but Jay cut him off.

"I don't give a shit; you'll find a ride. Now give them to me."

Jay's voice left little room for argument, and Grady decided not to test his luck. "Violet has them," he finally admitted before stumbling away from them, back toward the party.

Violet jumped when she heard her name. She felt like she'd been eavesdropping on the two of them. "Oh . . . yeah . . ." she seemed to be saying to herself as she held up the keys and then dropped them into Jay's outstretched hand.

For a moment, she wasn't sure what to say to him. Finally she opted for the obvious. "Thank you." It kind of said it all.

Jay pocketed Grady's keys and walked over to his mom's car. It was the car she must have heard pulling up while Grady was trying to attack her with his disgusting tongue. He opened the passenger-side door, and without so much as a glance in her direction, he turned that same commanding voice on her. "Get in the car, Violet."

And that was it . . . the end of her brief thrill at seeing Jay tonight.

His demanding tone, which she had appreciated when it was directed at Grady, felt like sandpaper rubbing against her already frayed nerves when he used it with her. All of the gratitude that she'd felt just moments before fragmented like shards of irreparable glass, and Violet narrowed her eyes at him. The entire week without him, missing him and craving his company, seemed to melt away . . . and now *she* was the one who was furious.

"Are you kidding me? You don't give me the time of day for the past week and then you want to come around and start giving me orders?" She put her hands on her hips, daring him to argue with her. Her cheeks seared as her temper burned fiercely. "I don't think so, Jay. That's not how it works."

Suddenly she wanted to go back to the party . . . to go back to her *real* friends, the ones that hadn't given her the silent treatment all week or disregarded her very existence. She turned on her heel and started back toward the house, following the trail of loud music that reached all the way down the street.

Jay didn't follow her. He didn't try to talk her into staying. It hurt her feelings that he didn't pursue her, begging her forgiveness for behaving like such a jerk.

But on the other hand, she decided, she'd made herself pretty clear, and Jay had certainly proven that he was capable of stubbornly standing his ground. And despite her wounded ego, no matter how relieved she'd been that he'd shown up when he had, there was *no way in hell* that she was going to let him start telling her what to do now.

She didn't look back to see if he was watching her leave.

She was too afraid of what she might see if she did. . . .

That Jay wasn't coming after her.

CHANCE

WHEN HE FIRST SAW THE GIRL WALKING ALONE *down the narrow, darkened street, he nearly overlooked her.*

It was too soon, he told himself. He had just buried one, and not enough time had passed to create the frenzied desire he usually craved.

But there was something about her . . . she looked lost . . . in need.

He slowed his car, way . . . way down, *watching her progress as she made her way through the night, tripping as if she were incapable of watching her own steps. She never looked back. It was as if she was oblivious to his very presence, despite the unnatural beam of his headlights filtering away the darkness from her path.*

And then he realized it, like the dawning of the first morning's light, clearing the way for the day. She needed him.

Almost as much as he needed her.

He moved his car closer, easing up behind her, careful to keep her in his sights should she become alarmed . . . frightened by his proximity.

The silhouette she created in his headlamps was the very essence of youth. Her movements, clumsy with inattention, were graceless and inelegant in a way that was lost in womanhood. Her body was still supple; her skin would be soft.

He cast sideways glances at the parked cars around him, watching for anyone who might be watching his approach.

There was no one.

He reached her, still without notice on her part, and he pulled his car silently alongside her.

She looked up then; her innocent, tear-filled eyes stared at him hauntingly, stirring his desire into a scorching frenzy. Recognition cleared them as she stopped walking then, and the tears were replaced by supplication.

He exited the car, moving fluidly now as the dance began again.

Few words were exchanged, mostly from him, and within the span of a heartbeat, he had slipped a comforting arm around her shoulder and led her to the passenger's side. . . .

All while she gazed up at him with unguarded gratitude.

CHAPTER 16

VIOLET HATED THE ANGRY TEARS THAT BURNED her eyes as she stumbled over an unseen rock on the ground in front of her.

She wished that she could just go back in time, to that moment. She wished that she had just gotten in his car when he'd commanded her. Even as angry as she'd been at him, she couldn't help thinking it would have been better than this . . . this lonely walk through the chilly darkness, berating herself with second thoughts and what-ifs. Better than the rejection that seeped like venom through her every pore.

She hated Jay at that moment, for making her feel so vulnerable and weak. She wasn't supposed to be that girl, she had never been that girl before . . . needy . . . and pathetic.

By the time the car was pulling up beside her, she didn't have time to wonder why she hadn't noticed it before. She hadn't heard the sound of the tires across the ancient asphalt with its gravel-filled potholes, or even noticed the headlights that blanched the blackness into pale shadows.

She turned her head sideways, squinting slightly, to get a look at who was inside.

When she saw him there, behind the wheel, she stopped walking, trying not to look so thankful as she blinked away the tears.

She heard the door opening, and before she could catch her gratified breath the driver was out of the car and she was in his arms.

She wanted to breathe, to inhale his lethally musky scent, but she couldn't find the air around her. She was suffocated in the strength, *the warmth*, of him.

Time seemed irrelevant at that point; it could have been seconds or hours. It didn't matter. She didn't even realize she'd been crying again until he pulled away and leaned down to kiss her wet cheek.

And then his lips moved softly, gingerly, tracing a path to hers. Electric shock waves, which started below her stomach and shot upward, made her tingle and burn as his mouth caressed hers.

She'd imagined this moment so many times, dreamed of him holding her like this for so long.

Violet sighed, sinking farther against him, forgetting

herself . . . forgetting her anger and her hurt, losing herself in the moment.

Jay kissed her, hard, and long, and deep. And she kissed him back, matching his intensity. He banished any trace of doubt that might have remained.

Violet was acutely aware of her own heartbeat, fluttering in strategic pulse points throughout her body, and echoing its heady rhythm through her veins. She was flushed and shivering at the same instant. She could smell the intoxicating heat coming off him in waves.

When his mouth left hers, she felt bruised and raw. She could still feel his touch on her lips.

He looked down at her, his eyes as glazed as her own, his voice thick with barely restrained desire. "Get in the car, Violet."

This time instead of sounding like a granite command, it sounded like warm silk wrapping around her. And instead of bristling against it, she just nodded as she stared at his beautiful face, unable to think of anything but the wonderful things his lips had just done to her.

They didn't move for a long moment, they just stood there, looking at each other. His gaze moved to her mouth and then lazily back to her eyes, as if he were memorizing her.

Somewhere in the distance, but probably closer than it seemed, Violet heard a car driving away. But she didn't bother looking up, because she had other things on her mind.

Jay had come back for her.

CHAPTER 17

VIOLET STAYED AWAKE FOR MOST OF THE NIGHT, thinking over and over again about what had happened. She wanted to remember every tiny detail, capturing it forever in her memory so that she could recall it again at a moment's notice.

Jay had kissed her.

Finally.

And not just any kiss. It wasn't one of the sisterly kisses of their childhood. There was nothing childlike about it. He had finally closed that chasm that had been growing between them since the end of the summer.

Finally.

Violet could hardly stand it. She was excited . . . elated . . . electrified all at once.

But along with those feelings came the others, the insecurities and the doubts. The questions of what his sudden appearance last night really meant. What the kiss really meant.

They hadn't talked about it at all during the ride home. They didn't talk about anything; the charged silence between them seemed to speak volumes. But there were no repeat performances, even as he walked her up to the door to make sure that she got inside safely. He hadn't held her hand or even touched her again. And now, in the morning's light, she couldn't help but wonder if he had simply been overwhelmed by relief that she was safe, that he had saved her before Grady had gone too far. Had he merely been reacting to a sudden surge of adrenaline . . . kissing her on impulse, without thinking it through?

She hoped not. She prayed not.

She pushed those negative thoughts away, remembering instead the feel of his soft lips against hers. And the heat of his body pressed, heart to heart, with her own.

By morning she was both exhausted and exhilarated.

She finally gave up chasing sleep and peeled herself from the rumpled warmth of her bed at just after seven o'clock. She could smell the rich scent of coffee brewing from downstairs and felt drawn to it.

Her mom was in the kitchen by herself. She didn't say anything about Violet coming home last night.

Violet looked around, a little surprised. Her dad was usually the early riser; it was her mom who could sleep until nearly noon. "Did Dad go to work already?" Violet asked, knowing that he often went to the office on Saturdays to catch up on his work without the weekday commotion.

Her mom looked haggard and weary, and she pulled her steaming mug closer to her, hugging her hands around it as if drawing strength from its warmth. "No," her voice croaked, and then she cleared her throat and tried again. "No, your uncle Stephen picked him up about a half hour ago."

Violet hesitated only briefly as she reached into the cupboard for one of the mismatched coffee mugs that littered the shelf. She found her favorite one, a faded ceramic mug with a garish picture of the Golden Gate Bridge splashed across it. Her parents had brought it home from a vacation before she was born, and she found the time-crackled paint charming. "Why?" she asked as she filled her own mug and reached into the fridge for the vanilla-flavored creamer. She was generous with it, turning her coffee a pale, milky tan.

When her mother didn't answer right away, Violet turned toward her to see what was the matter. "What is it?"

Her mom sighed, looking suddenly older . . . and worn out. She shook her head for several seconds before speaking, but she couldn't avoid it forever. "Another girl." Her voice cracked with quiet frustration. "From Buckley. From White River, Violet."

Violet hovered where she was, half standing, half sitting, in the chair beside her mom at the kitchen table. "Who?" was all she could manage, too stunned by the news to move.

"Mackenzie Sherwin. She's a little younger than you."

Violet froze. That name. She *knew* that name.

"Is she a friend of yours?" her mom asked, placing her own chilled hand over Violet's as Violet sank like a stone into the chair. "She was at a party last night, and then no one saw her again. Do you know who she is?" she asked again.

There was no point in lying. Even if they weren't bound to discover the truth about where she'd gone last night, which they definitely were, this was no time for lies.

"I saw her last night," Violet admitted, raising her eyes to meet her mom's. "I was at the same party."

Violet watched the looks that played across her mother's face, from the dawning flash of anger as she realized that Violet had lied to her about where she'd been, to the fleeting panic that it could have been her own daughter, to relief. And, finally, to acceptance. She must have decided, like Violet had about the lying, that this wasn't the time for reprimands. Although Violet knew that it would come . . . later.

"There's a search party. They're combing the woods to look for the girl. They can't rule out the possibility that she just wandered away in the night and got lost. The reports coming in are that she was drinking pretty heavily."

Violet thought about Mackenzie Sherwin. She could picture the younger girl who had thrown up in the bushes and then spent the rest of the night wandering in and out of the party with her own vomit drying in her hair. She could barely walk upright when Violet had last seen her.

"What if she's not lost?" Violet asked, hating the question even as it poisoned her lips.

"They can't rule that out either. They have every cop in the area looking for evidence, while half the city is combing the woods around the Hildebrands' house looking for that poor girl." Her mom squeezed Violet's hand before letting it go. "Since you were there, your uncle Stephen might want to talk to you."

"I'll get dressed and go over there," Violet decided.

Her mom looked up, as if surprised by the declaration. "No, Vi. I think you should stay here today. . . ." She didn't finish her thought, but Violet could hear the unspoken words that hung in the air . . . *where it's safe.*

She thought about holing up in the house again, watching the clock and waiting, not doing anything productive, and she just couldn't take it. And then she wondered if she would sense anything when she got there . . . a new echo maybe. She pushed away the troubling thought.

"No, Mom. I'm gonna go talk to Uncle Stephen. Maybe something I saw, *anything*, can help them find her." She was surprised by her own conviction, but she knew she hadn't yet convinced her mother, who was still wrestling with her own silent fears. "Don't worry, Dad's there. I won't do anything without his permission."

Violet waited for her mom to say something, holding her breath and willing her mother to agree to let her go.

When she did finally speak, her words were unsteady and filled with defeated fatigue. "I'd feel better if Jay was going with you," she said.

Me too, Violet thought without giving her words voice. *Me too.*

★ ★ ★

Violet wasn't sure what she'd expected to find when she turned down the road toward the house where she and her friends had partied just the night before. She had assumed there would be small groups moving around the area, calling out to the lost girl in hopes of finding her, misplaced among the thick stands of tall trees that practically overcrowded and dwarfed the few homes in the area.

But it wasn't just a few Good Samaritans helping a missing neighbor. This was a full-on search-and-rescue operation. It had the feel of organized chaos, with emphasis on the *organized* part.

Violet had to park her car much farther away than anyone had the night before, when they were just a bunch of teenagers converging on the semi-isolated house. And people were still arriving behind her. While ahead of her, emergency vehicles, both police and fire, hovered around the entrance to the forests that lay beyond.

Men and women, young and old, volunteers and professionals, all dressed in brightly colored vests, many of them carrying walkie-talkies, moved in smaller groups in all directions, efficiently combing the endless landscape with deliberate order. It was like nothing she had ever seen before. They were like a swarming sea of fluorescent vests, bobbing and shifting in steady progression.

Violet made a quick scan of the area as she walked toward the mass of people, to see if she could spot her father or her uncle in the throng of rescue workers. But if they were there, they were lost among the crowd.

She approached what seemed to be the central hub of activity. Groups grew larger as more people arrived, waiting to be told what they could do to help. She recognized some of the people among them, parents of her friends, neighbors, people who worked at stores in the area, and even one of the teachers from her school.

A woman was passing out the neon-colored vests, while another was taking down the names of the volunteers and organizing them into search teams, each with a leader who was assigned a walkie-talkie. A man with a bullhorn was shouting out orders about where to check in and instructions on how to proceed once they got started. Everyone was handed a black-and-white flyer with a picture of the missing girl, and Violet was glad to replace the mental image she had of the stumbling, incoherent girl from the night before with this smiling photo.

She waited with a crowd of people who were hanging around one of the many uniformed police officers; she was hoping he might be able to tell her where she could find her uncle. Other people shouted out questions all around her.

How long has she been missing?

Was this where she was last seen?

Do they think the killer might have taken her?

Do they expect to find her alive?

Violet tried to push her way to the front of the gathering, to get the officer's attention, but it was like swimming upstream, and she found herself making backward progress instead as she was squeezed toward the rear of the group. She didn't want to yell out and draw attention to herself, so eventually she just pried herself free from those looking for answers.

She wondered if coming here had been a mistake. Maybe she shouldn't have been so adamant about trying to help. But she felt guilty, riddled with a sense of at least some degree of responsibility for being among those who had last seen the girl . . . and one who hadn't bothered helping her when she'd so obviously been in need.

She drifted around, feeling a little like a wayward snow-flake caught in a breeze, finally landing near the cluster of volunteers who were busy checking in.

"Are you already assigned to a team?"

Violet looked up, caught off guard by the woman passing out vests. "No," she answered, thinking to tell the woman that she wasn't planning to join the search but never quite finding the words.

The woman handed Violet a vest and another woman assigned her to a team. She was introduced, only briefly, to her team leader, a man who was probably in his late fifties or early sixties. His gray hair was cut high and tight, army style, and he looked like he'd done a tour or two in some branch of the military. He handled his walkie-talkie like a seasoned veteran.

Surprisingly to Violet, however, especially since he gave the air of a man who had seen some action in his day, she sensed nothing at all from the über-militant team leader. John Richter carried none of the imprints of death she would have expected.

Maybe he wasn't so tough after all. Or maybe he'd just been lucky.

The no-nonsense team captain took the lead, reading the coordinates on the map he held and piloting them to the area they'd been assigned to search, which was circled in red Sharpie. There were five other members of her team, two women and three men. Violet didn't know anyone in her grouping, and she didn't really care. That way she didn't feel the need to make polite chitchat.

The farther they walked, passing other teams as they scoured the area, and moving deeper and deeper into the damp, darkening woods, the more ominous it all began to feel. Violet wasn't afraid, but she was definitely troubled by what they were doing out here. She had the foreboding sense that this was an effort in futility, that they were out here simply to rule out the possibility that Mackenzie had wandered away from the party and had gotten turned around among the trees . . . when it seemed so obvious to Violet, and probably to almost everyone around her too, what had really happened to her schoolmate.

He had gotten her.

Violet could hear the others, in all directions, calling out Mackenzie's name. They passed a few men who were carrying long wooden poles that looked like unpainted broom handles, and she could only imagine what they were meant to prod or uncover.

She followed her group until they reached their designated coordinates, and they were ordered by John Richter to fan out, keeping one another in their sights but spreading wide enough apart to cover as much ground as possible.

Violet moved with careful steps, losing herself in the process of the search. The familiar, reassuring smells of the woodlands drifted around her. The Christmassy smell of the fir trees surrounded her, along with the dank, earthy scent of fallen autumn leaves left to decompose. The air was moist and thick with the kind of misty precipitation that was common this time of year in the Pacific Northwest. It seeped through Violet's clothing and her shoes, until it was pressing itself damply against her skin and chilling her all the way to the bone.

While she explored she was aware of several weak echoes around her, which she generally assumed were long-dead animals buried in the underbrush of the thickly overgrown forest floor. They were easy enough to ignore under the circumstances.

Other teams moved past and around them, moving in larger circles, widening the search and covering more and more area. The sheer number of people involved in looking for Mackenzie Sherwin seemed endless, and Violet took some amount of comfort in the fact that so many people were trying . . . that so many people cared.

She hoped beyond hope that their efforts would be rewarded.

But she wasn't holding her breath.

She heard the musical ringtone of a cell phone, and even though the sound was far away, she instinctively patted her pocket to feel for hers and realized that she'd left it back in her car. Her mom would be pissed. It probably didn't matter, though, since she doubted she would have gotten reception out here anyway.

She climbed up, and over, a rotting log that was lying in her way. Her hand touched the slippery film on top of it as she maneuvered it, and when she was on the other side she wiped her hand against her jeans to rub away the slick sensation. She thought of Grady, trying to cram his greasy tongue down her throat last night, and she nearly gagged.

It was the first time she'd thought about what had happened to her, so close to this very spot, since she'd left her house that morning. It had been a nice reprieve, not to be consumed by the instant replays that had run over and over in her head, keeping her awake all night long.

But she let herself think of Jay. And of the kiss. And suddenly the damp chill that had been clinging to her evaporated in a wave of heat that started in her belly and spread like an uncontained blaze, flushing her from cheek to toe.

She realized that she was smiling now, and she had to force it away, not wanting anyone to see her as she searched in vain for the missing girl, grinning like the village idiot.

The cell phone was still ringing in the distance.

Violet looked around, trying to figure out which direction it was coming from, and realized just how easy it would be to get lost out here. All alone, in the dead of night.

Violet couldn't help but hope that was what had really happened. And that today, with the light on their side, they would find Mackenzie Sherwin, cold and hungover, confused and grateful to be rescued.

She heard another voice calling out for Mackenzie, and she looked around her.

She could no longer see the woman with the too-red hair, the team member that she'd been assigned to keep within visual range. She'd lost track of herself, and of where she was supposed to be searching, and she realized that she'd been moving without thinking, like a sleepwalker.

The sound of the phone grew slightly stronger, and she realized that she'd been following it. Searching for the source. *Drawn* to it . . . against her own will.

She could see another team's members, not too far away, and realized that even though she was breaking the rules by wandering off on her own, she still wasn't lost. It wasn't like she was out here on her own. This morning, the forest was swarming with dozens, maybe hundreds, of people. She wasn't alone.

She heard it again, only slightly louder, and she wondered why it was still ringing.

An ear-piercing bellow broke through her concentrated silence, and Violet jumped. She felt foolish when she realized that it was just another searcher, moving between the trees to the right of her, calling out the missing girl's name. She silently chided herself for being so skittish.

That was when she realized *why* she was so skittish . . . so jumpy.

It was the cell phone.

But it wasn't really a cell phone at all.

The sound that she'd been following, the sound she'd been drawn to, the very one that had pulled her away from her own search team as she wandered closer and closer to it . . . it was never a cell phone.

It was the sound of bells.

The spectral sound of Brooke's bells.

Far away, muffled, obscured over the distance . . . but growing clearer . . . stronger.

Her heart pounded violently, and her feet suddenly felt like they were mired in quicksand that was slowly sucking and pulling her down. She was afraid to struggle, afraid to move or even breathe, for fear of being dragged beneath the surface forever.

A thought flashed through her head that maybe *she* had never been moving closer to the sound at all, but rather *he* was out here and moving closer to her. She wasn't sure whether that was good news or bad. This was a man she'd been hunting. A man she'd been determined to find. A killer who needed to be stopped.

But why would he be out here? Now, of all times? Was he part of an assigned rescue team, searching through the forest and pretending *not* to know the fate of this poor girl? Or of all the others before her?

And, now, he was out here *with* her?

She suddenly felt trapped, and she wished that her father were here. Or her uncle Stephen. Or Jay.

And then the sound grew fainter, and Violet knew that could only mean that he was moving away from her. An unexpected panic settled over her as she realized that she could lose him. He could still get away from her, and they would be no closer to ending his reign of terror than they had been yesterday or the day before that. And no closer at all to finding Mackenzie Sherwin or Hailey McDonald, both of whom were still unaccounted for.

Violet moved then, stumbling in an effort to keep up with the sound of the bells . . . not wanting to lose his trail. She caught herself before she actually fell and was practically running before she'd fully recovered. She passed through areas being searched by other teams and felt a little like she was trespassing on their assigned coordinates, but that didn't slow her down. Thankfully no one seemed to notice her as she rushed past them.

She barely watched where she was going, concentrating only on following the sound of bells that was resonating, louder and louder, as she drew closer to the man carrying it. She didn't bother planning what she would do when she found him, when she could see into his face and *feel* the imprints he wore like a tainted uniform woven from his monstrous deeds.

She was more afraid of *not* finding him. Terrified that she would lose him inside the vast, crowded, overgrown woodlands.

She didn't even see the man in front of her until she had run smack-dab into him. The impact knocked the wind out of her in a breath-stealing *whoosh* as she collided against his rock-solid chest. He caught her with one strong arm before she could fall backward from the force of the collision.

She was too stunned to be immediately embarrassed.

"Whoa! Are you okay?" he asked, not releasing his grip right away, probably afraid she was too klutzy to stand on her own two feet. He looked down at her with genuine concern.

"Do you need some help?"

Violet didn't recover quickly, and she looked up at him in confusion, still processing what had just happened. "I . . . uh, I . . . I guess I'm okay," she stuttered, wondering at the buzzing sensation in her head. Had she actually hurt herself when she'd so gracelessly run into this man?

He let go of her cautiously, watching her for any sign that she might not be ready to stand on her own.

"Er, thanks." She started to feel the lagging humiliation wash over her.

She took an unsteady step back and saw that, beneath his orange vest, he was wearing the standard-issue uniform of the Buckley Police Department. He was one of her uncle Stephen's officers.

She didn't recognize his face, and she silently hoped that *he* didn't recognize *her*, especially since she'd practically run him over.

"Sorry about that," she offered lamely.

"Don't worry about it. Did you need something?" he asked her. He raised one eyebrow, studying her. "Did you find something?"

Violet had the sudden, inexplicable feeling that she shouldn't tell this man anything, and she wondered a little at why she would feel that way. "No," she stammered, uncomfortable about lying to a cop. "No, nothing like that. I was just . . . leaving."

He looked down at her, and she wondered if he believed her. She wasn't even sure that she'd been moving in the right direction if she *had* actually been leaving.

She met his gaze, smoothing her face into what she hoped looked like a convincing smile. "Thanks, by the way," she said, trying to laugh at her own clumsiness. "You know, for catching me."

He smiled back and reached out to pat her on the shoulder. She felt the vague buzzing again, and she realized that it was coming off him. An imprint, probably . . . not all that unusual for someone who carried a gun for a living.

"Anytime," he responded. "Just take it easy. Oh, and keep an eye on where you're going—it can be dangerous out here."

His warning hadn't really been necessary. Everyone who was out here this morning knew just how dangerous it could be.

But Violet knew, better than anyone else, what the *real* danger in the woods was today.

She thanked him again and moved away as casually as she could, trying to maintain the appearance that she was calmer than she felt, all the while focusing to stay tuned in to the sound of the haunting bells that were still too far away from her. Once she was sure she was out of the officer's sight, she sped up again, paying little notice to where she was stepping.

The sweetly melodic sounds drew her closer . . . seeming to pull at her from the inside out.

She came upon it quickly, much more quickly than she'd expected, thinking that it was farther away . . . so distant. But now she was sure he was nearby.

198

She slowed down, only now noticing that her shoes were muddy and the lower half of her jeans were soaking wet and filthy. She wasn't cold, she wasn't even afraid, but she was shivering, and her teeth were nearly chattering as she shuddered all over. She thought that it must be the anticipation, the adrenaline coursing through her as she approached a killer, still not knowing what she would do when she saw him.

She looked around. The bells were nearly deafening here, louder even than they'd been at Brooke's grave site. A volunteer moved past her, but she knew when she looked at him that he wasn't the source of the echoes.

Violet was sure, beyond any doubt, that she would recognize the killer immediately when she saw him.

She slowly scrutinized the area now, searching for something that no one else knew how to find. She moved in and out of stands of evergreens and stepped around the giant ferns that sprang up from the damp, shadowed forest floor.

She passed other searchers, as voices called out from all directions, but nothing could penetrate the musical chimes of the bells.

She saw the oil-slick echo, like the one that had come off the dead girl in the lake, clinging to him before she saw anything else. It seemed to glow, shimmering over him in slippery ripples that danced over his skin, obscuring the rest of him from her immediate view.

Violet felt as if her airway were squeezing shut, making her feel unexpectedly light-headed.

It was him.

Brooke's bells . . . the oily sheen from the body in the lake . . . both *attached* to him. And there were other echoes too . . . *tastes* . . . *and smells* . . . *and colors.* There were too many for Violet to differentiate one from another, as they created something less innocuous than the staticky white noise created by those who had been laid to rest. Instead he carried them, in all their furor, parading them around like a bonfire that signaled to her.

She almost couldn't believe that she'd never *sensed* him before.

He didn't see her, and amid the chaos of the search, with all the activity in the area, she stood out no more than any one of the hundreds of volunteers in the woods this morning. She drew back, only a little, to watch him, unnoticed from behind the wide trunk of a tree.

His back was to her, and she could see that, beneath the imprints of death, he was wearing the same exact vest as the other searchers that milled around the forest. He had joined the search for Mackenzie Sherwin. *But to what end?*

He turned sideways, and she glimpsed his face. Violet observed him. Only his behavior was different from the other volunteers. He was there, wearing the conspicuous vest, but he wasn't searching. He wasn't really even moving. He hovered . . . *waiting* . . . in the same place.

No one else seemed to notice, because to their eyes, and with their attention on other matters, there was nothing out of the ordinary about him. He wasn't young and he wasn't old. He was neither attractive nor unattractive. His bland expression looked passive enough. And Violet thought that he could probably live his entire life in anonymity, barely given a second glance. He certainly didn't look like a killer. He blended perfectly.

She waited for anything unusual to happen, noting that he moved slowly, if at all, but never actually left his spot.

It was as if he were standing guard.

And then it hit her. And she saw it so clearly then that she couldn't believe she'd missed it before.

One of the colors, a sparkling, radiant green that he wore like an aura, shining through even the oily sheen that painted him, was also coming up from the ground at his feet. It shimmered brilliantly, hovering over the sediment on which he stood. Coming from the spot he was guarding.

There was a girl down there.

That was why he was here among the searchers, camouflaged like a chameleon in plain sight. To make sure that the girl in the ground was never unearthed.

Violet stumbled backward, nearly tripping over her own feet in an effort to escape him. She covered her mouth with her hand, stifling her own terrified yelp as she caught herself before she fell, and then froze, praying that he hadn't noticed the sound of her clumsy feet crushing the twigs beneath her. Suddenly everything she did seemed too loud to her . . . each carefully plotted step she took echoed loudly off the trees, each labored breath she took was like an explosion. She tiptoed away, but even that seemed too obvious, and she told herself that she needed to act normal . . . to behave as though nothing had happened, and to sneak away unnoticed.

He never even looked up from his position.

Once she was far enough away from him, she looked around for help. It would have been too much to even hope to see her father or her uncle standing nearby. She wished she had her cell phone. She wished she had her pepper spray with her . . . and she cursed herself for leaving both of them back in her car.

She stumbled recklessly, no longer following the echo of a lost soul, but evading a killer. She was afraid now. Afraid as she had never been before, and she looked around for someone—*anyone*—that might be able to help her.

A woman in a vest appeared from around a thick cluster of dormant blackberry bushes, and Violet practically fell on top of her, not realizing how panicked she was.

"Where's your team leader?" Violet asked hoarsely, grabbing the surprised woman by the sleeve. "I need to find someone with a walkie-talkie."

The woman looked shocked by Violet's unexpected ambush, but she didn't hesitate. "He's . . . over there," she said, pointing. "On the other side of those trees." But Violet was already gone, rushing off in the direction the woman had pointed.

She knew she looked wild. She *felt* wild. But she had just found the killer. She had just stood, practically within arm's reach, of the man who had murdered God only knew how many girls.

And she had just detected another body. Maybe Mackenzie Sherwin's.

She saw the man ahead of her, with a map in his hand, and she knew he was a team leader. She couldn't see his walkie-talkie, but she was certain that he had one. Another man stood beside him, and they were talking when Violet exploded on them.

"You have a walkie-talkie?" she asked, sounding breathless even to herself.

The stern-faced man looked at her, taking note of the volunteer vest she wore before answering her. "You're not on my team."

"I need you to call for help. I need you to ask for Stephen Ambrose."

The man placed his hand over his pocket protectively. Violet was sure that was where his walkie-talkie was stashed. "Where's your team, young lady?" he asked with authority.

Violet was suddenly angry, her fear eclipsed by something more potent as she lost her patience. "I need you to tell someone to send Chief Ambrose out here. Tell him *Violet needs him*!" she demanded. She couldn't believe this guy was giving her a hard time about teams—they were all out here for the same reason: to find Mackenzie.

A look of irritation flashed across his face as he slowly—hesitantly—removed the walkie-talkie from his pocket. He eyed her suspiciously, gauging whether he should be following the orders of a hysterical kid demanding to see the police chief.

"*Now!*" she screamed at him when he took too long. And then she fell to her knees. She looked up at him, pleading now. *"Please!"* she begged the man. *"Please . . .* call my uncle and tell him I need him."

Something, either in her actions or her words, must have gotten through to him, because he was suddenly on the walkie-talkie, telling whoever was on the other end that he needed to get in touch with Chief Ambrose, and that it was an emergency. When he was finally patched through, it wasn't her uncle on the other end but one of her uncle's police officers who was acting as an intermediary for the chief on this chaotic day.

The team leader in front of her repeated what she'd told him, only pausing to ask her to state her name again, to make sure he'd gotten it right. The man was asked where he was and he repeated his coordinates twice. The officer on the other end told the team leader to wait a moment, and there was an extended silence that ensued.

Violet shivered there, staying where she was on the ground, unable to find the strength to get back up again. She thought that she should feel uncomfortable, huddled at this man's feet, while they waited for word from the other end. But she was too tired, and too afraid, to care what any of them thought of her.

Finally there was a crackling sound from the walkie-talkie that filled the silent space, and Violet heard the words she'd been waiting for.

Chief Ambrose was on his way.

Violet leaned forward, putting her face in her hands, and started to cry tears of relief.

CHAPTER 18

BY THE TIME HER UNCLE REACHED HER, VIOLET
felt only a little more in control of herself. She was still terrified
by the secret she was carrying, but her resolve had returned,
strengthening her will and building an outer wall of composure. She had stopped crying and she was pacing around in
circles while the team leader stood impassively, waiting to see
how this played out.

She ran toward her uncle when she saw him heading like
an unstoppable force in her direction. His arms closed up
around her, and she felt safe at last.

She didn't want to waste any more time, and she couldn't
afford for anyone else to hear what she knew. "He's here," she

whispered against her uncle's chest.

He didn't let her go, and she thought that his grip might have even tightened a little bit. "What are you saying, Violet?" he asked, even though she thought he knew *exactly* what she was saying.

She pulled away, just enough to breathe but not enough to be overheard by listening ears. "I saw him. He's just over there." She nodded her head in the direction from which she'd come.

Her uncle Stephen stiffened like a statue, and Violet thought that he was probably deciding what to do next. "Are you sure?"

She nodded.

He mulled that over for a minute. "Have you sensed *her*?" He seemed to have a hard time asking the question. "Mackenzie Sherwin?"

Violet wasn't sure how to answer that, so she answered the only way she could. She kept her voice to a pale whisper. "There's someone there . . . buried. And he's watching over the body." She swallowed, only half wondering what she and her uncle looked like right now, huddled together and exchanging whispered words. "I think he's making sure that no one finds her there."

He chewed his lower lip as Violet looked up at him, watching and waiting to see what he planned to do. He looked down at her and it was no longer her uncle staring down at her, it was the police chief of a town terrorized by the disappearances of its own children. His resolve was matched only by her own. "What does he look like?"

Violet shook her head, wishing she could tell him. "I don't know, really. Just ordinary-looking, I guess. I only knew it was him. . . ." She struggled for the right words, and as always when she tried to put her *feelings* into words they somehow seemed inadequate. ". . . You know, because of what I *sensed* around him."

"Violet! *Violet!*" The shouts were from her father as he came crashing toward where she and her uncle stood.

He pulled Violet away from his brother and buried her in an embrace that was as comforting as her uncle's had been but in a completely different way.

"Oh my God, I'm so glad you're safe," he breathed against her head. "*What* are you doing out here? How long have you been here?"

Violet silently glanced at her uncle for help. She knew that her dad was going to freak out when he realized what she'd really been out there doing . . . and what she'd discovered.

Her uncle winked at her but offered no rope to save herself with. "By the way, I let your dad know you were here." And then he looked over her head to her dad and, all business again, he said, "We need to talk."

Normally this would have been the time when Violet was brushed aside so the adults could speak in private. But her father refused to release her, and everything her uncle had to say to him was the direct result of what Violet had just confessed. They moved away from the prying ears of both volunteers, who had begun to gather with the appearance of the police chief, and away from his own officers, most of whom he'd brought along with him when he'd gotten his niece's distress call.

Stephen Ambrose quietly repeated what Violet had told him, about what she'd seen, and with each word she could feel her dad's heavy arm tightening around her shoulders protectively until she felt as if she might splinter apart beneath his iron grip. Her dad asked almost the exact same questions her uncle had but directed them at his brother instead of at her, as though by pretending Violet wasn't there he could somehow shield her from reliving the experience.

When they were finished with their hurried whispers, her uncle told her father the plan he'd come up with. Her father didn't like it a bit.

"Greg, I need you to bring Violet with us . . . back to where she saw this guy," her uncle said in his no-nonsense, chief-of-police voice.

"No way, Stephen. This is my daughter we're talking about. She's not going near that monster again. It's bad enough she ran into him once." Violet was surprised by the icy tone in her dad's voice, especially since he was normally so soft-spoken and calm.

"Look, all she has to do is make sure we're getting the right guy. She doesn't even have to say anything; she can just squeeze your hand and then you can let me know." Her uncle's voice was tactfully diplomatic as he appealed to her father's resolute sense of justice. "After she does that, you guys take off, head back to the house, and I'll meet up with you later. No one will ever know that Violet was involved at all. But we need to catch this guy . . . we need to stop him before he strikes again. And Violet's the only one that can point him out." He waited to see if his words had the impact he'd been hoping for, and then he said, "Surely, as a father, you don't want this maniac doing any more damage than he already has."

Neither of them spoke for a moment as they faced off, each standing their ground. Violet thought that maybe her father would win this one. She could feel every muscle in his body tightly wound as he stood toe to toe against his younger brother.

And then she felt him give, relaxing just slightly, so slightly that if she hadn't been standing right beside him, she might have missed it. "That's all, Stephen. No one knows it was her. And we won't wait around to see what happens."

Her uncle nodded, agreeing to her father's terms, and then he looked down at Violet. "Are you okay, Vi? Can you do this?" he asked her.

"Of course." It was what she'd wanted all along . . . to catch this guy.

It took Chief Ambrose all of three minutes to update his men, and another ten to have the volunteers who'd been hovering around them discreetly pulled back from the area. He used only the officers he'd brought with him when he'd come to find Violet, and he told them nothing except that one of the volunteers thought they'd seen something suspicious.

His plan was simple, and it was to be executed quickly and quietly. He didn't want trouble. There were too many civilians in the vicinity, and he wanted to make sure that no one was hurt.

When they were ready, her uncle Stephen gave the signal for his men to follow. Nobody questioned why Violet and her father were tagging along behind the police chief and his officers.

It was all over in a matter of minutes, at least her part of it.

Violet found the man again easily, the one they were searching for. He was in the exact spot where he'd been when she'd first encountered him, hovering over the body of an unnamed dead girl.

Violet squeezed her dad's hand as hard as she could, and her dad gave her uncle the signal that confirmed that this was, in fact, their guy. Looks were silently exchanged between the men who worked for her uncle, and then Violet felt herself being half dragged by her father back through the trees, past the volunteers who were unaware of the drama unfolding deeper in the woods and toward the very epicenter of the search-and-rescue efforts. She clung to him as strongly as he did to her, neither wanting to let the other one go for a moment.

When they emerged into the opening at the edge of the forest, Violet heard her father breathe a heavy sigh of relief as though they had just cleared a minefield and come out unscathed. And she supposed that, in a way, they had.

"Will Uncle Stephen come by later to tell us what happened?" Violet asked as they approached her parked car. She handed her keys to her dad.

"He'll come as soon as he can, but it may take a while," he answered her honestly. "This is big, Violet. *Really* big, and he's going to have to explain to everyone how he found the guy."

Violet didn't care how he explained it, even if it meant using her by name, because this was it, this was the ending she'd been hoping and waiting for.

They had the killer.

The next few hours went by in a blur for Violet.

She escaped to her bedroom as soon as was humanly possible, which was almost immediately, since her dad would need some time to talk to her mom. He would need to explain what had happened this morning out in the woods behind the Hildebrands' house and then to try to calm her down afterward. And Violet didn't want to be anywhere near them during that conversation, knowing that her mother was going to have a fit about what she'd done . . . hunting for a killer all by herself.

She waited until she was away from the prying eyes of her parents before checking her cell phone for messages. It was something Violet had been dying to do ever since she and her father had gotten into her car and she'd heard the phone's vibrations, alerting her that she had missed calls.

She flipped it open and scrolled through the call log. She realized that she'd been holding her breath, hoping to see Jay's number. His was the only number she'd wanted to see, and even though it was noticeably missing from the list, there *were* two numbers that she didn't recognize.

She checked her voice mail and the automated voice told her that she had fourteen voice messages.

She listened, erasing each message after she'd listened to

it, her frustration mounting with each disappointing message that wasn't from Jay. When she was finished she tallied the calls in her head.

Chelsea had left one message. One was from her mom, wondering if she'd found her dad and what time they thought they'd be back. *Twelve* were from Grady, who apparently had been the one to call from the two unknown numbers, probably on the chance that Violet had been screening her calls. She hadn't been, but only because she hadn't had access to her phone, otherwise she would have.

None of the messages were from Jay.

Grady's messages had been pathetic, teeming with profuse apologies and lame excuses about his having had too much to drink. Admissions of guilt and explanations were a common theme throughout all twelve of his messages, as he first asked, and then begged for her to call him back, so he could tell her just how sorry he really was. As though he hadn't already said it at least a dozen times.

But Grady was the last person Violet wanted to talk to today.

She heard voices coming from downstairs, and at first she thought that her parents must be arguing, probably about her, because they were talking so loudly. But when she heard another voice, one that didn't belong to either her mother or father, she thought that maybe her uncle had stopped by to give them an update.

She jumped up and raced down the stairs.

And then she stopped where she was, too surprised to take another step.

In the kitchen, her dad and Jay stood huddled together, talking quietly, keeping their voices low—their tone was serious. Violet was surprised by how much Jay seemed to belong there, in that setting.

Neither one looked up right away, even though Violet was certain that they both knew she was watching them. And something about the way they purposely avoided looking at her made her acutely aware of the fact that she was the subject of their private conversation.

She knew her father must be telling Jay about that morning in the woods. She hated that they were talking about her, ignoring her.

Jay glanced up at Violet, and there was something about the expression on his face that made her pause. He gave her a look that told her, without saying a single word, that he wasn't at all happy about what she'd done, and that he had plenty to say to her once he got her alone.

And there was *something else*.

It happened just as he was turning his head back toward her father: Violet could have sworn—and she would have bet money on it—that she saw Jay smile. Just a little one . . . almost unnoticeable, maybe completely imperceptible to anyone but her. She was sure that her dad had missed it entirely, as he continued his discussion without taking a breath.

And that single, nearly undetectable smile melted her.

She watched the two of them as they talked like that for several more moments. She wondered just how much of what had happened her dad was actually sharing with Jay and what he was leaving unsaid.

It wasn't a secret that Jay knew about Violet's "ability," but Violet couldn't recall a time, not one single, solitary instance, when her parents had spoken about it in front of him. There had always been an implicit agreement that it was to be kept tucked away in silence . . . in the same way that all really good family secrets are. It was the skeleton in their closet.

She was surprised when she saw her dad hold his hand out formally to Jay. It was more like a gesture between two businessmen than one she would have expected between her father and her best friend.

But without hesitation, Jay took it and they shook hands. And then her dad looked at her and he nodded. It was as if he was telling her that everything had been worked out, even though Violet had no idea what that meant. He then quietly disappeared out the back door, heading toward her mom's studio, where Violet assumed that her mother was busy working out her frustrations on her art.

Suddenly self-conscious about being left alone together, Violet decided to deflect the attention away from *them* by asking Jay to explain what he and her father had been talking about so seriously. She walked into the kitchen feeling nervous and unsure of herself. "What was that all ab—"

But before she could even finish her sentence, Jay had taken two long, ground-eating strides and gathered her up into his arms as his mouth covered hers possessively.

The kiss was hungry and passionate, and Violet was swept up immediately, wanting more . . . *demanding more*. He eased her down, just enough so that she was standing on her tiptoes, as she pressed herself against him, straining to get closer as her hands wound around his waist and pulled the back of his shirt toward her. She felt dizzy, in a good way—*in the best way*—and she let herself go with it, enjoying every moment, every enticing stroke of his tongue against hers. His hands moved restlessly, around her shoulders and down her back, then tracing their way back up to the nape of her neck, where his fingers tangled teasingly into her hair to draw her closer.

He pulled back, only slightly, moving his lips gently across hers, and she could hear his breath coming in ragged gasps. She knew that she was breathing just as hard and unsteadily as he was, and she could feel an unnamed frustration like she'd never felt before churning angrily within her.

"What were you going to say?" he asked, and she could feel him smiling his crooked smile right up against her inflamed lips.

She had no idea what he was talking about. He might as well have been speaking some obscure foreign language at that moment.

He didn't wait for her to regain herself and answer his question. Instead he took pity and stopped teasing her, squelching the irritation she'd felt when his mouth had left hers. She surrendered to the onslaught of his deep, fervent kisses and vaguely hoped that he was as undone as she was. She never wanted this feeling to end.

She was only dimly aware that they were moving, that he was maneuvering her through her own home, as he stroked, and touched, and explored her with his firmly gentle hands.

It wasn't until he was easing her down that she realized they were in her bedroom, and that he was lowering her onto her bed.

She felt the mattress shift heavily beneath their weight as she clung to him, and she gave only a fleeting thought to the fact that her parents were home . . . somewhere downstairs . . . before the delicious caresses of his tongue made her lose all coherent thought again.

His hands were as restless as hers, and Violet had no idea how long they were lying there like that, on her bed, their hands searching each other with frenzied passion. She felt as though she couldn't get close enough to him . . . as though these were the only moments they would ever have together, and they needed to take advantage of that precious time.

But then their kisses became something infinitely deeper . . . they took on a languid, unhurried quality, as they began to learn the feel and taste of each other. She ran her fingertips along the coarse hairs of his arms and reveled in the feel of lean, sinewy muscles beneath the thin layer of his T-shirt. She liked the way the two of them fit together, perfectly, like individual halves of a whole.

For a moment their mouths parted, and Jay looked down at her. Violet's lips curled in a half smile as she gazed at him; his hair was wildly disheveled, and she studied him. She craved the touch of his swollen lips against hers, and her desire flared hotly. When the building frustration was too much to take, she closed the distance between them, letting her lips drift lazily over his as she breathed into his open mouth, teasing him. He grabbed her tightly again, dragging her close, his breathing reckless as he possessed her mouth with fierce pleasure.

She wanted more than just this. She wanted more than the kissing and the touching . . . her body ached for much, much more. She pressed herself against him, moving her hips forward and enjoying the electric feel of his body against hers as she felt him physically reacting to the movement. She closed her eyes tightly as he rocked back against her, and shock waves spread like lightning throughout her entire body. She moved again and felt herself straining to be closer and closer to him, craving him like a drug. The mounting tremors within her were, in turn, blissfully stimulating . . . and infuriatingly lacking.

And then Jay pulled away from her, shifting his weight so that their hips were no longer touching, and the effort seemed nothing less than monumental as he groaned against her parted lips.

Violet was stunned, and too dazed by her body's reaction to think clearly, let alone speak. He wrapped one arm around her neck possessively and pulled her head against his shoulder, as if silently telling her that they needed to stop.

Violet had to fight the urge to feel insulted by his putting on the brakes so abruptly. But even as inexperienced as she was, she knew that this couldn't be easy for him either.

He reached out with his free hand and captured one of hers. Lazily he stroked her palm with his thumb as their fingers entwined, their hands playfully and tenderly caressing, while they lay there recovering.

Violet felt spent. She was exhausted in a way that she never had been before. She felt emotionally drained, but at the same time she was intoxicated by Jay's nearness, and she knew that even if she closed her eyes right now, sleep would be impossible.

She breathed in the delectable languor of just being in his arms.

After a while, she felt like she could speak again. "You didn't call," she said, testing the waters between them.

Without even seeing his face, she knew he was smiling. "I know."

"It hurt my feelings."

He kissed the top of her head, pulling her a little closer again. She melted against him. "I'm sorry," he whispered softly. "I wasn't sure what to say."

Violet was so absorbed in the feel of him against her that now she was the one who wasn't sure what to say. After a moment she whispered, "Grady called to apologize."

It was the wrong thing to say. She knew it as soon as the words were out of her mouth and she felt him stiffen against her. She wished that she could take the words back as soon as they were out there, but she knew she and Jay couldn't ignore the subject forever. Eventually they were going to have to talk about what had happened last night.

"He left twelve messages, all of them telling me how sorry he was for acting like such a dick. His words, not mine." She leaned up on her elbow, so that she was looking down at Jay.

She blinked, trying to stay focused on talking instead of . . .

other things. "I haven't called him back," she said.

That seemed to relax him a little, that simple nothing of a reassurance, as though there was ever a doubt that she wasn't exactly where she wanted to be at this very moment. As if there was even the slightest chance that she would rather be with Grady than Jay. He squeezed her hand, still holding it, and pulled her down so that she was leaning over his chest.

"Kiss me again," he challenged, only half joking.

It was so weird to hear him say that, to hear those words out loud. *They had kissed.* More than once. More than a lot. They had passed the point of being "just friends" by a long shot.

She leaned down and gave him a dry, sisterly little peck. And then she leaned back up again and smiled at him innocently. She wished she could make a halo appear above her head for effect.

Jay made a sound at her that was like a growl, and then he pulled her down . . . hard. He flipped her over so that she was lying on her back and he was poised above her, and taking full advantage of his upper hand, he moved his lips over hers with a feather-light touch, in a way that was anything but innocent. Until she parted her lips and let him kiss her again . . . completely . . . thoroughly. She heard herself moan, and she could feel the throbbing of her own pulse flickering hotly through her veins.

He lifted his head and stared down at her, rubbing his thumb across her lower lip. "That's what I was talking about. A *real* kiss."

She thought that he was probably trying to gloat, but she

219

was more than a little pleased with herself that he sounded as shaky as she felt after the kiss.

"Is this weird?" she asked with a satisfied sigh.

Jay shook his head. "Nah," he answered, rubbing his hand along the sensitive skin of her arm. "It was gonna happen eventually. I'm just glad it's finally out there. . . . I was getting tired of waiting."

Violet was confused. *Out there?* What the hell was that supposed to mean? *It was going to happen eventually?* How could he have known what was going to happen?

She wiggled out from beneath him. "What do you mean, you were tired of waiting? Waiting for what, exactly?" She propped herself back up on her elbow as she interrogated him, waiting for an answer.

He let the questions linger between them for longer than he needed to, deliberately teasing Violet as she waited impatiently. But when he finally did answer her, it proved to be well worth the minor annoyance. "I was just waiting for you to want me as much as I wanted you." His words were quiet but carried one hell of an impact. "I knew we were going to be together; it was just a matter of time. I kept hoping that you would figure it out. But for a smart girl, you're a little dense, Vi. I kept bringing up Lissie Adams, and showing you the notes she was leaving me, hoping that you'd get pissed enough to finally admit how you felt about me."

Lissie Adams. Just hearing the other girl's name made Violet bristle enviously, causing her to shiver. She rubbed her arms protectively and hoped that Jay didn't notice.

"What makes you think I was feeling anything?" she asked him suspiciously, as if he'd somehow read her mind. If she had been the kind of girl who kept a diary, she would have sworn that he'd picked the lock and read it word for word.

He grinned at her. "Because you did," he stated matter-of-factly. "I know, because I did, and there was just no way that you didn't feel it too."

She didn't bother denying it and instead asked, "So you *used* Lissie to make me jealous?" She tried to sound indignant, but it was difficult when what she really wanted to do was dance around her room triumphantly. She wondered what Lissie would think if she could see them now, together on Violet's bed.

"No, I *tried* to use Lissie. But apparently you're more pig-headed than I gave you credit for. I thought for sure that would do it. Instead, it backfired on me, and you agreed to go to the dance with . . . *someone else.*" He gritted his teeth, probably without even realizing it, as he choked out the words, unable to actually say Grady's name. "And when I realized you were going with *him*, I figured the only way I was going to get to see you that night was to ask Lissie to go with me. I figured I could sneak in at least one dance with you."

Violet couldn't help it—she giggled. Just a little. It was just too much. The whole thing. Jay trying to trick her into revealing her feelings for him. Grady trying to kiss her last night. And then this . . . now . . . she and Jay cuddled up together on her bed . . . *making out.* It was crazy.

"You think that's funny, huh?" He seemed a little bent

that she was laughing at him.

"Joke's on me, I guess," she said, serious now. "I get to sit at home, while you and Lissie Adams go to Homecoming." She tried to sound like it was no big deal, but the truth was that it stung more than she wanted it to.

Jay reached up and wrapped his hand around the back of her neck. He pulled her toward him, staring her in the eye as they closed the distance between them. Violet felt an agonizing thrill at just being so near him again. "I called her last night to cancel after I dropped you off." His voice was thick and husky, giving her chills. "I told her I was going to the dance with you instead."

Violet thought her heart was going to burst. It was exactly what she'd wanted to hear for weeks, maybe even for months. But she wasn't about to let him off the hook that easily for his devious little game. "Sorry," she offered with mock sincerity. "I have a date already. Besides, I don't remember you *asking* me."

He narrowed his eyes at her, as if daring her to argue the point. "*I'm* your date. Grady can go to hell, for all I care. Maybe Lissie'll go with him and he can paw on *her* all night."

They were nose to nose, and mouth to mouth. Violet was intrigued by this side of him . . . the confident, no-nonsense side, refusing to take no for an answer. She leaned forward and sighed as her lips barely brushed against his. "Fine," she exhaled in sham defeat. "I'll go to the dance with you . . . on one condition."

His lips moved into a smile right against hers. "Anything."

She gazed into his eyes as she licked her lips, purposely touching his lower lip with her tongue. That simple contact released a million nervous butterflies within the pit of her stomach. "Tell me what you and my dad were talking about."

Jay jerked away from her as if she'd just slapped him. And Violet realized that she might as well have. He sat up quickly, as if his mind had suddenly cleared from the sensuous haze, and abruptly the teasing grin was wiped clean from his face.

"Never mind," she blurted, trying to backpedal. "Forget I said anything." She wanted to go back to where they just were. But it was too late. The determined set of his jaw told her that.

"No," he said harshly. "I think we should talk about this, Violet." Even the way he said her name was suddenly hard and angry. "Your dad told me what happened today . . . out in the woods. He told me that you tracked down the guy who's been killing all the girls around here . . . that you put yourself in danger." Violet couldn't tell if he was angry or annoyed . . . or both. He ran his hand through his messy hair in an agitated gesture that indicated he was getting all worked up. "And it's not like it was the first time you've done that. Trouble seems to follow you wherever you go, and you're the only person I know who doesn't seem to care. I don't even want to think about what could have happened to you if I hadn't shown up last night while Grady was . . . *assaulting you*." He paused as if it really was too much to think about, and then he continued to rail at her. "You can't even go to the mall safely. I made a promise to your parents, and you just wandered off without even telling me where you were going." His voice was suddenly too abrasive, and it felt to Violet like he was scratching his nails across a chalkboard.

She bristled against the accusation in his tone, and suddenly he wasn't the only one who was upset. "And *you* didn't speak to me for a week!" she lashed back at him. "What was *that* all about? I spent the entire week waiting for you to stop ignoring me. And all because I didn't bother to *check in* with you? You don't get to tell me what to do! You're not my father, you know."

"Thanks for clarifying that, Violet," he said sardonically. "It would be creepy if you got your boyfriend and your father confused."

Violet practically jumped when he said the word *boyfriend*. Obviously she'd noticed that they'd gone beyond just friendship, but she hadn't been entirely sure what that meant for them. Apparently Jay had it all figured out.

But that didn't mean he could push her around.

"Don't you get it? Without me, they might never have found this sicko. And now, because of what I can do, he's done . . . *finished*. My uncle Stephen probably already arrested him after we left there this morning." She was sitting away from him now, angry, and even a little hurt, that everyone made it seem like she'd done something wrong. "I won't apologize for that. I can't. I'm glad he finally got caught, and I hope he rots in jail!"

She didn't even realize that she'd been yelling until she heard a knock on her bedroom door. From the other side, her

224

dad's soft-spoken voice was laced with concern. "Is everything okay in there?"

She bit her lip in frustration and tried to calm down. She was suddenly self-conscious of the fact that she and Jay were on the bed together, even though they'd been there, together like that, hundreds, maybe even thousands, of times before. And it had never bothered her then, when they were still *just friends*; but somehow with her father just a few feet away, especially right after they'd been making out, she felt like they were doing something wrong.

"We're fine, Dad!" she called back, trying to sound cool and composed. And then she glared at Jay for his part in making her shout to begin with.

They listened to the sound of her father walking away, and Violet noticed that even his footsteps were soft and unobtrusive.

There was a long silence once they were alone again. Words that needed to be said, and maybe some that didn't, were like invisible fireworks exploding in the empty space between them.

Jay was the first to give in.

He reached out and took her hand, wrapping it tightly in both of his. "Look, Vi, I don't know exactly how to say this, but I don't want anything bad to happen to you. I don't think I could handle it if something, *or someone*, hurt you." The tone of his voice was still immovable and stubborn, despite the sweet sentiment lurking behind it. He squeezed her hand, though . . . firmly, as if emphasizing his point. "I know it's selfish, and I don't really care if it is, but I'm not gonna stand by and let you put yourself in danger, even if it *is* to catch a killer." He eased up on her throbbing fingers, and his voice got all husky and rough again. "I can't lose you," he explained, shrugging as if those weren't the most wonderful words she'd ever heard before. "Not now that I finally have you."

She felt tears prickling in her eyes, and she blinked hard to try to stop them from coming. She was completely over-whelmed by what she'd just figured out . . . she'd realized it even before he'd finished talking. She knew what it was that he *wasn't* saying while he lectured her about safety.

He loved her.

Jay Heaton, her best friend since childhood, was *in love* with her. He didn't say it, but she knew that it was true.

And the part that really freaked her out, the part of it that caught her completely off guard, was that he wasn't in it alone. Because even though she'd been denying it for a long, *long* time, it had always been there . . . waiting just beneath the surface of their friendship. And now that it was out, there was no going back.

And it was so weird to even be thinking it, but . . .

. . . *she was in love with him too.*

CHAPTER 19

IT WAS ANOTHER RESTLESS NIGHT FOR VIOLET, but this time it had nothing to do with Jay. Well, that wasn't entirely true, it had a little to do with Jay, but there was something else interrupting her sleep. Something that made her feel unsettled . . . troubled . . . that sixth sense that something wasn't quite right in her world. And even though she had no idea what it was supposed to mean, she had learned not to question her intuition.

She gave a valiant fight, though, tossing and turning, and repositioning herself as she drifted in and out of the uncomfortable slumber. She'd dozed; she was sure that she'd caught little catnaps here and there, because she had dreamed. They were segmented and incomplete, extremely unsatisfying dreams that were cut short before they could even begin, but they were dreams nonetheless.

It wasn't until well after her digital alarm clock finally said seven o'clock, which to Violet was torturously early, that she reluctantly called off her battle with sleep and surrendered to the fact that she was awake—*wide awake*—and finally got out of bed.

She should have been ecstatic today. This was the fairy-tale ending she could only have imagined a few short months ago. Not only had she stopped a killer, using skills that no one else possessed, but she finally had Jay all to herself. No more sharing him with all the other girls at school.

And yet, instead of being elated, she felt worn down. Even the absolutely breathtaking possibility of seeing Jay again today had little impact on her washed-out energy level. She was sure that he was half the reason she was so exhausted.

By the time he'd left last night, after spending hours getting to know each other all over again, in ways they never had before, it was nearly midnight, and she was completely sapped. She felt like she'd been through the wringer yester-day . . . emotionally speaking anyway.

That didn't mean she wanted to skip the seeing Jay part; in fact, it was probably the only part of the day that Violet *didn't* want to skip. It just meant she was exhausted.

She showered before going downstairs, hoping it might revive her, and it did . . . a little. And by the time she stumbled her way downstairs she was actually feeling halfway human again.

Her mom and dad were at the table. And so was her uncle Stephen.

And if Violet thought she was exhausted, it was nothing compared to the way her uncle looked. His eyes were rimmed in red and bloodshot throughout, and the deepening circles beneath them were heavy and dark. It made her own eyes water just to look at him, he was so grizzled and worn.

He held on to a travel mug, which Violet could only assume was filled with the darkest, nastiest coffee that could be consumed and still be considered a liquid. That was the way her uncle liked his coffee: police-station black.

"Hi, Uncle Stephen." She acknowledged him curiously, pulling out a chair at the table. She wanted to ask a million questions about what had happened after she'd left yesterday, but from the look of him, she decided to wait and see why he'd stopped by. She doubted this was a courtesy or social call, since the only thing he should be visiting right now was his bed.

He nodded at her but didn't say anything right away, and from the look on his face, and the raised eyebrows cast in her father's direction, it was obvious that he was deferring to her dad to explain his surprise appearance this morning.

Suddenly that nagging sixth sense that had been toying with her all night clamped its razor-sharp teeth around her and wouldn't let go.

Something was wrong.

She looked from her uncle, to her dad, and then to her

mom, who Violet was sure was still harboring a grudge over being lied to . . . something she hated more than almost anything in the world, especially coming from her own daughter. She shook her head at Violet, telling her with a weary look not to come to her for help, not this time. So Violet glanced back to her dad again. The tension was almost palpable.

When her dad finally spoke, his normally calm demeanor was rigid and strained. "Your uncle was at the station all night. Since yesterday afternoon they've been gathering all the information they could and trying to tie up as many loose ends as possible. They don't want to make a mistake on this one, so they're being very thorough."

"Uh-huh . . ." Violet said, letting her dad know that he was taking way too long to get to the point. "What about a confession?" she asked, directing her question to her uncle. "Did he admit to anything?"

Her uncle Stephen nodded, bleary-eyed. "Everything. He confessed to doing all kinds of horrible things to those poor girls. He confessed to more than we asked him about. Apparently this has been going on for years, all over the state." He looked up to her dad, as though asking his permission to go on, and when her dad nodded his approval, her uncle dropped a bomb on her. "He even confessed to killing the girl you found."

Violet was confused. Of course he'd killed the girl she found; she knew that much the instant she saw the oily sheen on him yesterday in the woods.

The look on her face must have said what she was thinking,

because her uncle clarified, "No, Violet, not the one in the lake. The other girl. The one you found when you were eight, out in the woods by the river. That was his first victim. He told us that when she'd been found so soon after he'd dumped her there, it spooked him. He thought he'd done a better job of hiding her than that. And he probably had. He had no way of knowing that an eight-year-old girl with a special knack for finding bodies would come across her, buried there. He said that when she was found, he decided to branch out farther from home to find his victims, so for years he's been looking for girls in every county but our own."

Violet wasn't sure which question to ask first, so she picked the one that seemed the most obvious, the one that bothered her the most. "So, *where does he live?*"

She saw her mom shudder across the table from her, clutching her robe and pulling it tighter around her as if staving off a phantom chill. Violet looked back to her uncle.

"He lives here in Buckley. Well, just outside of town. He has about twenty acres of farmland between here and Enumclaw. He's lived there most of his life," Uncle Stephen explained. And then, as if he were angry at himself for not finding the killer sooner, he added, "Right under our noses."

Violet understood why her mom looked so shaken. It was close. *Too close.*

But after seeing the man yesterday, Violet knew exactly why he didn't need to bother moving from place to place, why he didn't worry about anyone being suspicious of him. He could live anywhere. He was invisible. Or he might as well be. Ordinary. Plain. Normal . . . or at least *normal-looking* anyway. There was nothing about his bland appearance that made him stand out. There was nothing about his harmless facade to cause suspicion or alarm.

"So, if he's confessed already, why are you here?" Violet asked. It was the next-most-obvious question she could think of.

More glances were exchanged over her head. She wished they would just spit it out.

Until they did. And then she wished they'd take it back again.

It was her dad this time. "They need you again, Violet. Uncle Stephen's here to ask for your help."

"*Why?* You've got him. He confessed. It kinda sounds like a no-brainer." She looked around the table. "What else is there?"

Her uncle took another long drink of the thick black ooze he called coffee before answering her. He dropped his head back and stared up at the ceiling for a moment. "It's the girl," he finally admitted, dropping his chin again and rubbing eyes that looked more like they were hemorrhaging than blood-shot. "We exhumed the body, from right where you said it was, and we've already been able to identify her."

"The girl from the party on Friday? Mackenzie Sherwin, right?" Violet asked, finally feeling like she had a grasp on the conversation.

"No, Vi," her mom corrected, speaking to her for the first time since Violet had gotten home yesterday. She reached over the table and squeezed Violet's hand. Her eyes were starting to fill with tears. "It was Hailey McDonald." Her voice broke.

Violet felt as though she'd just been punched in the gut. It wasn't like she hadn't suspected that Hailey was dead; it was just that, for some strange reason, actually hearing the words, and knowing that *she* had been so close to the girl's dead body, was just *too, too* terrible. Hailey was someone she'd known.

"Okay . . ." Violet struggled to keep her words coherent. ". . . So I still don't get it. Why do you need me if he confessed?"

"Because he's confessed to every one of them, and to more, but not to Mackenzie Sherwin," her uncle explained tiredly. "He refuses to take responsibility for her disappearance."

"Maybe he wasn't responsible," Violet offered, as if she were the first one to think of it. "Maybe she really *did* just wander out into the woods and get lost. Maybe she's still alive."

He shook his head. "He's lying," her uncle insisted adamantly. "I don't know why, but he's lying about her. I think he knows exactly where she is, and he doesn't want us to find out. I feel like we're missing something—something important—but I just can't pin it down yet. We've already executed a search warrant on his property and tried offering him deals in exchange for her location. He claims he doesn't know, but he's full of shit. Sorry, Vi."

Normally the sound of her uncle swearing would have made her giggle; it sounded so strange and unnatural coming out of his mouth. He was the only person Violet knew who sounded dorkier swearing than her dad. Her mom, on the other hand, had a mouth like a sailor, and only barely tried to conceal her love of curse words. But now wasn't the time, and this wasn't funny.

"Maybe he didn't have a chance to move her to another location yet. We'd like to take you out to his house to see if you can, you know . . . *feel* . . . anything there. Perhaps help us find Mackenzie."

Violet looked up at him with wide eyes and, without blinking, stated out loud what they all knew to be true. "You know I can only find her if she's dead."

There was no real plan once they got to the killer's house, but Violet knew what was expected of her. She was there to search for echoes.

Violet had been comfortable with her ability ever since she was a little girl. She'd even been kind of okay with accidentally stumbling onto the two human bodies she had found in her life. Three, including Hailey McDonald's. And she definitely hadn't shied away from looking for the killer when she thought she could help.

But this . . .

This was different. This was gruesome.

She was purposely looking for a dead girl. This would not be chance . . . no random discovery.

There were only a few officers at the site, and they were all too busy doing other things, searching for clues and gathering evidence, to even notice she was there. Violet trailed behind her uncle, letting him lead her at first through the house, which was small and dark and dirty, and then leading him as they walked the extensive property, which was sectioned off into several pastures by low wooden fences. Her dad followed right behind them.

It was eerie being here . . . knowing that she was standing in the very places that a killer once had. Seeing where he ate, and rested, and lived.

She stopped several times, feeling old echoes that were faded and weak from the passage of time. Violet was sure they were nothing . . . at least nothing that the police were interested in. She could only assume that cats hunted rats, coyotes killed chickens, and men slaughtered livestock. At least those were some of the reasons she imagined for finding echoes on a farm.

But her uncle tagged each spot anyway, marking it with a small orange flag that he stuck into the ground. They wouldn't start digging until after she'd gone. It was one of the many contingencies placed on this plan by her father. She was to get in and out as quickly as possible, with as few people, even her uncle's own officers, aware that she'd ever been there.

She knew before they were even finished searching that Mackenzie Sherwin wasn't here. Violet would have known, as clearly as she would have heard Brooke's bells or seen the rainbow sheen of an oil slick; it would have been fresh and strong.

If Mackenzie was dead, she was dead somewhere else.

HUNTED

FROM WHERE HE STOOD HE COULD SEE THE
weathered facade of the aging farmhouse. He had seen this house hun-
dreds of times before. But this time—today—he studied it through
different eyes.

He stayed out of sight, watching as the officers came and went,
taking photographs, tagging evidence, and carrying corrugated boxes
from inside the house out to their cars. This house, the one he'd visited
so many times before, had become a crime scene. Or at least, part of
a criminal investigation.

He still didn't understand where they'd gone wrong or how
they'd been caught. Well, maybe he hadn't actually been caught,
but the effect was just as catastrophic for him.

They'd been stopped . . . he and his partner.

Their perfect killing spree had ended.

So he watched and waited, to make sure that there was no way they could tie him to any of this mess.

He wasn't entirely surprised to see the police chief pull up in his unmarked, city-issued vehicle. It might as well have had PIG *emblazoned across the side of it, as conspicuous as it really was. But it wasn't the chief's presence that caught his attention; it was the ordinary-looking sedan that followed right behind it. Actually it was the passenger inside the sedan that had him on alert.*

He had seen her before . . . the pretty girl from the search party yesterday.

He'd noticed her out there in the woods, admiring her even then . . . her youth . . . her innocence, while the entire community searched for a girl who would never be found. At least not alive, anyway.

Had they been out there alone, just him and the girl, without all of the rescue workers and volunteers, things might have ended very differently.

He froze in place while he watched her, a skill he had mastered after years of military training, surveying and analyzing the scene before him.

He'd learned later, after that chance encounter with the girl, that she was Chief Ambrose's niece. And until this very moment, he hadn't given a second thought to the fact that she happened to be there when they'd discovered his partner, while he'd been standing right where he'd been ordered to stand, making sure that no one searched that spot too closely.

And yet here she was again. Strange coincidence.

He watched as she led the police chief, and a man he assumed was her father, around, the three of them speaking quietly among themselves. He saw how Chief Ambrose marked the spots where she pointed.

This was wrong, something was wrong about her being here today. And was it really just a coincidence that she had been there yesterday too? She knew something, but how? How could she know anything . . . and still be alive to tell it?

He wasn't sure, but he couldn't take any chances. They'd already captured his partner; he couldn't let them find him too. He knew what he had to do.

He was going to have to stop her. Silence her. Once and for all.

It was the only way he could stay safe. It was the only way he would be free to hunt again.

The chief's niece would have to die.

CHAPTER 20

THE NEXT MORNING WAS STRANGE FOR VIOLET.
She was nervous about going to school. She even got up and
checked the school's website, hoping that classes had been
canceled due to both the discovery of Hailey McDonald's
body and the still-unexplained disappearance of Mackenzie
Sherwin over the weekend.

No such luck, and Violet knew that the school would,
instead, be overrun once again by the grief counselors, as they
tried to soothe the raw nerves of a student body that mourned
for not one but two of their own.

But that wasn't why she was nervous.

She was anxious about seeing Jay again. At school. In front

of their friends. And in front of their non-friends, among whom Lissie and Grady were definitely now included.

As it turned out, Violet hadn't seen Jay since Saturday night. He'd called her on Sunday to tell her that he was going with his mom to his grandparents' house, which was two hours away. So this morning Violet wasn't sure what to expect. She kind of hoped to keep it a secret, this new relationship of theirs, at least for a little while . . . until she could sort it all out in her head. But she had no idea what Jay had in mind.

It was odd for her, pulling into Jay's driveway that morning, the same way she had countless times before. She saw the door open, but instead of Jay, his mom poked her head out the door and waved enthusiastically at Violet. Jay pushed past his mom, who was smiling conspiratorially at Violet and practically ignoring her own son.

Violet waved back, feeling sheepish. *She knows*, Violet thought. *Jay's mom knows.*

Jay had no intention of letting her keep it a secret.

The low hum of butterflies she'd been feeling all morning became a violent flutter.

Jay slid in, as casual as ever, and kicked his backpack out of the way at his feet. He stretched back in the seat and grinned at her. "Ready?" he asked, as if sensing her hesitation and teasing her about it.

She slumped down a little in defeat and put the car in reverse. "Do I have a choice?" She tried not to, but she knew she was pouting.

He chuckled and cupped her chin in his hand affectionately,

stroking her jaw with his thumb. And then he flashed his dazzling smile at her.

"Not if I have any say about it," he answered, laughing.

School went exactly as Violet thought it would: weird. It wasn't her best, and it wasn't her worst, day ever. It was just *weird*.

Jay was true to his word, deciding not to hold anything back. And it started the second they got out of the car, when he claimed her hand and refused to let go, even when Violet tugged and pulled to try to get it away from him. He ignored her mute protests and held on tight, smiling more to himself than to her, and paraded her right into the school like that.

Not that they'd never held hands before, because they had. But this was entirely different, and Jay was hell-bent on making sure that everyone knew it. And just in case anyone wondered what the hand-holding actually meant, he made sure to clear things up for them by planting a big, albeit very satisfying, kiss on her lips, right in the middle of the hallway. Violet didn't try to pull away from that; in fact, she was dismayed to find herself leaning into him, craving more, and not caring—at least at that moment—who might see them together.

Unfortunately that person turned out to be Chelsea. Chelsea, of all people, along with Claire, who happened to walk up at that very inopportune instant.

"Well, well, well," Chelsea said in an *oh-so-innocent* voice. "Look what we have here, Claire-bear. It's old Jay and Violet."

The unconceived smile was embedded deep in her voice. "Only, and correct me if I'm wrong, this looks a little more than friendly, don't you think?"

"I never kiss my friends like that," Claire replied, blank-faced and serious, oblivious to sarcasm.

Jay's answer was to pull Violet closer, wrapping his arm around her waist. Violet cringed.

Chelsea cocked her head at Claire. "I was just trying to make a point."

Claire looked confused. "What point?"

"*Seriously, Claire?* That Violet and Jay are dating now." She glanced away from poor confused Claire and flashed a gloating look to the couple in front of her. "It's about time, by the way. I think everyone will thank you for putting us all out of our misery. I, for one, was completely fed up with watching you two lovesick puppies pining over each other. Seriously, it was disgusting."

She grabbed Claire by the sleeve of her snug, body-hugging hoodie and led her down the hallway, toward their first-period class. Violet watched in stunned silence, processing everything that Chelsea had said to them, as Claire bounded along in Chelsea's commanding wake.

Jay decided that it was his turn to gloat. "You *pined* for me?" he asked, stupid grin and all.

Violet hit him on the arm. "Shut up!" She shook her head. "I'm pretty sure she was talking about *you* anyway."

Chelsea's lack of surprise over the spreading news that Violet and Jay were dating was almost exactly the same as everyone else's, only most people had the decency to keep their knowing comments to themselves. Apparently Violet was the only one who hadn't seen it coming, and that included Jay, who claimed that *they*—as a couple—had been inevitable.

The only thing that took some of the attention off the new Jay-Violet pairing was the fact that most of their classmates were talking about Hailey McDonald's death and Mackenzie Sherwin's disappearance. But the biggest news of the day, the buzz at school that overshadowed almost everything else, revolved around the capture of the man responsible for killing so many girls.

That didn't mean no one noticed Violet and Jay. They definitely got their fair share of attention. But it wasn't until lunchtime that Violet became acutely, and uncomfortably, aware of just how much notice they were getting.

Grady had made it easy on her, steering clear at every possible meeting point. Violet wasn't sure whether he was avoiding her or, more likely, Jay. But where he had previously been wagging his tail and waiting for her, now he was noticeably absent. And thankfully so.

But Lissie Adams had no such qualms about remaining in the background, unnoticed. Unlike Grady, who had everything to be ashamed of, Lissie was obviously pissed off that she'd been cast aside by Jay. And it was easy enough to decipher that she blamed Violet.

Violet was sitting at her usual lunch table with Claire and Jules. Chelsea and Jay hadn't shown up yet, and Violet was being bombarded by questions from Claire about how she and Jay had hooked up. She wanted details, every last juicy one of them. Violet did her best to redirect the conversation, which wasn't particularly hard when she was talking to Claire, who was infinitely more interested in talking about herself than anyone else. But unfortunately Jules wasn't about to let Violet off the hook so easily, and instead of letting Claire be sidetracked by Violet's deflections, she kept steering Claire back on topic.

"So, Violet, is Jay a good kisser?" Jules asked.

"Yeah," Claire sighed dreamily. "I bet he's a good kisser. Is he?"

Violet glared at Jules, who was having a hard time chewing her mouthful of sandwich while she laughed.

"What'd I miss?" Chelsea asked as she sat down next to Jules, practically pushing Claire out of her way. Claire barely noticed.

Jules answered for them. "Violet was just going to tell us if Jay is a good kisser." She grinned at Violet with bread stuck all in her teeth.

"I think *I'd* like to hear the answer to that question." The voice from behind Violet felt like dull razor blades scratching down her spine.

Violet closed her eyes, trying to decide how she should handle this. She finally plastered on her best fake smile and stood up to face Lissie Adams, and her little lapdog "best friend," who was always tagging along behind her. Lissie was glaring at Violet.

"Hi, Lissie," Violet sighed, for lack of anything more intelligent to say, as she waited to see what the older girl wanted from her.

She didn't have to wait long. Lissie's perfectly perky mask had been cracked, and she was practically seething venom at Violet. "Do you think you're better than me? Because you're not. And just because you managed to convince Jay to go to Homecoming with you, by doing *God-knows-what*, that doesn't make you any better than you were last week."

Chelsea stood up from her seat. "Screw you, Lissie. You want to say something to my friend, then you're saying it to me too. You can either get your liposuctioned ass outta here, or we can take this outside."

Violet put up her hand to stop Chelsea before things went too far. "It's okay, Chels, she can say whatever she wants." And then she looked back at Lissie, who was still glaring at Violet like she wanted to strangle her. "I didn't set out to *steal* your date, Lissie. It's just . . ." She paused, trying to get the words right. "It's complicated with Jay and me." That wasn't exactly as smooth as she'd hoped for. "Anyway, I'm sorry if I messed up Homecoming for you, but you can't really think this is *my* fault."

Lissie opened her mouth, but then she seemed to freeze in place, and a perfectly bland smile replaced her vicious sneer. Violet didn't need her "special abilities" to know from the insipid look on Lissie's face that Jay had joined them and was standing right behind her now.

His voice was deceptively casual. "Hi, Lissie." He was standing so close to Violet that he was practically pressed against her back.

Lissie looked suddenly self-conscious, something she

probably wasn't accustomed to, and she cocked her head to the side, her voice brimming with phony flirtatiousness. "Hey, Jay. Violet and I were just talking about the dance."

Jay had the good sense to sound genuinely remorseful. "Yeah, about that, I feel really bad, Lissie."

Lissie batted a hand at the air, blowing off his apology. "Don't be silly. I already told you it's no big deal." She leaned forward and seemed to forget that Violet was standing right there. Her voice became throaty and was overflowing with suggestion. "Like I said, maybe some other time." She flashed a seductive smile over Violet's shoulder to where Jay was standing, and then she sauntered away, wagging her hips provocatively back and forth.

Violet stiffened. And then she cringed. She hated the brittle stab of jealousy she felt.

Jay, the mind reader, whispered in her ear, "Don't worry about her. If she wasn't such a bitch I might have felt sorry for her. But all in all, she made it pretty easy."

Violet smiled, and then relaxed, enjoying the warmth of him against her back.

"God, I hate her kind," Chelsea muttered as Violet tore herself away from Jay to sit down again.

The rest of lunch was fine, but Violet was even more aware of the fact that *curiosity* wasn't the only interest that she and Jay were piquing today. And that Lissie wasn't the only one who seemed to be put out that they were a couple. She began to notice little looks, sometimes not so subtle ones, from the other girls around her. They ranged from envy to resentful anger and fell everywhere in between. Violet probably should have been uncomfortable from all the negative vibes being thrown her way, but she wasn't. How could she be, when every time she looked at Jay, and he was grinning back at her with more than a small dose of desire in his eyes, little thrills shot through her like electrical shock waves?

When she wasn't thinking about Jay, Violet was consumed with frustration that there were still no answers regarding Mackenzie Sherwin's disappearance. And even though she wasn't tortured by the same physical discomforts that had seized her in the wake of encountering Carys Kneer—the girl from the lake—she was haunted by the disturbing knowledge that Mackenzie was still out there somewhere. And that no one knew whether she was alive or dead.

In the meantime, Violet's skin was growing thicker by the day, as she grew immune to the gossipy whispers and the fleeting—and sometimes not so fleeting—daggers that were shot her way by the other girls who envied her new status as Jay's girlfriend.

She did her best to avoid running into Lissie, or any of her "backup dancers," as Chelsea liked to call the blonde automatons that followed Lissie around all day. But by Wednesday, rumor had it that Lissie already had another date for the dance, and the word was that *she* had dumped *Jay* rather than the other way around.

Jay didn't seem to care what anyone said, and he made it more than clear who he would rather be with.

Grady, on the other hand, she still hadn't dealt with. He seemed to be avoiding her like the plague. He sent a few more apologetic text messages, and Violet responded to them, letting him know that even though she thought he'd acted like a jerk, she wasn't going to hold it against him. What she didn't say was that Jay was still mad at him. But Grady probably knew that, which was why he was giving Violet as wide a berth as was humanly possible.

She and Jay settled into a nice pattern. School during the day and then doing homework at her house afterward. And, of course, "doing homework" meant making out in Violet's room until both of them were tense with frustration and they had to take a break from each other just to get their sanity back. That was when the *real* homework was done.

She kept waiting for her parents to notice how much time they were spending in her bedroom and to say something, but they never did. Not that she was complaining; their ignorance meant she and Jay could continue with their extracurricular activities without interruption.

But on Thursday afternoon, after only about an hour of "studying," Violet's mom tapped on the door.

Violet shot up, not wanting her mom to walk in and catch them all tangled up together. Jay hopped off the bed as quietly as possible, and Violet rushed to the door, cracking it open to see her mom on the other side holding out the phone.

"Jay's mom wants to talk to him."

"Er, thanks, Mom," Violet mumbled, taking the phone and trying not to sound incredibly guilty. She hoped that her messy hair wasn't a dead giveaway to what they'd been doing.

Violet's mom gave her a curious look, and Violet was sure that her mom was finally going to say something, but then she seemed to change her mind, and she left them alone again.

Violet handed the phone to Jay, who seemed remarkably composed considering they'd almost lost their closed-door privileges.

They'd lost them before, once when they were eight and Violet's mom had walked in to find them playing a game of "I'll show you mine, if you show me yours," which at that point consisted of Violet flashing her flat-as-a-pancake chest at Jay. Her mom had come in while the bottom of Violet's shirt was pulled up in front of her face. They never got far enough for him to show his.

Violet listened to Jay's end of the conversation and knew, even before he'd hung up, that he had to go home. His mom needed his help at the house.

Jay didn't bother explaining, he knew he didn't need to, he just got up and crossed the room, pulling her as close as he could and kissing her with unrestrained tenderness . . . which led to barely restrained passion. She ended up clutching his shirt just to keep her balance. What was it with her?

He said he'd come back if he could, and then he was gone. His absence was almost tangible, and Violet missed him almost immediately, and then she chastised herself for being *one of those girls*. You know, the ones who can't function without their boyfriends around, and when they weren't together, that was all they could talk about. It was gross, really, and she definitely did not want to join their club.

She really didn't have much homework—not *real* homework—and she decided that it might be a good time, with nothing better to do, to go for a run. After all, she hadn't really taken advantage of her newfound freedom since the killer had been captured. She glanced outside to make sure it hadn't started raining, always a possibility in the Northwest, and she decided to go for it, stripping out of her jeans and into a pair of track pants and a sweatshirt. She redid her ponytail, which was a total mess after rolling around on her bed with Jay for the past hour, and she slipped on her running shoes.

She stopped at her mom's studio to tell her where she was going, invigorated by the idea of getting some fresh air and exercise, especially after being on lockdown for the past few weeks.

And then she made her way out of the driveway and toward the familiar path, glad—for the moment, anyway—that Jay's mom had called him away.

PREDATOR

HE COULDN'T BELIEVE HIS LUCK.

The chief's niece was leaving her house. All by herself.

He'd been watching her for several days, waiting for an opportunity when she was alone, but it never came. Day in and day out, someone was always with her. Her boyfriend never seemed to leave her side, and when he did, her parents were home.

It had begun to wear on his nerves, and then this . . . his lucky break.

He moved after her, keeping close to the trees, where he blended best, hidden from her view. He maintained a good distance, not wanting to frighten her. At least not yet, while she was still so close to home . . . so close to help. He needed to isolate her, to move her away *from safety, and then he would strike, eliminating her.*

His practiced feet moved stealthily, noiselessly, and despite her steady pace, he had no trouble keeping up with her.

He was exhilarated to be on the prowl again.

CHAPTER 21

VIOLET SHOVED THE EARBUDS INTO HER EARS and pressed the button on her iPod until she found the song she was looking for. It was easy to fall into step, despite the weeks that had passed since she'd last run. The weather was holding out nicely, although the lack of crispness in the air and the dreary gray cloud cover wasn't very promising. But for now, at least, the rain was held at bay, and Violet wasn't about to let a decent afternoon go to waste.

She watched her feet move steadily over the gravelly terrain until she fell into an even rhythm. She found herself getting lost in the music as she ran, inhaling and exhaling with the cadence of her steps.

She wasn't surprised that she couldn't see the mountain today; the low clouds obscured any trace that it had ever even existed, blotting the image completely from the skyline. She ducked beneath the canopy of the trees, following the trail she'd run so many times before and enjoying the feel of the threatening moisture in the air against her skin.

And then something suddenly invaded her sense of calm. She paused the music and listened.

It was strange when an echo came to her, especially one that wasn't exactly an auditory echo, like now. Not to say that she couldn't *hear* it, she could . . . kind of. But it was much less a sound than it was a feeling. A high-pitched squeal that was nearly beyond the range of her ears . . . more like a resonance, a dark vibration, than an actual noise.

Either way, it was there. And it was clear and strong. And it was definitely close.

Her first thought was that there was a body nearby. The intensity of it didn't speak to *what* it was so much as *when* it might have been left behind. She pulled the earbuds out of her ears and slowed way down, and then came to a stop as she tried to decide how best to handle this. She thought about trying to locate the echo, right here, right now, but the idea of potentially uncovering another body—another girl, maybe even Mackenzie—out here on her own, all by herself, was more than a little alarming to Violet. Her previous reactions had not been a good indicator as to how she might respond.

On the other hand, she knew this trail by heart, and she could easily find her way back here if she went to get help.

She glanced around her, to make sure she knew exactly where she was, and decided to go back.

She turned around and started jogging again, this time slower, her senses heightened and straining to keep in touch with the shrill, almost inaudible, screech.

That turned out to be easier than she'd expected.

It followed her.

Her chest tightened, and her heart rate doubled as she glanced around her. She ran a little faster, concentrating on the echo more than ever.

It was definitely moving, getting closer to her even as she should have been moving away from it.

And then it hit her. It wasn't an echo at all. It was an imprint. Which meant it wasn't a body she was sensing. It was a predator.

Her first thought, besides getting home faster, was that it was an animal of some kind. Coyote or wolf . . . maybe even a bear that had caught her scent as she'd trespassed into the forest. But whatever it was, it was closing the gap quickly, and Violet was desperately afraid that she might never make it out of the woods alive. Home was too far away.

She needed to shorten the distance, even though that would mean leaving the trail. But she was being hunted now, she knew that with a certainty that she couldn't explain, and she didn't have much choice. The space between her and her predator was rapidly disappearing.

She lurched slightly to her right, stepping off the fairly cleared pathway and into a sea of lush green ferns and brush that seemed to spring up from every square inch of ground. Stinging nettles clung to the bottom of her pants with their cutting barbs, and she had to lift her feet higher to outmaneuver the obstacles in her way. But adrenaline had kicked in, along with her fight-or-flight reflex. She felt like her airway was clearer and wider, and her steps had become easier rather than more difficult.

Whatever was prowling through the woods followed right behind.

Violet could hear her labored breathing, punchy with each hard footfall, as she concentrated on finding her way. She glanced back, quickly, only to see nothing in pursuit. But she knew better than to trust her eyes. It was there. There was no doubt in her mind that it was coming after her.

And then she tripped, not all the way, she didn't fall to the ground, but she'd stumbled . . . hard. Just as her knee grazed the ground, at the very moment that her fingertips shot out to catch herself in case she actually fell, her head turned, just slightly, to the right . . . and that was when she saw it. Or rather, *him*.

She regained her balance more quickly than she would have thought possible, and before she could think through her decision she instinctively turned to her left and ran as fast as she could. The problem was, now she was running *away* from her house. But in that instant, it didn't matter; all that mattered was getting away from the man who was following her . . . *hunting her*.

She tried not to linger too much on the details, concentrating instead on where she should go and how she was going to get away from him. But the image of him, flanking her at that moment, was haunting. He was dressed in camo-gear, which to Violet was more reminiscent of the military than of hunters she had seen. Even his face had been painted, army green with black smudges circling his eyes. But the most disturbing part of all, the most alarming part, was the imprint he carried with him.

He was a killer. And he was after her.

She heard his footsteps eating up the ground behind her, as he gave up being stealthy and discreet. They sounded like thunder. She ran as fast as was humanly possible through the tangled ground cover, beneath the expanse of towering trees.

She heard the river, and she knew she was getting closer to it. But that was bad . . . really, really bad. It meant she was going in the wrong direction, and the river, if nothing else, would provide the worst kind of roadblock, trapping her between it and the man chasing her.

Far away, another sound penetrated her terror. She tried to listen to it, but it was gone too soon, before she had a chance to make out what it was exactly.

She squeezed her way through branches that lashed out at her, whipping her face and arms. She was grateful that her feet kept finding a solid place to land, terrified that at any moment she might stumble again and lose any advantage that she might have in getting away from the man pursuing her. But she was growing tired now, winded, and panic was making it harder and harder for her to think clearly.

The sound was there again, louder this time. It was distinctly different from the shrill resonance coming from her predator, but still, she couldn't decipher it.

She ducked left to avoid a huge cedar tree in her path and heard the heavy, nearly deafening footsteps of the man behind her. She twisted right then, hoping to use the tree between them to cut off his direct path.

This time, when she heard it again, she knew what it was. A voice rang out through the dense woods. She felt a surge of hope, even though it was still too far away for her to hear the words called out or to tell who was behind them.

Without thinking, she yelled back, as loud as she could manage with her chest now constricting tightly, practically squeezing her throat closed with panic. *"HELP! HELP!!!"* she screamed as hard as she could, but it came out hoarse and disjointed. She couldn't wait around to see if she'd been heard.

Her toe caught against something sticking up from the ground, and her footstep stuttered, but not enough to really slow her down. She didn't know how much longer she could keep this pace, or even if this pace was enough to keep him at bay behind her. Her lungs were burning with the fiery strain, and the stitch in her side was pinching tightly.

The voice came again. Louder, much louder now. She could hear the words . . . and she recognized who it was.

"Vi-o-let!" she heard Jay's voice calling out to her. *"Vi!"*

She wanted to cry with relief, not sure that she should even *be* relieved to hear him. Maybe his presence only meant that the killer tracking her down would carry two more imprints out of the woods today. But she couldn't help reveling in a moment of sheer delight at the sound of his voice.

"Over here!" she yelled. *"I'm over here!"*

A group of trees stood in her way. She dodged between them, or thought she had, until she felt her shoulder slam hard against one of the immovable trunks. It practically knocked the wind out of her. And this time she stumbled, slowing way too much. She tried to regain her speed, not looking where she was going as she broke through the cluster of trees and bushes, and by the time she realized that she'd reached the edge of a bluff leading down to the river, it was too late.

The fall was long, and hard, and happened so fast that Violet could only make out the blur of green, brown, and gray on one side and the distorted icy rushing waters of the river on the other. She felt her ankle twist beneath her as she landed at the bottom. She hit the ground with a surprisingly loud thud that forced every ounce of air from her body. Her head ached, although she couldn't tell if she'd hit it or not. Her body felt battered and defeated.

She opened her eyes, only briefly, expecting to see the camouflaged man in hot pursuit, taking advantage of her incapacity to finally catch up with, and kill, her. She looked up to the spot where she'd fallen from and she saw no one.

The imprint was gone.

When her lids became too heavy to hold open any longer, she let them flutter shut again.

And she dreamed.

Of Jay.

CHAPTER 22

WHEN VIOLET AWOKE, SHE WAS CONFUSED. Disoriented, like the strange sensation of waking up in a bed that wasn't your own and then struggling to remember where you'd fallen asleep.

Only this time, Violet was pretty sure she hadn't fallen asleep in the back of an ambulance.

The details of how she'd gotten there were hard for her to grasp and felt like scraps from a dream—or a hallucination— pieced together in incomplete segments.

She remembered running. . . .

And being chased.

And a voice calling out to her.

She tried to sit up, only to find that she was fastened to the stretcher and her neck was being held immobile by a huge brace strapped around her.

She remembered falling, a memory made more clear by the pain shooting up from her ankle. She assured the paramedic riding with her that her neck was just fine, but he insisted that she stay put, and no amount of pleading on her part could change his mind.

"How did you find me?" Violet finally asked him, giving up on the idea that he would release her.

"Some kid called it in, said he was your boyfriend. He's coming right behind us." He waved his metal clipboard toward the rear doors of the vehicle as if Violet could see out of them. She couldn't of course; she was strapped to a gurney. "I think he thinks the sirens are for him too."

Violet closed her eyes. *Jay* had *been there, it hadn't been a dream after all. He'd come looking for her.* She didn't allow herself to think about what might have happened if he hadn't.

Relief spread through her, insulating her in the knowledge that she was safe now. She kept her eyes closed and concentrated on the sounds of the wailing sirens to distract her from the throbbing pain in her ankle.

She was embarrassed by all the attention she drew when the ambulance pulled into the emergency bay at the hospital. Jay met her inside, and never left her side, holding her hand silently—reassuringly—throughout the triage process, where she was cleared from the restraints. And when she was finally wheeled back to a room with long curtains hanging down to separate one bed from another, Jay pulled a chair close to her.

He captured her hand between both of his and touched her fingertips to his lips. "Are you okay?" he finally asked, seeming to breathe for the first time since she'd seen him.

She felt guilty for causing him to look so troubled. "I'm fine, really. I think I just twisted my ankle a little. It's nothing. As soon as my parents get here, we can go home."

She hated being in the hospital. She'd already felt several imprints moving around her. She doubted those who carried them were murderers exactly, but Violet was certain that echoes attached to those who administered lethal doses of painkillers too . . . even when it was done to give the dying a more peaceful passing.

Jay's mom was a nurse and carried an old, faint imprint of her own. Violet had never asked Jay about it, but when she'd told her mother once, her mom had explained that sometimes it was too much to watch someone suffering when they died.

"What were you doing so far off the trail, Vi?" Jay continued to cup her hand tenderly.

She didn't answer him. This wasn't a question she wanted to discuss yet—especially not with Jay. She asked him a question of her own. "I thought your mom needed you. How come you came back?"

She didn't tell him how grateful she was that he had. Or why.

It was enough of a diversion to keep him occupied for a moment. "She only needed me to let her into her car. She locked her keys inside, and I had her spare with me. But by the time I got back to your house, your mom said you'd gone for a run. I was gonna try to meet up with you on your way back and walk with you, maybe sneak you behind the bushes for a few minutes." He smiled at her before turning more serious. "And then I heard you yelling for help . . . and crap, Violet, it scared the hell out of me. How did you fall, anyway? What were you doing down by the river?"

She heard her parents then, before she saw them, and their chaotic arrival saved her from answering Jay's questions. She could hear them at the nurse's station outside her door, asking about their daughter's condition, still questioning one of the nurses as they dragged her into the room with them.

Violet assured her parents—in the same way she had Jay—that she was fine. That it was just a fall, some bruises and scrapes, nothing to worry about. And still, no one seemed to believe her.

After a full workup, and a painful, and humiliatingly unsuccessful, attempt at standing on her own, she was sent down to Radiology for an X ray on her right ankle. By the time Uncle Stephen arrived with Aunt Kat, Violet was ready to make a run for it. Only she doubted she could get very far.

On the other hand, her uncle was *exactly* the person she wanted to see right now. She had been biding her time until she could tell him what had really happened to her. But now that he was there, she wasn't sure how to start. So she waited for the right moment.

He ruffled her hair as he came in, all uncle and no cop about him now. She far preferred her uncle to the chief; he had inherited the sense of humor in the family, while her father got the receding hairline and mad skills with numbers. "Geez, Vi, you didn't need to break your own leg to get out of going to the dance with Grady Spencer. A simple 'no' would have been just fine, I'm sure."

Apparently no one had noticed that Jay had barely let go of her hand for a second. His thumb was now tracing lazy circles around her palm, and he answered her uncle's teasing comment without looking away from Violet for even a split second. "She's not going to the dance with Grady," he announced, smiling at her mischievously, and for a moment Violet forgot how to breathe. She hoped she never got used to how a simple look from him could turn her into a blithering idiot.

"Really?" her aunt Kat asked, her eyes narrowing as she glanced from Violet to Jay, and then down at their intertwined hands. Clearly she wasn't going to let the comment pass unnoticed. "Why is that?" she asked in a voice filled with unspoken meaning.

Stephen Ambrose looked at his wife curiously, a little slow to catch on, which was sad, really, considering it was his job to seek out clues and solve mysteries.

Jay answered Kat without missing a beat. "Because she's going with me." He winked at Violet, whose cheeks had flushed to a brilliant shade of scarlet. She wasn't entirely sure she was ready for this.

Violet saw her mom and Aunt Kat exchange meaningful glances.

They knew, she realized. And now her uncle did too.

Uncle Stephen gave Jay his best *I'm-keeping-my-eye-on-you*

264

look, but a quick "Hmm" was the only sound he made.

How much embarrassment could one person possibly survive?

There was a moment of awkward silence, made even more uncomfortable by Jay's refusal to look anywhere but at her. He reached out and brushed his finger along her cheek. Violet almost forgot to care that everyone in the room was looking at them.

Her uncle Stephen cleared his throat, and Violet jumped a little.

"So, what exactly happened, Vi?" Suddenly the police chief was back in the room with them.

Violet pursed her lips. She wasn't sure where to start, but she knew it needed to be said. "Well," she began, "I went for a run." She paused to chew her lip, trying to put her words in the right order. "Anyway, I thought I, you know, *heard* something. An echo."

"Really?" her uncle asked. "Do you think it was a body ... a *person*? Did you stop?"

Violet shook her head. "No, it wasn't that, exactly." She cursed herself for being such a chicken, but she was afraid of how everyone was going to react if they knew she'd been followed—and very nearly captured—by a man who had obviously been chasing her. "I ... it wasn't a body." *Spit it out, already!* "It was a man."

The words didn't have quite the impact she'd expected, and she knew from the clueless looks on their faces that she was going to have to explain it to them.

"Someone was following me," she stated, and finally she had their full attention. Before they could bombard her with questions, she plunged ahead. "It was a man, and he was carrying an imprint on him. That was how I first knew he was there. He was hiding, wearing camouflage so I couldn't see him, and he was . . . following me while I ran." She paused to take a breath, feeling a little light-headed now that she was in the middle of her explanation. "When he realized that I'd seen him, he started to chase me. I knew I needed to get off the trail to try to get home faster, but I got turned around and ended up heading toward the river instead." She looked at Jay gratefully, fresh tears stinging her eyes. "That was when I heard you calling for me."

Violet glanced up. Everyone was watching her uncle, who was pacing now. He seemed to be deep in thought. It wasn't quite the reaction she'd expected from him.

"What is it?" her dad asked his brother.

Stephen didn't hesitate. "I knew we were missing something" was his only explanation at first.

"Missing *what*?" Violet's mom rounded on her brother-in-law like a protective mother bear. "If you know something, then tell us . . . now!" she demanded.

Her uncle looked torn, but his familial obligation won out. "Look, Maggie, I'm not even supposed to be talking about this. We're in the middle of a *murder investigation*, and the things we uncover are confidential. I could be compromising the case just by discussing it with you." He sighed then, having gotten it out of his system, and continued. "But we've been following a lead based on evidence we recovered at the

266

suspect's home." Violet thought it sounded strange to call him a "suspect" when she knew exactly what he'd done—what he'd *confessed* to doing—to those girls. As far as she was concerned he was the *killer*, not the suspect.

Her uncle went on: "I was hoping we were wrong, but it looks like it might be true after all." He shook his head, as if he were having a hard time believing it himself. "We were starting to suspect that he wasn't acting alone, that he might have had a partner." He held up his hand when Violet's dad was about to interrupt him. "I know what you're going to say, but up till now it's been more speculation than fact. We have no idea who this accomplice might be or even if there *is* an accomplice at all. My detectives are going over phone records and following every lead they can, but most of them have been dead ends. We've even enlisted the help of the FBI forensics to go through his computer. But so far, nothing."

"Until now," Jay challenged.

"Until now," he agreed, ignoring the accusation in Jay's words. "I'm sorry, Violet. If there was any chance, *any chance at all*, that I thought someone might come after you, I would never have kept this to myself. As it is, only a handful of men are even working on this aspect of the case."

"So then why Violet? How would this . . . *person* . . . know that Violet was involved?" Now it was Kathryn Ambrose who was criticizing her husband.

He shrugged. "That's just it. . . . I have no idea. It could just be a coincidence, but I doubt it. And if it's not, if somehow he knows about Violet, then we need to find him. Fast."

He sounded resolute now.

When the doctor came in with Violet's discharge orders, he explained that a bad sprain like hers could take weeks, even months, to heal properly, and that she would need to stay off her foot as much as possible. One of the nurses expertly wrapped the Ace bandage to the point that Violet thought her toes might not be getting enough blood circulation. Her parents were handed a prescription for some painkillers and heavy-duty-strength ibuprofen for the swelling. And Violet was fitted for crutches, which always sound like fun when you're little, but in reality chafe your underarms and make your muscles burn from the constant strain.

Her uncle was on his cell phone, ordering a round-the-clock police presence at Violet's house. And Violet could feel the walls closing in on her. Between her current inability to walk on her own, and the suffocating notion of being watched 24-7 ... *and not just by the cops,* she thought, as she glanced at the worried faces of her already overprotective parents, she could sense her world shrinking. She had just barely escaped being on lockdown, and now she was going to be in maximum-security solitary confinement.

Jay smiled at her encouragingly, taking in the ashen look of horror on her face, and she could practically read his mind as he imagined the two of them locked up together until this maniac who had hunted her in the woods was finally caught.

She supposed that, if she had to be in isolation, isolation with Jay might not be so bad after all.

CHAPTER 23

DESPITE LISTENING TO THE REASSURING WORDS
repeated by her parents, and by her uncle and even Jay, Violet
was having a hard time trusting that she was safe. They tried to
assure her that there was no way the man in the woods could
have known that she'd had any part in locating his victims—
or in the capture of his partner. That he'd come across her the
same way he had all of those other girls, by simple, random
chance. And that she'd just been in the wrong place at the
wrong time.

The extra safety measures were simply to prevent him
from coming back for her.

So she convinced herself that they were right, mostly

because it made it easier for her to get through each day. Having Jay around helped too.

The weekend passed peacefully, and after everything that had happened, Violet welcomed the reprieve.

The day after the incident in the woods was a Friday, and Violet stayed home, keeping her ankle elevated and iced. Jay reluctantly went to school, but only because his mother made him, so Violet was left on her own. Well, alone with her mom, and an armed police officer who was stationed out in front of her house.

She had meant to use the time to catch up on some reading. She had several books she'd been wanting to read, but instead she sprawled out on the couch surrounded by pillows and blankets, and spent the hours flipping channels between *Judge Judy*, *The People's Court*, *Maury*, and *Jerry Springer*, and rounded out her afternoon with *Dr. Phil* and *Oprah*. All in all, it was a complete waste of a day. At least until school got out.

Jay showed up after school with a bouquet of flowers and an armful of DVDs, although Violet couldn't have cared less about either . . . *he* was all she wanted. She couldn't help the electric thrill of excitement she felt when he came strolling in, grinning at her foolishly as if he hadn't seen her in weeks rather than hours. He scooped her up from the couch and dropped her onto his lap as he sat down where she had been just a moment before. He was careful to arrange her ankle on a neatly stacked pile of pillows beside him.

He stubbornly refused to hide his affection for her, and if Violet hadn't known better she would have sworn that he was going out of his way to make her self-conscious in her own home. Fortunately her parents were giving them some space for the time being, and they were left by themselves most of the time.

"Did you miss me?" he asked arrogantly as he gently brushed his lips over hers, not bothering to wait for an answer.

She smiled while she kissed him back, loving the topsy-turvy feeling that her stomach always got when he was so close to her. She wound her arms around his neck, forgetting that she was in the middle of the family room and not hidden away in the privacy of her bedroom.

He pulled away from her, suddenly serious. "You know, we didn't get much time alone yesterday. And I didn't get a chance to tell you . . ."

Violet was mesmerized by the thick timbre of his deep voice. She barely heard his words but rather concentrated on the fluid masculinity of his tone.

"I feel like I've waited too long to finally have you, and then yesterday . . . when . . ." He stopped, seemingly at a loss, and then he tried another approach. His hand stroked her cheek, igniting a response from deep within her. "I can't imagine living without you," he said, tenderly kissing her forehead, his warm breath fanning her brow. He paused thoughtfully for a moment before speaking again. "I love you, Violet. More than I ever could have imagined. And I don't want to lose you. . . . I *can't* lose you."

It was her turn to look arrogant as she glanced up at him. "I know," she stated smugly, shrugging her shoulder.

He shoved her playfully but held on to her tightly so that she never really went anywhere. "What do you mean, 'I know'? What kind of response is that?" His righteous indignation bordered on comical. He pulled her down into his arms so that his face was directly above hers. "Say it!" he commanded.

She shook her head, pretending not to understand him. "What? What do you want me to say?" But then she giggled and ruined her baffled facade.

He teased her with his mouth, leaning down to kiss her and then pulling away before his lips ever reached hers. He nuzzled her neck tantalizingly, only to stop once she responded. She wrapped her arms around his neck, trying to pull him closer, frustrated by his mocking ambush of her senses.

"Say it," he whispered, his breath warm against her neck.

She groaned, wanting him to put her out of her misery. "I love you too," she rasped as she clung to him. "I love you so much. . . ."

His mouth moved to cover hers in an exhausting kiss that left them both breathless and craving more than they could have. Violet collapsed into his arms, gathering her wits and hoping that no one walked in on them anytime soon.

The weekend progressed in pretty much the same fashion. Chelsea stopped by once, to check on Violet, which was actually kind of sweet. Sometimes it was easier to be around Chelsea outside of school, when she didn't have an audience. She brought Violet a couple of magazines, some beef jerky, and two packs of gum, all wrapped in a brown paper bag . . . stuff she'd gotten from a convenience store on the way. It was her version of a bouquet of flowers.

The rest of the time, Violet's parents were around, but they were never really *around*, leaving Violet and Jay on their own for the most part. When it got late, Jay would help Violet up to her room so she could go to bed; then he would head home, only to be back first thing in the morning. Her parents had agreed to let him take Violet's car back and forth, so he could come and go easily without having to tie up his mom's car all day.

The only news from Uncle Stephen was that there was no news. They'd gotten no further in determining who the mystery man following Violet in the woods had been. Violet felt bad that she couldn't help the police in identifying him, since he'd been wearing camouflage makeup when he'd chased her, and all she could really tell them was that he was tall.

By Monday, Violet couldn't avoid the real world any longer, and it was time to face school again. Pretty much everyone in school had heard about what had happened to her, although none of the details were exactly right, and Violet didn't bother correcting them.

It was Homecoming Week, which also meant it was Spirit Week, the most important week of the fall quarter. And Violet's perilous escape from an unknown assailant got lost in the shuffle of Homecoming rallies and pep assemblies, along with the impending announcement of the Homecoming Court and anticipation over the game and dance the coming weekend.

Violet had a hard time being overly excited, knowing that she wouldn't be able to participate in any of the activities outside of school. She wouldn't be allowed to go to the game, and even if she could convince her parents to let her attend the dance on Saturday night, there was no point. On crutches she would only be able to sit on the sidelines and watch anyway.

It was too bad, because her dress was amazing . . . and she would have liked to see Jay in a suit.

She tried not to be too disappointed, and it was made a little easier for her when the Homecoming Court was announced and Lissie Adams was named Homecoming Queen after garnering the most votes from the student body. Several of her perky little sidekicks were named "Lissie's princesses." It was enough to make Violet feel ill, and to make her feel much better about not being able to attend the game, where Lissie would be crowned at halftime, or the dance, where Lissie would be the center of attention.

Jay was a huge help at school, and he carried Violet's backpack as she hobbled from the car to her first-period class. If she'd have allowed him, he probably would have carried her. As it was, he got special permission from the Attendance Office to leave all his classes early so that he could help Violet get from one class to the next.

By the end of the first day, Violet's arms were killing her, and Jay insisted on making her wait at the curb while he got her car. Queen Lissie surprised Violet by appearing out of nowhere as soon as Jay had disappeared from sight.

"Hey, Violet," she said, as she eyed Violet's bandaged ankle and the crutches with spiteful superiority. "Walk much?"

The two bleach-blonde girls with her giggled at their queen's lame attempt to make fun of Violet's injury.

She wanted to smack that superior smirk off Lissie's face. But she couldn't think of a clever comeback, so she finally just mumbled, "Shouldn't you be polishing your crown or something?"

Lissie smiled sweetly past Violet, waving her fingertips at Jay as he pulled the car up to the curb where they stood. Her face was the picture of serenity, as if she hadn't been mocking Violet while he was gone, but under her breath she got in one last barb at Violet's expense. "Jealous?" But it was a little hard to be overly offended when it was so far from the truth.

Violet didn't bother responding, and Jay bounded from the car to help her inside.

He gave the briefest of glances at Lissie, barely acknowledging her presence as he gently eased Violet onto the seat. For good measure, and Violet was sure it was premeditated, he gave her a long, sweet kiss before closing her door.

Violet was surprised at how quickly she responded to his touch, even when she knew it was more for Lissie's benefit than for hers. But she had to suppress a triumphant smile when she stole a quick look at the other girl's disgusted expression before Jay put the car in drive and left Lissie standing there, gawking after them.

"Sorry about that," he said apologetically as he concentrated on maneuvering through the busy parking lot. "I've been so worried about strange men following you around that I forgot how dangerous Homecoming Queens can be."

Violet smiled at him. "That's okay. That kiss was a nice touch, by the way. Sheer genius."

"Yeah, that one just came to me," he chuckled.

"Maybe you can show it to me again . . . later," she said playfully.

He reached over and gave her leg a squeeze, his eyes never leaving the road. "I like the way you think, my friend."

"Is that how it is now, we're back to *just friends*?" Violet asked, raising her eyebrows at him challengingly. "I'll remember to keep that in mind next time we're 'doing homework.'"

He was suddenly serious, his tone determined. "We'll never be just friends again, not if I have anything to do with it." And then with conviction he added, "I love you too much to go back now, Vi."

It was still strange to hear him saying things like that. The words sounded so foreign to her ears, but her heart responded, as if it had been waiting a lifetime to hear them, by beating erratically.

They spent the evening watching one of the movies that Jay had rented, snuggled up on the couch together, while her mom popped a frozen lasagna into the oven for dinner. Of course.

They ate together at the table that night, she, Jay, and her parents. They talked carefully around one another, avoiding the conversation that seemed to hang ominously over them: the glaring lack of headway in finding the man who'd been after Violet. Violet actually preferred it that way, the *not* saying it, almost as if not speaking the words out loud somehow erased what had happened to her . . . at least to some extent. She knew that was foolish thinking, and she tried to ignore the fact that she carried the grim reminder of how real it was all day long as she limped from place to place.

She was afraid to organize her disjointed worries into an actual, articulated concern. But ignoring it didn't make it go away, and she couldn't help wondering if *he* was still after her. It was a question that had begun to haunt her thoughts more and more frequently as the police, and even the FBI forensics team, seemed to be getting nowhere in figuring out who she'd seen out in the woods that day.

When Jay left that night, Violet collapsed onto her bed in a state of exhausted apprehension, trying to convince herself that her worries were unfounded, that she was probably just a casualty of being in the wrong place at the wrong time. Just like all those other girls had been.

So why couldn't Violet push away those nagging thoughts, the ones that hovered around the fringe of her consciousness, telling her it was no accident that he'd been out there that day? Why couldn't she shake the feeling that *she* was the reason he'd been lurking in the dark cover of the forest? That he'd been waiting for her?

She got up and double-checked her window, making sure it was locked, and glanced down to see the officer in his car, leaning back in his seat, settling in for his shift. She bounced in two hops back to her bed after first trying to put some pressure on her foot, only to be disappointed that it still wouldn't support her weight without sending a jolt of pain all the way up her leg. She nearly fell over after the excruciating attempt to stand.

She settled in, struggling to shut off the disturbing thoughts that raced around inside her head, until she finally fell asleep, where they haunted her dreams instead. In them she was hunted by a stalker so dangerous, and so mysterious, that even her subconscious couldn't give him a face. His unrevealed image pursued her with unrelenting stamina, finding her wherever she hid, while she ineffectively struggled to elude him. His determination knew no bounds.

Violet woke in the night feeling like her chest was being crushed beneath the panic that settled over her. She convinced herself, after checking her window again, and making sure the cop was still awake outside, that it was just a dream. That her faceless assailant couldn't stay that way forever, that eventually he would be caught.

But until that time, Violet knew she would be fearful of closing her eyes for too long.

The next few days were hard for Violet. She felt like she was sleepwalking through school, and restlessly fighting against sleep each night. It was impossible to hide the strain from Jay, who had become increasingly attentive, recognizing what was bothering her even before she was able to voice it out loud.

"You know they're going to find him, right?" he finally offered one afternoon.

"I know," she answered, but even she knew that her voice was too bright, and her response too quick, to be sincere.

His voice was serious when he asked, "Do you, Vi? I think it's bothering you more than you want to admit. I think you're scared."

She was annoyed that he'd figured it out so easily. She thought she'd been keeping up appearances fairly well, only to find out that she was completely transparent. She wondered if her parents were as perceptive as Jay was about her fears. "I know," she said again. This time her voice was tinged with defeat. "I just can't quit thinking about it—about *him*. I was so scared, Jay. And if you hadn't come looking for me . . ." She trailed off, unable to even imagine what might have happened out there . . . alone with her assailant in the shadow of the trees.

Jay's jaw clenched tightly, as if the image was too much for even him to bear, but his voice was considerate. "I know you're afraid. But they *will* catch him, and until then, I'm not gonna let you out of my sight. No one's going to let anything bad happen to you." He didn't say it, but Violet heard the word *again* hanging there behind his words.

But she still felt better just hearing his reassurances, like she wasn't alone.

"I'm okay. I think all this isolation, and all the extra security stuff, is just starting to wear on me. I'm going a little stir-crazy being cooped up all the time." She tried to explain her sulky mood. "Especially with Homecoming this weekend. The idea of sitting around here, while everyone else is out having fun, just sucks."

He didn't react the way she'd expected him to react. She'd expected some more sympathy, and maybe even some suggestive comments about the two of them being left alone together. What she didn't expect was for him to smile at her. But he did. And it was his sideways smile, which told Violet that he knew something she didn't.

"What?" she demanded adamantly.

He grinned. He was definitely keeping something from her.

"Tell me!" she insisted, glowering at him.

"I don't know . . ." he teased her. "I'm not sure you deserve it."

She punched him in the arm for making her beg. "Please, just tell me."

He laughed at her. "Fine. I give up. Bully." He pretended to rub his arm where she'd hit him. "What if I were to tell you that . . ."—he dragged it out, making her lean closer in anticipation, his crooked smile lighting up his face—". . . we're still going to the dance?"

Violet was speechless. That wasn't at all what she'd expected him to say.

"Yeah, right," she retorted cynically. "My parents barely let me go to school, let alone go to the dance."

"You're right, they didn't want you to go, but we talked about it, and even your uncle Stephen helped out. The football game was definitely out of the question; there are just too many people coming and going, and there're no restrictions for getting in. But the dance is at school, in the gym. Only students and their dates can get in, and your uncle said he was already planning to have extra security there. So, as long as I promise to keep a close eye on you ... which I do"—his voice suggested that the last part had nothing to do with keeping her safe, and Violet felt her cheeks flushing in response—"your parents have agreed to let you go."

She glanced down at her ankle, double-wrapped in Ace bandages, and completely useless. "But I can't dance." She felt crestfallen.

He slid his finger beneath her chin and lifted it up so that she was staring into his eyes. "I don't care at all if we dance. I just want to take my *girlfriend*"—his emphasis on the word gave her goose bumps, and she smiled—"to Homecoming."

They stayed there like that, with their eyes locked and unspoken meaning passing between them, for several long, electrifying moments. Violet was the first to break the spell. "Lissie'll be there," she stated in a voice that was devoid of any real jealousy.

Jay shook his head, still gazing at her intently. "I won't even notice her. I won't be able to take my eyes off you."

Violet was glad she was already sitting, because his words made her feel weak and fluttery. The corner of her mouth twitched upward with satisfaction. "Not if I have any say in it, you won't," she answered.

CHAPTER 24

IT DIDN'T TAKE LONG FOR VIOLET TO ADJUST TO the idea of going to the dance. In truth, Saturday night couldn't come fast enough.

Friday went by in a blur of activity. There was a huge pep assembly at school that took up the last half of the afternoon. The entire football team was introduced, to a frenzy of cheers and screams from the student body watching from the bleachers. Violet wished more than ever that she didn't have to miss the game, but she understood all too well why she couldn't go. Still, it was easy to get swept up in the fervor of school spirit.

When the Homecoming Court was announced, Violet

felt a moment of insecurity. Lissie gracefully swept out on to the hardwood floor of the gymnasium like she'd been born for this role. Violet glanced inconspicuously at Jay, wondering why on earth he would have picked her over the stunning Lissie Adams.

But he wasn't looking at Lissie. All of his attention was focused on Violet instead, and he caught her fleeting look in his direction.

"She's not half as beautiful as you are," he promised, in answer to her silent doubts.

She nudged him lightly with her shoulder. "Shut up." But she couldn't keep the smile off her lips as she said it.

"Knock it off, you guys. Get a room, for God's sake!" Chelsea squealed at the two of them above the clamor of the crowd in the bleachers.

When the assembly was over, Jay became a human barrier between Violet, who was wobbling along on her crutches, and the throng of students in their mass exodus to get away from the school. In the parking lot, car horns were blaring loudly and windows were rolled down, despite the cool autumn weather, and the air was filled with shrieks and battle cries. The game was going to be thunderous tonight.

Jay drove Violet home, where she thought he'd be staying with her for the evening, so she was surprised when they got to her house and Jay's mom was waiting for him in the driveway.

"Where're you going?" she asked, trying not to sound too upset that he was leaving.

He shrugged noncommittally, and Violet had the impression that he was being evasive on purpose. "I have some things I need to do. I'll see you tomorrow, okay?"

Violet tried to hide her disappointment as he helped her inside, carrying her backpack over one shoulder and keeping one hand protectively at the base of her back, just in case she lost her balance.

He kissed her good-bye, and then kissed her again, and then again. Pretty soon five minutes had passed, and Jay's mom honked her car horn out in the driveway.

"'Bye, Violet," he whispered against her cheek, his voice thick with desire. "I love you."

She watched him leave, still reeling from his kisses.

The night without Jay hadn't been a total loss . . . except for the devastating loneliness . . . and the overwhelming desire to be at the Homecoming Game with all her friends . . . and the crushing boredom.

She started a book she'd been planning to read. Stopped. Tried another. Gave up on that one too. And finally worked her way down the stairs to hang out with her parents. When they went to bed, which was barely at the crack of ten o'clock, Violet was left on her own once again.

It took some doing, but she finally managed to fix a bowl of microwave popcorn and actually get it to the family room, eventually giving up on the crutches and hopping—carefully—from one room to the next. She was exhausted by the time she reached the couch again. So when the tapping started, so faint that she wasn't sure she'd even heard it at first, she tried to convince herself that it was nothing.

But it didn't go away, and in fact it got louder, and pretty soon Violet knew that she couldn't just ignore it. It was coming from the front door.

She was a little afraid, even though she told herself that she shouldn't be. There was a cop out there, facing the entrance. And her parents were right upstairs; all she had to do was yell and they'd come running.

She finally got up, which was not a small feat in itself, and decided to at least look through the peephole before deciding whether or not to answer it. She didn't move quickly, for obvious reasons, and the tapping continued in intermittent spurts, not really getting louder but remaining fairly constant.

Despite self-reassurances, her heart was beating too fast and her mouth was suddenly too dry. She tried to concentrate on sensing anything unusual coming from the other side of the door.

When she finally reached it, she bent forward and looked through the peephole.

Jay was grinning back at her from outside.

Her heart leaped for a completely different reason.

She set aside her crutches and quickly unbolted the door to open it.

"What took you so long?"

Her knee was bent and her ankle pulled up off the ground. She balanced against the doorjamb. "What d'you think, dumbass?" she retorted smartly, keeping her voice down so she wouldn't alert her parents. "You scared the crap out of me, by the way. My parents are already in bed, and I was all alone down here."

"Good!" he exclaimed as he reached in and grabbed her around the waist, dragging her up against him and wrapping his arms around her.

She giggled while he held her there, enjoying everything about the feel of him against her. "What are you doing here? I thought I wouldn't see you till tomorrow."

"I wanted to show you something!" He beamed at her, and his enthusiasm reached out to capture her in its grip. She couldn't help smiling back excitedly.

"What is it?" she asked breathlessly.

He didn't release her; he just turned, still holding her gently in his arms, so that she could see out into the driveway. The first thing she noticed was the officer in his car, alert now as he kept a watchful eye on the two of them. Violet realized that it was late, already past eleven, and from the look on his face, she thought he must have been hoping for a quiet, uneventful evening out there.

And then she saw the car. It was beautiful and sleek, painted a glossy black that, even in the dark, reflected the light like a polished mirror. Violet recognized the Acura insignia on the front of the hood, and even though she could tell it wasn't brand-new, it looked like it had been well taken care of.

"Whose is it?" she asked admiringly. It was *way* better than her crappy little Honda.

Jay grinned again, his face glowing with enthusiasm. "It's

mine. I got it tonight. That's why I had to go. My mom had the night off, and I wanted to get it before . . ." He smiled down at her. "I didn't want to borrow your car to take you to the dance."

"Really?" she breathed. "How . . . ? I didn't even know you were . . ." She couldn't seem to find the right words; she was envious and excited for him all at the same time.

"I know, right?" he answered, as if she'd actually asked coherent questions. "I've been saving for . . . *for forever*, really. What do you think?"

Violet smiled at him, thinking that he was entirely too perfect for her. "I think it's beautiful," she said with more meaning than he understood. And then she glanced back at the car. "I had no idea that you were getting a car. I love it, Jay," she insisted, wrapping her arms around his neck as he hoisted her up, cradling her like a small child.

"I'd offer to take you for a test-drive, but I'm afraid that Supercop over there would probably Taser me with his stun gun. So you'll have to wait until tomorrow," he said, and without waiting for an invitation he carried her inside, dead bolting the door behind him.

He settled down on the couch, where she'd been sitting by herself just moments before, without letting her go. There was a movie on the television, but neither of them paid any attention to it as Jay reclined, stretching out and drawing her down into the circle of his arms. They spent the rest of the night like that, cradled together, their bodies fitting each other perfectly, as they kissed and whispered and laughed quietly in the darkness.

At some point Violet was aware that she was drifting into sleep, as her thoughts turned dreamlike, becoming disjointed and fuzzy and hard to hold on to. She didn't fight it; she enjoyed the lazy, drifting feeling, along with the warmth created by the cocoon of Jay's body wrapped protectively around her.

It was the safest she'd felt in days . . . maybe weeks. . . .

And for the first time since she'd been chased by the man in the woods, her dreams were free from monsters.

CHAPTER 25

THE DAY OF THE DANCE WAS LIKE A DREAM.

Violet woke up alone. She realized that Jay must have left sometime during the night, and she'd stayed where she was, curled up contentedly on the couch, basking in the warmth he'd left behind.

As she stretched and finally forced her nebulous thoughts to clear, she remembered Jay's new car. She was thrilled for him all over again as she easily recaptured his image in her mind's eye, that childlike enthusiasm on his face as he showed off his new toy. She smiled to herself at the memory of it. She couldn't wait to ride in it, with Jay behind the wheel.

She couldn't wait to go to the dance.

She spent a lot of the day fielding text messages from her friends . . . and forcing herself *not* to call Jay, allowing the expectancy to build to a crescendo, the suspense filling her senses as intoxicatingly as any narcotic. She was giddy by the time she was slipping into her dress.

Her mom made several appearances, camera in hand, to take pictures of her getting ready. It seemed to be exactly what they needed as a family, something to take their mind off all the tragic and frightening events of the past weeks. Even her father, who still had reservations about her going, couldn't stop telling her how beautiful she looked when her mom dragged him in to see Violet all dressed up.

Her dress was simple enough: a soft, flowing, black jersey fabric with a narrow Empire waist and a halter top that created a V-shaped neckline. The crisscrossing straps in back held up a scoop of fabric that ended in a soft wave, exposing a generous length of nearly bare skin from her shoulders to below her midback. It clung to Violet's body in all the right places, and the hem all but covered her strappy sandals, for which Violet was now grateful, knowing that it would also cover the ugly, unavoidable ankle brace she would be forced to wear.

The effect was not only elegant but dramatic.

Violet felt like a princess.

Not like one of Lissie's band of nauseatingly counterfeit princesses, but like a real one. From a fairy tale.

A really, *really* sexy fairy tale.

Her mom helped Violet to pin back her hair, leaving wisps of strategic curls to fall loose, framing her delicate porcelain face perfectly. And for the first time, probably ever, Violet was grateful not to have the same stick-straight hair that all the other girls had. Her eyes were striking, with smoky charcoal liner and a luscious coat of lash-lengthening mascara that outlined the flecked emerald green of her irises. The color in her cheeks had little to do with the makeup she wore, since she was flushed with excitement.

Her dad poked his head in just as her mom was crouching down to help her fasten the tiny buckle of her shoe, the final touch.

He whistled approvingly. "I'm starting to have second thoughts again. I'm not sure I should be letting you out of the house like this." He smiled, but his eyes were tearing up a little, and Violet knew that he was comparing her to the little girl she once was.

Her own eyes started to burn, and she fanned her hands in front of them. "Stop it, Dad! You're gonna make me cry too."

Greg Ambrose took a cleansing breath and composed himself before announcing, "Jay's downstairs waiting."

With her father on one side, and the handrail on the other, Violet descended the stairs as if she were floating. Jay stood at the bottom, watching her, frozen in place like a statue.

His black suit looked as if it had been tailored just for him. His jacket fell across his strong shoulders in a perfect line, tapering at his narrow waist. The crisp white linen shirt beneath stood out in contrast against the dark, finely woven wool. He smiled appreciatively as he watched her approach, and Violet felt her breath catch in her throat at the striking image of flawlessness that he presented.

"You . . . are so *beautiful*," he whispered fervently as he strode toward her, taking her dad's place at her arm.

She smiled sheepishly up at him. "So are you."

Her mom insisted on taking no fewer than a hundred pictures of the two of them, both alone and together, until Violet felt like her eyes had been permanently damaged by the blinding flash. Finally her father called off her mom, dragging her away into the kitchen so that Violet and Jay could have a moment alone together.

"I meant it," he said. "You look amazing."

She shook her head, not sure what to say, a little embarrassed by the compliment.

"I got you something," he said to her as he reached inside his jacket. "I hope you don't mind, it's not a corsage."

Violet couldn't have cared less about having flowers to pin on her dress, but she *was* curious about what he had brought for her. She watched as he dragged out the moment longer than he needed to, taking his time to reveal his surprise.

"I got you this instead." He pulled out a black velvet box, the kind that holds fine jewelry. It was long and narrow.

She gasped as she watched him lift the lid.

Inside was a delicate silver chain, and on it was the polished outline of a floating silver heart that drifted over the chain that held it.

Violet reached out to touch it with her fingertip. "It's beautiful," she sighed.

He lifted the necklace from the box and held it out to

her. "May I?" he asked.

She nodded, her eyes bright with excitement as he clasped the silver chain around her bare throat. "Thank you," she breathed, interlacing her hand into his and squeezing it meaningfully.

She reluctantly used the crutches to get out to the car, since there were no handrails for her to hold on to. She felt like they ruined the overall effect she was going for.

Jay's car was as nice on the inside as it was outside. The interior was rich, smoky gray leather that felt like soft butter as he helped her inside. Aside from a few minor flaws, it could have passed for brand-new. The engine purred to life when he turned the key in the ignition, something that her car had never done. Roar, maybe—purr, never.

She was relieved that her uncle hadn't ordered a police escort for the two of them to the dance. She had half expected to see a procession of marked police cars, lights swirling and sirens blaring, in the wake of Jay's sleek black Acura.

Despite sitting behind the wheel of his shiny new car, Jay could scarcely take his eyes off her. His admiring gaze found her over and over again, while he barely concentrated on the road ahead of him. Fortunately they didn't have far to go.

Even the parking lot at school had an entirely different feel as the cover of night began to fall in a sheer dark curtain, allowing the distant twinkling of the stars to break through the dusky sky. Violet could hear the music migrating out from the open doors of the gymnasium as couples paraded into the dance.

Jay patiently led Violet inside, showing his student ID, and then helping Violet with hers, to the two teachers manning the door and checking identifications. Once inside, Violet was surprised at herself. She had expected her hypercritical eyes to devour everything and mentally tear it to shreds, from the cheesy décor to the dorky DJ playing the music and trying to be "hip" to what the kids were into. Right down to the obnoxious and unpleasant Queen Lissie.

But she didn't. She kind of liked it, in *all* of its tacky splendor.

She let Jay lead her to the photographer, a man in a cheap suit with a greasy comb-over-style hairdo. They had their picture taken in front of a backdrop of draped tulle in shades of pink and red, and flanked by freestanding white—probably Styrofoam—pillars that were meant to look Greek and tragically romantic. Instead, they looked tragically shabby, as if they might crumble at any moment from years of overuse. But Violet didn't care about any of it; she could hardly breathe whenever she glanced sideways at her arrestingly handsome date.

When they were finished they saw Chelsea and Claire. Actually, the two overly wound-up girls came running right *at* Violet, screaming with excitement to see her. As if they didn't see her every single day.

"Oh . . . *my* . . . God, Violet! You look *amazing*!" Claire gushed at her, and Violet tried not to be insulted by the insinuation that it was so far-fetched for her to look good.

And then Jules walked up with her date, a senior from

another high school, and Violet almost didn't recognize the tall, leggy bombshell towering over her. Jules wore an almost sinful black dress with a bustier top that left little to the imagination and no room for a bra of any kind. Before this moment, Violet hadn't even realized that Jules *had* boobs, let alone full-on cleavage.

"Wow!" Claire breathed, unable to say anything beyond that single word. And suddenly Violet wasn't so insulted, because Jules's transformation had actually left Claire, the girl who always had something to say, completely speechless.

The music was loud, and the bass was up way too high, making everything from floor to ceiling vibrate. They had to raise their voices just to hear one another.

"Yeah, Jules!" Chelsea said in a voice thick with envy. "Go away, you're making the rest of us look bad." She winked at Jules's date wickedly. "I bet you just want to eat her up, don't ya?"

He stared at Chelsea with bewilderment and glanced back at Jules for help.

"Just ignore her," Jules explained over the noise from the sound system. "She doesn't get out much."

Chelsea tried to look hurt by Jules's words, but she couldn't quite pull it off. "I'm just sayin', Jules, he'd better watch his back tonight, or I might be trying to take you away from him." Chelsea loved to play the potentially *bi-curious* card, even though everyone knew she liked boys far too much to go to bat for the other team.

"Gross!" cried Claire, who wasn't pretending at all. Claire

hated it when the conversation deviated too far off her straight and narrow path. The operative word being *straight*.

"Don't worry, Claire-bear," Chelsea soothed condescendingly. "I'm not going to hook up with Jules." She wrapped her arm around Claire's waist and then said suggestively in her ear, "I'm much more likely to make a move on you."

"*Eww!*" Claire shrieked, shoving Chelsea away. "Get away from me!"

"Leave her alone, Chels," Jules interrupted. "Or you're gonna make her start her '*It's Adam and Eve, not Adam and Steve*' speech. And, sorry, Claire, but none of us really want to hear that."

Jay pulled Violet close to him as they listened to the familiar, playful bantering. He slid his arm around her waist from behind, and let his lips gently tease her earlobe while no one was paying attention to the two of them. Violet wanted to turn around right there, in his arms, and forget this whole *dance thing* altogether.

"Hey!" Chelsea's voice interrupted them, and Violet jumped a little, realizing that everyone was staring at them. "Did you hear me?"

Violet leaned forward on her crutches and away from Jay, still feeling bemused by the close and intimate contact. "What?" she asked, trying to focus on what had been said.

"I said, 'I gotta pee.' Let's go to the bathroom," Chelsea repeated as if Violet were some sort of imbecile, incapable of understanding normal human speech.

"Keep it up, Chels, and none of us is gonna want to hook

up with you tonight," Violet promised jokingly.

Chelsea grinned at Violet. "I like the way you think, Violet Ambrose. Maybe you'll be the lucky girl I choose." And then she turned to Jay. "Don't worry, I've got her from here," Chelsea announced. Jules and Claire followed.

Violet laughed and glanced back at him. "I'll only be a few."

Jay gave her a skeptical look that no one else would have even noticed, as he assessed the three girls who would be escorting Violet. And then he finally nodded. "Okay, I'm gonna show these guys my car." He was beaming again. "I'll be right outside, but I won't be long."

Violet did her best to keep up with the trio ahead of her, but it was hard on one high heel and two crutches. Finally she yelled at them exasperatedly, "If you guys don't wait, I'm not going!"

They all three stopped and turned around.

Chelsea tapped her lovely silver shoe impatiently. "Hurry up, Violet, or I swear I'll take you *off* my list."

IN PLAIN SIGHT

SHE WAS EASY TO SPOT, THE GIRL, CHIEF AMBROSE'S
niece. She was the only girl at the dance on crutches.

She was pretty. Beautiful even, he thought longingly as he studied her. She had the air of a girl who had no idea how seductively
appealing she was to the men of this world. He liked that . . . her
innocence.

He'd been watching her since she'd arrived, keeping his distance in case she somehow managed to recognize him from that
day in the woods, when he'd chased her. He still couldn't figure
out how she'd known he was there. He'd been so careful, creeping
stealthily behind her, and then somehow, some way, she'd known,
and she'd run. But even then, he almost had her.

At least until her boyfriend showed up.

298

He knew, of course, that she hadn't seen his face out there. He knew that there was no way she could identify him. If she could have, she would have done it already. But there was no point in taking chances . . . not when he was so close.

It had been hard to wait, frustrating. He'd been forced to bide his time until those watching her slipped, letting down their guard just enough to give him a chance to move in quietly.

And here he was. At last.

The dance was turning out to be more fun than he'd anticipated. He felt like a kid in a candy store, as lovely young ladies floated past him in colorful shades of chiffon and taffeta. They looked like mouthwatering little confections. Only, he couldn't have any of them.

He could only have one of them. He just needed to be patient . . . to wait until he could get her alone.

None of them even seemed to notice him there, at their dance, barely affording him a first glance, let alone a second. He blended into the background, an everyday fixture that hardly deserved notice.

It was the perfect disguise. All dressed up as himself.

He kept a close eye on her, on Violet, on his Violet, trying not to have his attention sidetracked by the other blossoming girls all dressed up in women's bodies. He could smell their youthful essence, and it was distracting.

He observed his girl interacting with her friends, playful and carefree. He watched her boyfriend pulling her close, kissing her on the neck.

And then he saw her leaving. Not all alone, but not with her hovering date either.

He felt a blistering flash of energy course through him, and he *lifted himself away from the wall.*

He followed in their general direction but was careful to keep a good length of space between them.

Mentally he prepared for what he was about to do.

CHAPTER 26

THE GIRLS' BATHROOM, THE ONE CLOSEST TO THE interior gymnasium doors, was a central hub of activity, and as soon as they went inside, Chelsea changed her mind about being there.

"Come on. I know it's farther, but let's go to the one past the locker rooms. There's probably no one there." She looked meaningfully at a couple of senior girls wearing their fake-jewel-encrusted princess crowns and lowered her voice. "Where the workers are, the queen can't be far behind." And Violet couldn't help laughing at Chelsea's stupid bee analogy, as she pictured Lissie Adams buzzing around with a stinger sticking out of her ass.

They all agreed, even though they knew it would take forever to get there since they would have to wait for Violet. But this time no one complained.

Chelsea was right. The bathroom was deserted. But even way out here, they could still feel the floor vibrating from the deep bass coming from the gym. It was nice to be able to talk, just the four of them, especially since what they really wanted to talk *about* was the other girls at the dance. This way they didn't have to worry about whose feet were under the stalls or who might be eavesdropping on their conversation.

Chelsea, of course, was the first one to speak up. "Okay, am I the only one who noticed how *gi-mungous* Mimi Nichols's dress makes her ass look? Of course, you can barely notice it since her freakishly giant boobs are practically hanging out the top of it." Chelsea glanced at Jules and grinned. "No offense, of course," she offered, raising her eyebrows at Jules's chest.

Claire giggled, and Jules wrinkled up her face in disgust at Chelsea's teasing barb. "You're just jealous," she retorted, eyeing Chelsea's chest in return.

"Touché, Jules. Touché!" Chelsea admitted.

Claire wanted so badly to join in on the catty conversation, but she was terrible at finding other people's flaws . . . at least intentionally. Still, she gave it her best shot. "And what about Jennifer Cummings?" she asked accusingly, trying to mimic one of Chelsea's cutting looks.

They looked around at one another, wondering what it was that they weren't getting. Chelsea was the only one brave enough to ask, "What about her, Claire?"

"She does not even look kind of cute!" Claire stated, her face a mask of mock horror.

They all stared at her, not sure what to say.

And then once again, of course, it was Chelsea who broke the stunned silence. "I swear, Claire-bear, I am going to call your mom and tell her you need to start riding the short bus. You really need to start practicing your bitchy comments. What are you gonna do when we're not here to get your back?"

Claire rolled her eyes, too oblivious to be insulted, which was why she was the perfect friend for Chelsea, who was too insulting to be oblivious. "Geez, Chels, I don't even ride the bus."

Jules couldn't help herself; despite her best efforts to hold on to her detached cool, she started laughing. And pretty soon they were all laughing, even Claire, who still didn't realize what they were laughing at.

"You guys are so mean!" Violet charged accusingly. "Can't you just have fun and stop picking everyone apart?"

Chelsea looked disgusted. "You've gone soft, haven't you? Jay has made you soft!"

Violet rolled her eyes, smiling despite her best efforts. "Whatever. *Everyone's* soft compared to you."

"Ouch!" Chelsea pretended to be wounded. But again, she just couldn't pull it off.

They spent some time primping in front of the mirror, fixing stray pieces of hair and touching up lip gloss. Violet looked down at her bandaged foot and tried to wiggle her toes, which felt like they were being pinched in an unyielding vise. Her mom had obviously wrapped it too tight.

She sat down on a wooden bench that was bolted to the floor . . . in case some high school hooligan like herself decided to make off with it, she supposed. She set down her crutches, leaning them against the wall, as she assessed the damage to her throbbing foot. She wondered briefly if the stretchy Ace bandages could actually cut off her circulation. She only half jokingly hoped her toes wouldn't fall off.

"Ready?" Chelsea asked after using the bathroom, as if now that she was finished, they all should be.

"Mmm . . . not yet," Violet said, leaning down to loosen the wrapping around her ankle. She glanced up at her three best friends, who looked amazing in their dazzling dresses, and she felt guilty about keeping them away from the dance any longer. "You guys go ahead. I'm just gonna redo this and I'll be right there."

Chelsea looked a little skeptical about leaving Violet behind, the first hint of humanity she'd shown all evening. "I don't know. . . ."

"Go on, I'll just be a few minutes," Violet assured her.

"You sure?" Jules asked.

"Seriously. I'm right behind you," she said convincingly.

Violet watched them go before turning her concentration back to her foot. She carefully unrolled the bandage, breathing easier as she felt the restricted blood begin to flow more freely. She sighed out loud when she felt the last remnant of bandage slacken and then snap elastically off her swollen ankle. She could see the impression of the bandage in her distended skin. She leaned back, giving herself just a brief moment to savor the relief, allowing her foot to breathe a little.

She knew she needed to get on with it, before Jay got impatient and decided to come in after her.

She leaned down, suddenly glad that she wasn't strapped into a tight, corset-style dress like Jules was wearing. Honestly, she didn't think she'd be able to breathe in that thing, let alone bend over. She started to wrap the flexible fabric around and around, giving her foot a little more space than her mom had. The bench beneath her began to vibrate harder, as a song change meant even more of the insufferable bass, setting Violet's teeth on edge as she struggled to concentrate on what she was doing.

She heard the door, but she was almost finished, she almost had the last piece of bandage right where she needed it. She absently reached for one of the small silver clasps with the jagged teeth that would hold the binding in place. When the door opened, the music grew louder, as did the deep rumbling from the speakers. Violet assumed that someone else had the same idea that Chelsea had, about avoiding the overcrowded bathrooms nearest to the dance. She didn't look up to see who it was.

She fumbled with the first fastener, finally getting it right, and then reached up to grab the second where she had placed it on the bench beside her. Her fingers groped but found nothing there.

She glanced back at the bench beside her, moving only her eyes, but before she could find it, she was distracted. A hand reached out in front of her, holding the clasp out to her.

"Thank you," she said, her fingers momentarily brushing the warm skin as she reached out to take it.

And she froze, her hand feeling scalded by the brief contact. She looked up, again with only her eyes, and she gasped, instinctively drawing away her hand and holding it against her chest.

"You don't need it now?" the deep male voice asked her casually, as if it were perfectly natural that he was in the girls' bathroom with her.

She sat up, ignoring his question as she studied him, from head to toe, taking in every detail of his outfit . . . *his uniform*. She should have felt better, reassured by his presence, but she couldn't . . . not knowing what she knew. Not after touching his hand and *feeling* what she'd felt.

The shrill vibrations. The ones that had nothing to do with the pulsating beat coming from the dance. The same high-pitched, ear-piercing resonance she'd felt before . . . in the woods when she'd fallen. The day she'd been chased.

And she recognized him, not just by the familiar imprint he carried, but by his face as well. Although it wasn't from the day he'd followed her, tracking her like a wounded animal among the trees. She recognized him from a different day, the day that she, along with everyone else in town, had been searching in the woods for Mackenzie Sherwin.

She'd run into him that day, right before she'd located the killer, when she'd been following Brooke's bells. He was the officer she'd collided with.

He raised his eyebrows, as he watched all of this cross her face. Each of them scrutinized the other . . . she trying to figure out how he could possibly be the killer, one of her uncle's own officers . . . and he, trying to decide how she knew.

He spoke first, his curiosity getting the better of him. "How did you do it? When no one else could, how did *you* figure it out?"

Violet's mouth went dry as her mind raced through half a dozen options, some of which she ruled out immediately. Running was impossible. Screaming was futile all the way out here, especially with the DJ trying his best to rupture eardrums. Her cell phone was in her purse, but she'd left that with Jay since it was too difficult for her to carry. Crying . . . begging . . . pleading. All viable options.

And then she decided. *Lying.*

She did her best to look confused, praying that he didn't know as much as he seemed to. "What are you talking about?" Her voice was quivering. "Is something wrong, officer?"

He paused thoughtfully, seeming to consider her questions. He was tall, massive really, with broad, boulderlike shoulders that seemed to shrink the space of the restroom. His uniform stretched tightly across the wide expanse of his chest. He grinned at her, showing a glimpse of his white teeth, but still he remained silent.

Violet's heart surged violently. She decided to try another tack, in case he didn't know who she was. "Did my uncle send you in here?" she tried nervously. "Chief Ambrose?"

He took a step closer to her, if that was even possible. "You can drop the act." He skipped a beat, and then he added, *"Violet."* He said her name in a way that suggested that there was never a doubt; he knew *exactly* who she was. And then his voice changed, leaving no wiggle room when he commanded her harshly, "Stop toying with me. I'm asking the questions here. Understand?"

Violet jumped. Her stomach felt queasy, and she started to shake, unable to contain the shuddering fear coursing through her. She nodded apprehensively, her eyes wide.

"I did some digging," he finally explained, his voice oddly composed again. "You've been there all along the way. I'm not even sure that you know how far back you and I go." He stepped back in an informal manner, his body relaxing as he launched into his explanation. "I didn't realize it right away. In fact, I might never have realized it, if I hadn't seen you in action for myself." His gaze swept over her as she sat, transfixed, listening in frozen horror to the menacing tenor of his deep voice.

She had a hard time concentrating, separating his words and his voice from the high-pitched ringing reverberations he unwittingly carried. She could barely believe that she hadn't noticed it sooner, that she hadn't recognized the sound earlier when it was so close to her. How could she have missed it? Even if she had been deaf she should have noticed that sensation.

It was impossible to ignore now. He, of course, was completely unaware of it.

"I would never have suspected you if I hadn't been there that day, at my partner's house, when your uncle brought you out to look for . . . for what? Clues? Bodies? Of course, you must know by now that I had a partner. I doubt you thought it was a coincidence that I was in the woods with you when you had your"—he paused—"your accident."

Violet thought it was ludicrous that he would call it anything other than what it was. He had tried to attack her, and if it hadn't been for Jay showing up, he would have. "It wasn't an accident," she heard herself saying with more conviction than she would have thought possible under the circumstances.

He laughed at her. "It was, actually. That was *not* how I intended for things to end up. It was simply fortuitous for you that your boyfriend came along when he did." And then he added, as if boasting, "I could have killed you both out there, but I hadn't planned on using a weapon. . . ." He smiled at her. "And I really didn't want witnesses to what I was going to do, even the kind that don't live to tell about it. So I decided to wait. I wanted to have you all to myself."

"Why?" Violet asked, even though she already knew the answer to the question. Because she knew too much, and he couldn't risk being revealed.

He didn't bother answering her question. Instead, he kept talking. "After I saw you out there at my partner's house, pointing out spots that your uncle later ordered exhumed, I realized that somehow you knew where the bodies were buried. Even the ones that didn't turn out to be human." He raised his eyebrows. "Did you know that? That we found animals buried in those places?" He shrugged. "You probably already knew that," he said, more to himself than to her now.

"I was curious about you, so I started to go through the case files. I found something interesting. Your name, it showed up in only one place. *One place*," he announced, seemingly baffled by the solitary connection, as if he'd expected more. "You found my poor little lake girl. But you know . . ." he added, narrowing his eyes with the anticipation of a hunter targeting its prey. His eyes locked on to hers. ". . . She wasn't the first of *my girls* that you found."

His news wasn't a complete surprise; she'd known about the girl in the woods, the one she'd found when she was eight years old, and her uncle had already told her that the other man had confessed to killing the girl. But somehow imagining that these two lunatics had been hunting together for that long, that these psychotic killers had found each other in the first place, and then stayed together for over eight years, was appalling to Violet.

Her head was spinning.

This is crazy, she told herself.

He didn't wait for her to respond, and she didn't. He seemed to like flaunting his twisted prowess. Besides, what difference did it make if she knew? She doubted he planned on letting her get away from him again.

"That's right," he said, enjoying the game he was playing now. "The little girl who found the little girl. Of course, at the time I had no idea that you were involved, and according to the official records, you weren't. But the name listed in the

310

file was close enough. An Ambrose is an Ambrose, and your father's name was as indicative as your own would have been." He leaned closer to her, as if he was telling her a secret, even though they were all alone. "I wonder why he felt the need to leave your name out of it."

She didn't answer. She didn't need to; he wasn't really asking her a question. But his nearness was unnerving, and Violet found herself leaning back against the wall to get away from him.

He straightened up, his voice taking on a deceptively casual quality once again. "I didn't actually kill them, you know?" He watched her, waiting for her reaction.

She wasn't sure she should rise to his bait, but his cryptic explanations were wearing thin. And curiosity was a powerful emotion. He had no way of knowing that she could recognize the lie he spoke. "I don't believe you," she stated flatly.

"It's true. Or at least it *was* true. *He* was the one who killed them," he said, alluding to his partnership again. "I would find them and bring them to him. That was the part I loved, the hunt. That was the part that *did it* for me. After that, at least until it was time to dispose of the bodies, they were *his* problem." He said it as if the girls themselves were insignificant. And Violet believed that, to him at least, they were. Their lives meant nothing to him; they were simply quarry to track, useless once captured.

It suddenly made sense to her, why the other man had carried so many echoes on him, like a patchwork coat he wore all around him. She hadn't wondered before, but if she would have had time to process it, to think it through, she would have noticed it. That this man, the cop in front of her now, carried only one shrill echo.

So whose echo was it?

It was a question she couldn't ask.

But she didn't have to; he answered anyway.

"They'll never find her, you know, the girl they were searching for out in the woods." He smiled again, only slightly, and it made Violet's skin crawl as she studied him. "I was always so careful, dumping each of them in different locations, in different ways. Never the same place twice.

"But not this time, not *her*. She was my first kill, and this time they'll have no idea to look for her in the exact same spot where they found my partner, standing guard over the McDonald girl." His smile grew, revealing a flash of glistening white teeth. "And they'll never find you either."

CHAPTER 27

JAY STOOD AT THE EDGE OF THE DANCE FLOOR, still holding Violet's purse and scanning the darkened gymnasium, searching for her. He tried to ignore the panic rising within him. Something was wrong.

But when he saw Chelsea, dancing with her date, he was no longer able to contain it.

He interrupted the two of them on the dance floor. He didn't seem to notice that he was causing a minor scene. "Where's Violet?" he demanded, ignoring Chelsea's shocked expression.

"What . . . *Jay? What are you doing?*" she asked, her eyes widening at his unexpected outburst.

But Jay was too determined. "Chelsea . . . *where is she?*"

313

Chelsea stopped, momentarily stunned by the alarm she heard in his voice. "Relax! She's in the bathroom, fixing her ankle wrap. She'll be right back."

Jay looked up, in the direction of the restrooms, and felt himself relaxing when he saw the swarm of girls coming and going in clusters. Chelsea watched his reaction.

"Not that one." She corrected his mistaken belief that Violet was in there with the crowd. "We went down to the one past the locker rooms, so we could be alone."

Jay felt his blood turn to ice; he felt freezing fingers grip his heart with chilling dread. "You left her there? *Alone?*"

Chelsea shrugged, glancing rudely at a couple beside them who were staring now. They looked away, embarrassed to be caught in Chelsea's cutting gaze. "So what?" She turned back to Jay. "She'll be right back. Go get some punch, or maybe something stronger if it'll calm you down."

Jay searched the room, spotting one of the uniformed officers stationed near the entrance. His irritation with Chelsea turned to insistence, as he barked orders at her. "Go tell that cop to get help. Tell him where Violet is, and tell him to call her uncle!"

Chelsea was confused, but something in Jay's cryptic demands broke through to her, making her feel panicked without even knowing why. She didn't question him again; she just ignored her date, who was still standing there stunned by the conversation he'd just witnessed, and she raced toward the doors—toward the officer standing there—to get help for her friend.

Jay was already running the other way.

∗ ∗ ∗

The giant man in front of her reached out and captured a stray tendril of Violet's hair, rubbing it between his thumb and forefingers thoughtfully, and then he looked up as if he were genuinely sorry. "I'd love to sit here and chat with you, and believe me, I am enjoying myself. But we have to go." He spoke somberly, sadly. "It's time."

Violet shook her head. "I'll scream," she insisted, not sure what she really hoped to accomplish with the empty threat.

He seemed authentically disappointed. "I would snap your neck before anyone even had a chance to respond. Besides, Violet"—hearing her name on his vile lips made her visibly recoil again—"no one can hear you. And even if they did, I have a gun." He glanced down at his weapon. "I have to get rid of you or I lose everything. It's too late to go back now, right?"

Violet thought about her classmates . . . her friends . . . *Jay*. How could she allow any of them to be hurt by drawing attention to her . . . unfortunate predicament? She *wanted* to scream, to cry for help, but she couldn't. She wouldn't.

She stood up and reached for her crutches, feeling dead already. She had no other choice.

He led the way, holding the door open for her while she awkwardly shimmied through. He was sickeningly polite . . . and calm. He wasn't the hunter now, just the nameless executioner leading his prisoner to the gallows. There was no chase, no thrill in capturing her, at least not this time. She had made it far too simple for him.

CHAPTER 28

VIOLET'S ARMS WERE ACHING FROM TRYING TO keep up with him, but she refused to complain or even to slow down. His strong, calloused hand was wrapped tightly around the back of her neck, a warning to her of how fragile she was, how easily he could end her life should she try to get away from him at any point. She had a hard time imagining just how he thought she might escape, given the fact that she could barely walk, let alone outmaneuver him. But she kept her opinions to herself.

They were alone out here, in the long deserted hallway, heading toward the doors that led to the faculty parking lot. She could still hear the distant music, seemingly farther now and fading fast, in the background of her distressed thoughts.

She was worried, not about *if* she would die, as it seemed a certainty at this point. And although Violet had never been particularly afraid of death itself, she was worried about *how* it was going to happen. She prayed he would do it quickly, without making her suffer too much.

The other thought that haunted her in these last moments of her life, the one that bothered her even more than dying, was the idea that this monster, this madman, would wear her imprint on him for the rest of his life. Maybe longer.

The very idea made her feel physically ill, as she imagined sharing any part of her life's essence with him.

At first she thought she'd imagined it, the voice she heard coming from the other end of the hallway, from behind them. But it was too real, too perfectly beautiful, to be imagined. The moment her name was spoken, and she recognized who it was, her eyes began to tear up painfully.

It can't be him! Violet thought. *Anyone but him!*

"Violet?" His familiar voice was filled with confusion as he called out to her.

The hand around her neck tightened, and Violet followed the tactile cue and stopped. The grip was a threat in itself. They turned around in unison, the unbearably strong fingers never leaving the tender, already bruised flesh around her neck.

Facing Jay in person was nearly too much for Violet right now. She felt her frail heart splintering into a million lifeless shards.

He said her name again. "Vi?" He glanced up curiously at

the man escorting her, and he visibly relaxed a little. "What's going on? I was so worried. . . . I thought something might have happened to you." He waited for one of them to speak, and then he asked the obvious. "Where are you going?"

Silence ensued—the kind of void-filling silence that yawns endlessly until it becomes virtually impenetrable.

Violet wanted to build a bridge across the quiet chasm, but she couldn't find the words. They felt lodged behind the aching lump in her throat. She struggled with herself not to cry.

Suddenly the presence of the cop was not enough to make Jay feel secure. His posture stiffened, and he took a threatening step forward, his mouth set in a determined line. "What's going on?" he demanded this time.

Violet felt the iron grip squeezing forcefully, and she knew what was expected of her. Her mind raced, as she tried to think of something—*anything*—that would make Jay leave now.

"We . . . we're just . . ." She hated the way she stammered, and she ordered herself to get a grip. She wasn't saving herself here . . . she was trying to save Jay. She started again. "I asked the officer here"—she glanced up pleadingly at the rock-solid man beside her—"to take me to his car so I could call my uncle. My dad said he'd kill me if I didn't check in at least once."

Jay stood his ground. He knew she was lying to him, and Violet wanted to scream at him to just go away. "Here," he challenged, lifting her purse out to her and eyeing the officer's hand around the back of her neck. "You can use your cell phone."

She shook her head, no small feat with the jawlike grip

squeezing her. "No, I need to use *his* phone." Her voice had taken on a pleading quality, and she begged him with her eyes to believe what she was saying. She was losing her tentative grasp on the situation, and she didn't want Jay to get hurt. "Please, Jay, just go back to the dance. I'll be there soon." Her words broke, and she felt herself struggling to keep her composure. This wasn't the time to fall apart.

Jay took another calculated step forward, and the punishing fingers dug deeper into Violet's skin, biting at her fiercely. She winced. She didn't mean to, but the pain was so intense that it happened reflexively. There was nothing she could do to stop it.

That was all it took. That one nearly imperceptible recoil on her part, and Jay lunged forward. "Get your hands off her!" he yelled, his voice unmistakably filled with rage.

Violet couldn't move. She couldn't breathe. She hadn't wanted this; she simply wanted to disappear into the night, with this man she knew would kill her, and silently vanish. Forever.

That way no one else would get hurt.

She felt her neck jerk forward as the giant hand released her, shoving her away. If it hadn't been for the support of her crutches she would have toppled over.

Jay was already swinging his fist wide and hard, hitting the man who'd been holding her captive. His fist connected solidly against the man's jaw, and the officer's head snapped hard to the side from the impact. Violet felt a surge of hope blossom within her.

And then it incinerated into white-hot ash.

The officer remained upright, almost insultingly so, as if he'd never been struck at all. He sneered at Jay, his face hideously masked with contempt for the younger man. "You stupid little punk! You couldn't leave well enough alone, could you?" He approached Jay now.

She knew what he was going to do. She knew that now, like her, Jay had no chance of getting out of there alive.

She reacted without thinking.

Violet watched the arc of the metal crutch swinging widely before thudding sickeningly against the side of the cop's head. A metal wing nut, holding a long, pinlike bolt, struck his temple, gouging him deeply. He never saw it coming, and the force of the blow carried more weight than she would have thought possible, and she watched as he staggered sideways.

She saw him hit the ground. Everything seemed to happen so fast, and so slowly, all at the same time. The look on his face was that of complete surprise as he struggled to process what had just happened to him. Her ankle throbbed from the leverage she'd used to hit him with the crutch, but somehow she ignored the pain.

She couldn't think fast enough, but Jay was already grabbing her by the arm and dragging her down the hallway, back in the direction of the dance. But they were so far away, and every time Violet's foot hit the ground, fresh pain radiated up cripplingly from her ankle to her hip, nearly incapacitating her. He did his best to hold her up, pulling her against him, with his arm anchoring her around her waist, but she was lagging now . . . slowing him down.

They didn't look back.

And they didn't get far before the pain was more than she could bear. She slumped against him. "Jay, go get help," she whispered sadly. "You'll get there a lot faster without me."

"No way." He pulled her up again, dragging her into his arms so he could carry her.

"Don't, Jay," she insisted, crying now and struggling to make him set her down again. "You'll never make it with me. Please . . . just go!"

But there was no answer to give . . . because neither of them was going anywhere.

Violet felt the massive jolt jarring Jay from behind, and then she was falling . . . flying nearly, through the air. She landed with a dull, skidding thud against the industrial tiling of the school's vacant hallway. The sounds she heard bouncing off the walls around her were those of defeat.

She glanced up, trying to ignore the bright sting from her injuries. She scrambled to turn around, despite her own physical discomfort, to see what was happening behind her.

She heard it before she could see it.

The soft click. The menacingly quiet sound that made her throat constrict painfully.

Jay, who was lying facedown, had heard it too, and he slowly, warily, rolled over onto his back . . . careful not to make any sudden movements. He put up his hands cautiously, palms out and fingers spread, letting the huge man standing above him know that he was surrendering. That he was defeated.

The gun was all Violet could see now. It was black, and

from her position it looked like it could have been a child's plastic toy. But Violet knew better. This was not a toy that he expertly handled. And it was pointed directly at Jay.

The man holding it was bleeding; rivulets of oozing red blood trickled down the side of his face. He seemed somewhat off balance, and he staggered a little, probably from the blow he'd taken to the side of his head . . . but his aim looked perfect. *Dead-on.*

Violet could only whimper as she watched. "No! *Please, God, no!*" And then she was crying, "You don't need him. He can't hurt you. Please . . ." She crawled forward, meaning to block Jay, but she was moving too slowly. She felt like she was progressing in slow motion, like a bad dream where her feet were too heavy to make any real headway. She looked up at the man, and when she saw the look in his eyes, she realized that she was too late.

The sound of the gun was like a deafening crack, and Violet instinctively flinched, closing her eyes, her hands covering her ears at the same time that she started to scream. She heard a second shot immediately follow the first.

She opened her eyes just long enough to see the blood. Everywhere . . . blood. And she squeezed them tight again, unable to look. She knew she was still screaming, but she couldn't hear anything aside from the internal ringing that seemed to fill her head.

But her mouth was suddenly filled with the strangest sensation . . . the taste of dandelions. It was the bitterly familiar taste of childhood, of picking the weeds to make a yellow bouquet, and then later, when you put a finger in your mouth, you could still taste the caustic flavor of the dandelion milk clinging to your skin. Her tongue recoiled.

Violet realized, while she was being peeled up from the floor by strong hands, that the taste had nothing to do with picking flowers.

It was an echo.

A brand-new echo.

EPILOGUE

VIOLET LOOKED OUT THE WINDOW AT THE FIRST snowfall of the season. The thick, fluffy flakes came down through the darkness, casting a brilliant whiteness that radiated throughout the night sky.

There was something so refreshingly delicate about a new snow. It was like a rebirth.

And it meant that school would be canceled tomorrow.

She turned back to her room, as she reached behind her neck to remove the thin silver chain that Jay had given her the night of the Homecoming Dance. She rubbed the smooth finish of the heart before setting it gently into the black velvet box it had come in, trying, as she did every night, to blink back the hot tears that started to sting her eyes.

The night of the dance . . .

That was almost two months ago, but just thinking about it again made Violet shiver despite the warmth of her bedroom. She wrapped her arms around herself and rubbed at the goose bumps that broke out over her skin.

If she closed her eyes, she could still picture the vivid images that would be forever ingrained in her memories. But it was physically painful if she dwelled there for too long.

She was safe now, she had to remind herself of that, and there was something cathartic about remembering what she'd somehow survived.

She could easily recall the blistering sounds of the gunshots, and then everything seemed to blur together for her.

It was her uncle who'd found her and lifted her up from the floor. By the time she was aware of her surroundings, all hell had broken loose around them.

She remembered her uncle explaining how they'd finally figured out, almost too late, that it was one of his officers who was responsible for the deaths of all those girls—and nearly responsible for Violet's as well.

They'd found a receipt among the evidence collected from the farmhouse belonging to his partner in crime. The receipt was for a disposable cell phone; apparently that was how the two of them had communicated. When they traced it back, it led them right to the man who had worked both with, and for, her uncle for the past ten years. The GPS from his own patrol car confirmed his presence at several of the crime scenes . . . and many of which they'd been unaware.

Later, after her uncle had fired the shot that had killed the officer in the hallway of the school, they'd gone back to search the woods where they'd first discovered Hailey McDonald's body, and found Mackenzie Sherwin buried right where Violet said she would be.

Her neck had been broken.

But Violet had survived. Her uncle had saved her. And now he carried with him a new aura, *a new imprint*, that Violet found somewhat disturbing to be around . . . the bitter dandelion taste. But even that was fading, almost faster than it should have, and Violet found it bearable now to be around him for short periods of time.

There was a tap at her bedroom door before it opened.

Violet turned in time to see Jay coming in. His grin was mischievous and wicked at the same time. She practically leaped into his arms as he closed the door behind him.

He laughed against the top of her head. "I missed you too."

She lifted her face to his, and he kissed her, his arms pulling her closer.

"I just came to say good night," he said between hungry kisses.

"So say it."

He kissed her again, and then again, but he never said good night . . . or good-bye.

"Good night," she finally whispered when his lips left hers.

She was grateful every single day that Jay had only been

grazed by the first shot fired that night. Grateful that the wounded officer—the killer—in the hallway had been too dazed to fire straight. And even more grateful that her uncle had come around the corner in time to fire the second shot ... the deadly one.

Jay watched her, reading the thoughts clearly on her face. And then he smiled and lifted her into his arms, kissing her lightly on her forehead, her cheeks, her nose. "Maybe I can stay for a little while," he breathed as he finally found her lips.

Violet knew that everything was going to be all right now. Jay was safe. The killer was dead.

She curled into Jay as he pulled her down against his shoulder.

Everything was better than all right—it was perfect.

ACKNOWLEDGMENTS

To my friends John McDonald and Bryan Jeter, for advising me on all things police, fire, and rescue . . . thank you for lending me some credibility. Men in uniform rock!

To Laura Rennert, my super-amazing agent, for taking a chance on me even though I nervously confused the words "urban" and "rural" during our first (three-minute) meeting.

To the entire team at HarperCollins, including my oh-so fabulous editors, Gretchen Hirsch and Farrin Jacobs, for helping me polish *The Body Finder* into something that sparkles. I can't tell you how much I appreciate both your tact *and* your patience.

I also have to thank my mother, Peggy, for always telling me that I could be anything I wanted to be (you're such a mom!).

To my husband, for encouraging me to jump without a net. None of this would have happened without your endless encouragement. Thank you, thank you, thank you . . .

And to Amanda, Connor, and Abigail . . . *you guys really can be anything you want to be!*